Anton

Antonine Maillet was bo[...]
attended the universities o[...]
writing, she has educated and entertained the pub[...]
stories of her native Acadie. She has won several literary
awards, among them the Governor General's Award and the
Prix Goncourt, and is a best-selling author in Quebec and
France. Her work includes *La Sagouine*, which enjoyed
enormous success both as a novel and a play; the fantasy *Don
l'Orignal*, which won a Governor General's Award; and *Les
Crasseux*, a dialectical drama. Antonine Maillet lives in
Montreal.

George Reid

George Agnew Reid was born on a farm in western Ontario
in 1860. In spite of his father's opposition, he enrolled in the
Ontario School of Art in Toronto where he studied under
Robert Harris. At the age of twenty-two, he moved to
Philadelphia to study at the Pennsylvania Academy of Fine
Arts under Thomas Eakins. There he married a fellow student,
and together they traveled to Paris where they attended the
Academies Julian and Colarossi. After returning to Canada in
1889, Reid began teaching at the Central Ontario School of
Art and Design. A popular artist who sold well, he mainly
painted genre, historical, and landscape subjects. He died in
1947.

New Press Canadian Classics

Distinguished by the use of Canadian fine art on its covers,
New Press Canadian Classics is an innovative, much-needed
series of high-quality, reasonably priced editions of the very
best Canadian fiction, nonfiction and poetry.

New Press Canadian Classics

Hubert Aquin *The Antiphonary*
  Alan Brown (trans.)

Marie-Claire Blais *Nights in the Underground*
  Ray Ellenwood (trans.)

George Bowering *Burning Water*

Matt Cohen *The Expatriate*

Jack David & Robert Lecker (eds.) *Canadian Poetry.*
  Volumes One and Two

Mavis Gallant *My Heart Is Broken*

Anne Hébert *Kamouraska*
  Norman Shapiro (trans.)

David Helwig *The Glass Knight, Jennifer*

Robert Kroetsch *Badlands, The Studhorse Man*

Félix Leclerc *The Madman, the Kite & the Island*
  Philip Stratford (trans.)

Keith Maillard *Alex Driving South, Two Strand River*

Antonine Maillet *Pélagie*
  Philip Stratford (trans.)

Brian Moore *An Answer From Limbo*

Michael Ondaatje *Coming Through Slaughter*

Leon Rooke *Fat Woman*

George Ryga *The Ecstasy of Rita Joe and other plays*

new press CANADIAN CLASSICS

Antonine Maillet

Pélagie

Translated by Philip Stratford

PROPERTY OF THE
PUBLIC LIBRARY
ST MARYS ONT

General Publishing Co. Limited
Toronto, Canada

Translation © 1982 by Doubleday & Company, Inc

All rights reserved

No part of this book may be reproduced or
transmitted in any form or by any means,
electronic or mechanical, including photography,
recording, or any information storage or retrieval
system, without permission in writing from the
publisher.

Grasset and Leméac edition
published in 1979

Doubleday edition published in 1982

General Paperbacks edition
published in 1983

Published by arrangement with Doubleday & Company, Inc.

ISBN 0-7736-7052-1

Printed and bound in Canada

PROLOGUE

According to old Louis-à-Bélonie, a shoot of the Bélonie branch and a child of the cart like myself, the only survivors in the Massacre of the Holy Innocents were the Innocents who knew enough to hold their tongues. Let sleeping bears lie, he used to say, especially the one asleep on your own doorstoop. And that's why, when Acadie wrenched itself out of exile at the end of the eighteenth century, it quit its crib so quiet, with never a wail nor a shout, without even clapping its hands. It came home by the back door, and on tiptoe. And when the world got round to noticing, it was too late; Acadie already had springs in its shanks and its nose in the wind.

A nose, among others, like Pélagie-the-Grouch's, creeping out of the woods a century later just to sniff the wind a whiff, just to see what the weather was. It was fine; life could begin again. And the old bag hails the others to come out of their holes and take their place in the sun. She had heard the cry of the wild geese coming back from the south; they could begin to turn the earth again and to cast their nets into the sea.

"Bestir yourselves, you bunch of flabby asses!" Pélagie hollers. "No one here's going to spoon-feed you or tuck you in bed."

Pélagie-the-Grouch, third-of-the-name, liked to say that she descended in a straight line from her direct ancestors. And as if this aphorism weren't enough to convince the circle of pipe-slurpers seated in a half-moon round the *maçoune*—which some call the hearth—any wicked winter's night you chose she would take up her lineage from the start, from Pélagie, to Madeleine, to Pélagie, to herself Pélagie-the-Grouch, if for no other reason than simply to enrage the Després and the Gallants who, according to her, had no place among the deported passengers of the cart.

Bélonie, father of Louis-à-Bélonie and storyteller and chronicler by trade, would snigger at such amateurish delvings that couldn't even tell the going-down from the coming-back of this Deportation, and that couldn't have named for sure the schooner of Captain Broussard-called-Beausoleil, which, sailing the coast from north to south and from south to north, had done as much to gather up the tatters of Acadie as the famous cart and its forty-six followers. So much for Pélagie-the-Grouch!

And Ptui! into the hearth.

"That so? Well maybe it's on account of because they were high and dry down in the hold of that ship for the whole trip that none of them brazen-faced Bélonies ever noticed the shadow of our forefathers' cart rolling back home with never so much as a creak of the wheels?"

Bélonie wasn't ornery, no more than his father, than his grandfather or his forefather Bélonie, who hadn't hidden in the hold of a schooner—correction Pélagie—but had clung to the rack of the cart, the real one, right there beside that Pélagie, first-of-the-name, straight-line ancestor of Pélagie-the-Grouch who even after a hundred years hadn't yet pardoned her antecedent for welcoming that bastard into the family . . .

"Bastard? Bah! Why the very name of Bélonie still sets three-quarters of the country dreaming and gives the other quarter the shivers . . . And besides, I'm not ornery."

And he had no more to say to The Grouch.

But The Grouch needed no reply to understand, needed no explanations, nor history lessons on her own country. And she sent Bélonie and the whole hearth-circle back to their pipes.

"If you think you're going to get me to swallow that stuff, me!"

For a hundred years now they'd been passing the cart down from Bélonie to Bélonie to Bélonie, like an heirloom, when all the time the cart belonged to none other than her legitimate and unique master, Pélagie, first-of-the-name, LeBlanc by her man, who had come alive through the flames of Grand-Pré.

"And you still think you can tell me about my own ancestors' cart?"

Yes, still, and again, and again. For without these storytellers and root-delvers of Bélonies, sons of Bélonies, and the sons of sons of Bélonies, History would have rolled over and died at the end of every century. How many times had she stopped, stumbled, and collapsed on the edge of the road? And if it hadn't been for one of those Bélonies chancing by one winter evening . . . He sees her just in time with the death rattle on her, he picks her up, straightens her out, and brings her back, gasping but still warm, to the fireside. And there, by virtue of logs on the fire and spurts of spit in the flames . . . Ptuil . . . she's brought back to life, the bitch, and History goes on again.

And goes on today in the mouth of my cousin Louis-à-Bélonie who holds what he knows from his father, Bélonie-à-Louis who held it from his grandfather Bélonie, contemporary and adversary of Pélagie-the-Grouch, who received it from father to son from that very Bélonie, son of Thaddée, son of Bélonie-the-First who in 1770 feasted his ninetieth year sitting in the bottom of the cart of that same Pélagie, first-of-the-name.

After all that, just try to tell me, who every morning shine up my sixteen quarters of cart, that a people who can't read can't have a History!

To the memory of my mother,
Virginie Cormier

1

PROPERTY OF THE
PUBLIC LIBRARY
ST. MARYS, ONT.

Bélonie, first of the line of Bélonies to come through the Great Disruption, was a patched and peeled old codger when the oxcart rattled off on its way. And for the youngsters who clambered aboard he would unravel the legend of the Wagon of Death. He had seen it close up many and many a time, old Bélonie had; had heard it rather, yes, heard it, for no man living had ever seen that somber contraption with neither doors nor lamps, drawn throughout the world by six spanking black horses since the beginning of time.

"If nobody ever seen it, how come you figure it's black, that cart of yours?" Pélagie let fly smack in the middle of the old chin-wagger's forehead.

"Hee!"

. . . was the whole of Bélonie's reply. For like any good storyteller by trade he saved himself for his stories, Bélonie did, and never wasted saliva on foregone obstinacies. Who has eyes to see, let him see. No man alive has ever seen Death, yet everyone

knows him. Everyone knows the Devil with his horns, and
Saint-Michael the Archangel leaning on his spear, and the phantom black wagon without any doors drawn by three teams of
horses, so that's that. No more to be said.

All right, all right, that's that. But Pélagie knew who'd be the
first to have more to say on the subject. And with shouts of
"Hue!" and "Dia!" she got the oxen moving again. The Wagon
of Death could flounder in the swamps of Georgia for all she
cared; she, Pélagie, had a load of her own to drive in the cart of
Life.

"Jump aboard, Célina, and don't heed the old chin-wagger
there."

Célina pitched her sack in the chin-wagger's lap and straddled
the sideboard.

"Just you let me know when it's my turn to walk, Pélagie. I'm
no more decrepit than anyone here."

". . . No more decrepit, no, just a mite clumpier." Bélonie said
this without saying a word, smiling all the while at Célina
through the gaps in his teeth. But Célina stripped his thought to
the core.

"Were we bound to bring that one along?"

Yes, had to. Couldn't leave an old gaffer nearly a hundred all
alone in Georgia without living kith and kin. Pélagie wouldn't
have had the heart to leave behind this patriarch of the deported
Acadians, no, not if he had to drag his phantom wagon along
with him all the way to Grand-Pré.

"And drag it he will, I know him," chipped in Célina. "So long
as he don't get it into his head to harness our oxen to it. . . .
Bien le bonjour, young folks. Don't budge, I'll find room."

The young folks were Pélagie's three sons and her daughter
Madeleine who was already stowing Célina's gear away with the
bundles of clothes, the provisions, and straw pallets, all that was
left of the LeBlanc's worldly goods after fifteen years of Georgia.
They had sold everything: household linen and pewter mugs
rescued from the Disruption, furniture, poultry, sheep, even the
plank hut that had eased their exile and had kept the family from
drifting apart like so many others.

"Not me!" Pélagie had exclaimed, seeing her deported countrymen dropping like flies all along the coast of Georgia. "I'll plant none of mine in a foreign soil."

And from that day on, her first day on dry land after months and months in the troughs of thirty-foot waves that from the shores of Acadie had already swallowed up half her clan, Pélagie had sworn to her ancestors to bring back at least one full cradle to her own country. But her children had grown too fast, even little Madeleine born right in the hold of an English schooner, and when Pélagie was finally ready to get under way, her lastborn was fifteen. And as for a ship, all Pélagie could rig out was a cart.

A cart and three teams of oxen that had cost her fifteen years in the fields under a heavy southern sun and the boot of a brutal cotton planter who swung his whip with the same contempt on his black slaves and the poor whites. She, Pélagie Bourg, called LeBlanc, harnessed to the plough of slavery! She who had known prosperity and independence in the land of Acadie . . . yes, independence. For Acadie, tossed from one royal master to another, had managed to slip between the two and fool them both, going about its own business right under the old-country noses of Louis and George still sniffing the wind for spices. And without breathing a word, the little Atlantic colony had let the kings of France and England send back and forth their revised and corrected maps of Acadie and Nova Scotia, and had gone on happily cultivating its garden. It wasn't to last: The harvests were too good to be true. And the English soldiers, dreaming of a few country acres, began to covet those Acadian fields.

Exile is a hard chapter in the book of History. Unless one turns the page.

Pélagie had heard say that all along the coast, in the Carolinas, in Maryland, and further north, Acadians from Governor Lawrence's schooners, who like her had been dumped off at random in creeks and bays, were little by little resetting their roots in foreign soil.

"Quitters!" she couldn't help shouting up at them from across the Georgia border.

For roots are also one's own dead, and Pélagie had left behind, sown between Grand-Pré and the English colonies to the south, father and mother, man and child, who for fifteen years had been calling her every night: "Come on back! . . ."

Come on back! . . .

Fifteen years since that morning of the Great Disruption. She was a young woman then, just twenty, no more, and already with five offspring hanging to her skirts . . . four to be exact, the fifth on the way. That fateful morning had found her in the fields where her oldest boy, God rest his soul, had summoned her with his shouts of "Come on back! Come on back!" His cries clung to her eardrums. Come on back . . . and she saw the flames climbing the sky. The church was on fire, Grand-Pré was on fire, and the life she had let run free in her veins until then suddenly boiled up under her skin and Pélagie thought she would burst. She ran, holding her belly, leaping over the furrows, her eyes fixed on her Grand-Pré, that flower of the French Bay. They were already piling families into the schooners, pell-mell, throwing LeBlancs in with Héberts and Héberts with Babineaus. Bits of the Cormier brood seeking their mother in the hold where the Bourgs were calling the Poiriers to look after their little ones. From one ship to another Richards, Gaudets, Chiassons stretched out their arms toward fragments of their families on other decks, crying, "Take care of yourself! Take care . . ." their cries carried out by the swell to the open sea.

. . . So it is when a people departs into exile.

And she, Pélagie, with the shreds of the family she had managed to save from the Great Disruption, had landed on Hope Island in the north of Georgia. Hope Island! Only the good omen in the name had kept this woman, this widow of Acadie with her four orphans, alive. Hope was a country, a return to the paradise lost.

"Well, they sure lost their paradise, them Richards and Roys," Célina was quick to put in, her nose in the air. "How come they drowsed off all of a sudden, the slackers?"

Didn't drowse, no, chose. With regret, most of them, but chose just the same. Not everyone can start up again at the change of life, Célina. And start over at zero, groping, on foot. The farewells from the cart to Hope Island were not joyful, despite the smile spread on Bélonie's face and Pélagie's ringing words to her sisters in exile:

"I'll replant the barley you left there ripening and make you a soup of it when you decide to come home!"

And her neighbors wiped their eyes and chins on the backs of their hands, leaning on the men or children left them, while with a great "Hue-Ho!" Pélagie set her oxcart in motion.

But creaking in the very ruts of Pélagie's cart came the invisible wheels of the Wagon of Death. And old chin-wagger Bélonie picked up his story again right where Célina's clubfoot had marked a full stop.

". . . Now the wheels of this cart creaked, you see, to warn the living to clear out of the way, for it only came for the dead, the dying, and those marked by fate. That's the noise we heard at the death of the late Sirois-à-Basile Gautreau, last spring when he dropped from exhaustion in the tobacco field; and the night of poor Barbe-à-Babée's passing, you could hear it all up and down the Savannah River; and when the late *Espérance* was shipwrecked off the islands, the cart creaked all night around the shores of the Grande Echouerie . . ." After all that, just try to tell Bélonie the storyteller, the old man of Acadie, that the Grim Reaper isn't one of the family, or a close connection. And he explained to the youngsters, who were laughing from fright and the sweat in their eyes, that Death is the surest traveling companion a man can have. The only one you can count on at the very end to snatch you away from the dangers of life.

At this Pélagie took her whip to the oxen.

"Can't we hear a little small talk about the sun and the rain and get this cart set on a better course for our journey north?"

Célina lost no time in taking Pélagie's side.

"We going to have to endure this prophet of doom all the way home? The trip could be long, who knows, might drag on for months or years."

"Or generations," Bélonie snickered.

And he added a "Heel" just to keep true to form.

Ah! Phew! He was starting to grate on Célina's nerves. Getting Pélagie's goat too. Who was he to tote up the generations between the exile and the return? What Jeremiah had engendered him anyway? And had the old sorcerer forgotten that it only took a matter of months to come down?

The old gaffer screwed up his face.

"To come down south, they furnished the ships," he said without batting an eye.

Célina choked on her tonsils. Well, yes, sure! That's the way a deportation works, I'll have you know! They furnish you the schooners, if they have to. Just like they furnish the condemned man the rope and the gallows. Is that any reason to pine after their gallows and their ships? And what are we supposed to do now, go round tell the hangman to fix up our journey back?

"If there's anyone on board here finds we're not moving fast enough, they can always go shake up Governor Lawrence and ask him to outfit us a schooner."

"Shut up, Jeannot. You don't use that tone with the oldest old man in the land."

And Pélagie took back the reins from the hands of her son.

The cart had been rolling on its way for several days, its four wheels greased with sunflower oil turning briskly, its racks thrust like masts up into the sky, its floorboards pitching like the deck of a schooner at sea, when the lead oxen stopped abruptly, bringing the whole crew to a halt. Pélagie stood up. The rest waited.

"Why, it's La Catoune!" said Célina jumping down.

La Catoune indeed it was, that child from Beaubassin stranded in the wrong ship on the day of the Great Disruption. No one had ever been able to fathom the origin of this little girl, barely three, who by way of baggage had only a nickname, the Beaubassin she came from, and but one word in her mouth: "M'hungry!" She must have been passed from the deck of this schooner to the deck of that, for no one could explain how, in mid-ocean, she had turned up in the hold of the *Nightingale* transporting LeBlancs, Richards, Roys, Belliveaus, Bourgs, and bits of the Babin and Babineau families.

"Now where's she sprung up from like that?"

From Hope Island, surely, on foot, at a run. She must have run sniffing the oxen's trail like a dog. Like a cat. She was of the cat family, La Catoune.

"Hey! Get a move on, Charlécocol Can't you see she's worn out, the poor child of God?"

Yes, she was stretched out on the road like a wet cat, rasping and trembling all over. And Charles and Jacquot, Pélagie's twins, so merged in body and spirit that they came to be always called by the one plural name, together lifted up the child of God who, after four or five days without food, weighed no more than an angel.

"There, and now what do we do with her?"

Jean quickly seized Catoune from the arms of his pair of clumsy brothers and laid her on the hay in the bottom of the cart.

"Enough for seven's enough for eight," Pélagie answered, catching sight of Célina's puckered brow.

She had delivered the same verdict fifteen years earlier, the young Pélagie had, sharing her milk with every newborn child tossed up on the Georgia coast, to the point of putting the life of her own child in peril. Madeleine had cried for six months and then got used to the heresies of this mother who held that charity begins not at home, but with others.

So it was that little Catoune, who had never learned to split hairs, came to slide into the folds of Pélagie's skirts whenever she felt threatened. And threatened she must have felt often, ever since the very first days of the Incident. Pélagie remembered the little refugee thrown one day into the hold of the *Nightingale* and bleeding everywhere, yes, everywhere. It was Célina, healer and midwife, who had first taken care of her. And Pélagie looked after the rest, a rest that was to last fifteen years.

"Get some milk, Madeleine."

The whole cartload craned their necks. Milk? But where was a body to find milk on the frontier between Georgia and the Carolinas, in a foreign land, in a wagon pulled by six oxen? Even old

Bélonie stopped grinning an instant to stare at this thirty-five-year-old woman demanding milk from the stones of the fields.

Not from stones, Bélonie, from life. From life swarming everywhere around the cart as it had swarmed around their plank cabin for fifteen years, on the open sea for months, and for a happy century in Acadie. Life doesn't dry up just because it heads off on the road north, does it? Life's not more life around home than on the highway. The Hebrews crossed the desert, didn't they? And anyway, all life's a voyage, in a manner of speaking.

"What you're going to do is fetch some milk for us, Madeleine. We can't just leave this slave of the Good Lord to die."

And Madeleine obeyed.

"Heel . . ."

Yes, Bélonie, that morning Pélagie's cart was stronger than yours, laugh as you might. For within an hour Madeleine came back not only with milk but with the whole goat. And La Catoune was saved.

Without asking her daughter for details, Pélagie felt it was probably best not to linger, for soon some goatherd in a neighboring field would be counting his flock and . . .

"Hue-Ho!"

. . . and at any rate, Grand-Pré wasn't exactly next door.

Two days later La Catoune was laughing with the rest of them and joining in by ear, chirping and twittering like a bird, for the woodland spirit had never bothered to decant her soul into words. She babbled everything, Catoune did, but said nothing. And little by little, by bits, they guessed the true reason why she had run away.

It wasn't the first time she had disappeared, the little savage. All childhood long she had run wild in the woods and far into the marshes and along the dunes. To begin with, she would eat from bowls left out on the doorsteps by Blanchards, Richards, Roys, it little mattered by whom. But as she grew in appetite and stature, she would come more and more freely to Pélagie's table. Till finally Pélagie counted her as one of the cart. The

widow of Acadie wasn't one to abandon to exile the orphaned
child of her people. Catoune would return to her port of
Beaubassin.

But Catoune must have forgotten Beaubassin after years of
wandering, for the morning the cart departed she had disappeared.

"Take off like that at the very moment we get under way? It's
curious."

And Pélagie had waited for Catoune two whole days.

"Enough said, Charlécoco! You'd have sat up waiting for your
dog if your dog had took off."

Charlécoco looked sour; they'd never owned a dog.

But two days later:

"If Heaven wills it so for La Catoune, mustn't tempt God,"
says Pélagie. "Come on, my twins, harness up."

And the twins lost no time fixing the yokes to the animals and
the animals to the cart . . . and all the while La Catoune lay in
the wild hay sniffing the wind to see which horizon the cart
would lumber off to. For several days, weaving between the
bushes, cutting through the woods, she had followed, then out-
stripped the cart until she had fallen from exhaustion almost
under the front oxen's hooves!

"Now what could've got into her, the featherbrain!" exclaimed
Célina, raising two gaunt arms to heaven.

Nothing, except that in that little featherbrain there had never
been room for either security or guarantees. And La Catoune
was taking no chances on being sent back to the Richards, already established on a Georgia plantation.

Pélagie looked tenderly at this girl of less than twenty who
had set out alone, on foot, on an empty stomach, determined to
follow the deportees back to Acadie. And wiping her nose on the
back of her hand, Pélagie smacked a great lash of the whip on
the flanks of the oxen.

"If Beaubassin is still somewhere under the sun, you'll see it
again, my girl," says she.

And everyone understood that from now on La Catoune was

to have her own bowl and bundle of straw like the rest. For Célina it was clear as day.

"Anyways, who'd I be to kick?"

Which was her way of letting them know, right across the continent, that she too had boarded another's cart, and she knew it.

. . . From her earliest days she had ridden in others' wagons and lodged under others' roofs. For, unlike Catoune or the foundlings of the holds, Célina was orphaned not by deportation but by birth. Some whispered between their teeth she might be the product of a Micmac father and a witch or wild woman of the woods. But they held their long tongues in the old maid's presence, for shrew she might be, but healer and midwife too. And if you'd seen the last of the Savoys from Grand-Pré's kids stick a foot with six toes on it out of its mother's belly, why . . . you thought twice about peddling nasty gossip.

A vocation for midwifery is born in an odd way in Acadie. Like a naval career for the Swiss. A midwife goes hunting for dreams in the bellies of others, so they say, and they claim the trade is reserved for widows and barren women. But nothing proved Célina was barren. She'd never had a chance to prove it. She was down on her luck, that's all. Luck might have smiled on her at thirty-five as on so many others at that age when solitary or disadvantaged girls usually meet advantageous mates, it's customary in a country like ours given over more to luck than to reason. But Célina's luck had been swallowed up in the mass deportation and the poor girl rounded the cape of thirty-five in the hold of a schooner. What good then to go chasing after a destiny that has thumbed its nose at you? Even a clubfoot, offspring of a hypothetical father and mother, has her dignity. So Célina, when she set foot in Georgia, went back to foraging for new healing herbs and to bringing other people's children into the world.

Célina's plants were to be all-important from the start of the journey. To such an extent that a century or so later the storyteller-chroniclers of the dubious branch of the family were able to attribute to Pélagie very mixed motives in picking Célina up in her cart.

As if that were likely!

As if Pélagie-the-Cart, heroine of the ancestral return to Acadie, would have been able to entertain such intentions, or any intentions at all beyond the intention to return, I ask you!

And Pélagie-the-Grouch, her descendant in the following century, once again put all the laggards round the hearth in their place, swearing she'd write the history of the country herself if need be, the true history, the one of her own family, the branch deported to the south who, without her ancestor Pélagie's cart, would damn well have stayed there. So there!

According to my cousin, Louis-à-Bélonie, Pélagie-the-Grouch was probably right. His great-great-first-of-the-name could hardly, given the circumstances, have gone through all the gymnastics required of murky intentions. If she had taken the healer into her cart, it was because the healer herself was infirm, without parents or relatives, without connections of any kind, except to her plants. So Pélagie had taken the plants along with Célina.

And Old Bélonie for the same reasons.

"Heel . . ."

Naturally Bélonie must have his snort. What? Pick up an old maid without ancestors and a centenarian without heirs for the same reasons? Heel

"It comes to the same thing."

. . . The same thing? Hmph!

"If you could only come to reason and try to forget your Wagon of Death once in a while. We've all had our dead. Some more than others, everyone more than his share. And you can't blame the Good Lord for that."

Bélonie fixed Pélagie straight in the eye. Since when was he blaming anyone, eh? Everyone hauled his own cart, that's all, with his own kindred aboard. She carried her load of the living in a hardwood cart, and he, a ninety-year-old who had seen go down almost before his very eyes . . .

. . . No, Bélonie, you didn't see that . . .

. . . had seen the storm scatter the schooners and the cyclone strike and suck one down in its wake, the *Duke of Wellington* it was, and with it drag down all his descendants into the depths of the sea.

No, Bélonie!

. . . He wasn't accusing a soul, wasn't complaining or whining, but he'd surely earned the right to smile in his own way at the Grim Reaper who had followed him step for step since his first day of exile.

"Yet I know some, Bélonie, who've started life over after seventy!"

Bélonie kept on shaking his head. Would the stubborn never listen to reason? He hadn't given up on life, Bélonie hadn't, he was living proof of that, he'd just coupled on the other wagon, that's all. Two carts could move in caravan, couldn't they, eight wheels in the same ruts. As far as he, Bélonie, was concerned, he wasn't going back home alone, so put that in your pipe and smoke it.

"Old loony!"

But Pélagie cut Célina short. To each his own baggage and each his own fantasies.

If only Bélonie's cart didn't take the lead ahead of Pélagie's.

"Hue-Ho! Get on there! Hey for the north! And don't let me catch a one of you letting his head veer south."

Hee! . . .

He had scored a point, just the same, Bélonie had. And his cart followed on behind.

2

PROPERTY OF THE PUBLIC LIBRARY ST. MARYS, ONT.

"The first gulp's always the worst, buck up!"

At that the cart came up with a bump, all four wheels at once. It was hardly the time to talk about gulps when for weeks they'd been measuring out bread by the crumb and water by the sip. The image was poorly chosen, Pélagie; better to have spoken of cotton or tobacco. But Pélagie didn't choose her images, she had dragged them along with her all the way from her native land. A land of masts and shrouds, framed in bays, slashed with rivers and all walled round with *aboiteaux*.

Aboiteaux! The very word drove Pélagie wild and she whipped the oxen. How had a place like Georgia drained its fields without *aboiteaux?* All her childhood Pélagie had run free on those wide dikes that bordered the meadows and stole land from the sea. Her father used to tell her that in the old country where his sixteen quarters of ancestry came from, a land sometimes called France and sometimes Poitou, they had been water-clearers from father to son for generations. The sea is a sly one

and she must be taken by tricks and traps. She may rage and spit
and swallow up a whole dune of white sand in a mouthful, but
in the end she always tires and lets her waters die down. And
then it's the turn of the *aboiteaux* to avenge the land and save
the fields. With their clappers opening and closing under the
weight of the water, the *aboiteaux* send the sea back to its bed.
And there's time then to sow before the next flood tide.

All that water rose in Pélagie's veins in the heart of the Georgia desert! But calm, Pélagie, they'd overcome. It's always the
first gulp the shipwrecked find hardest to swallow.

"I'll accustom us yet. We've known worse in the past, and
we've overcome."

Worse? One after another the heads popped up from the box
of the cart. Worse than hunger and thirst?

Pélagie's eyes traveled round the cart, her gaze held by the
large white eyes, the thick lips, the flared nostrils drinking in the
air drop by drop, then fell on the thicket of Catoune's hair where
she sat crouched like an Indian, her eye riveted on the north.
Yes, Pélagie's head nodded, there's worse than famine.

"But that's no reason not to get out and find the spring," she
burst out, smacking the floor of the cart with the butt of her
whip. "Charlécoco, off with you, each to his own side, one north-
erly, one southerly, and bring me back a hand scoop of fresh
water."

"Huh?"

"None of your huh's, or groans, or surly looks. After the years
of the lean kine come the years of the fat. Let it never be said I
left us toiling between the two. Away with you!"

And the twins set off to the right and left, spitting, mutter-
ing, signing themselves backward and forward, and tapping the
rocks like water-diviners to let God and Pélagie know they
weren't to be taken for Moses.

Hmph!

If Charles and Jacquot had known the surprise waiting for
them behind the hill, or if they'd known their history better,
they'd have taken themselves for a couple of little pharaohs. But
all that Acadians of old Acadie knew about history were the chap-

ters passed round from mouth to ear by the hearth, and the kings of Egypt weren't part of the story. Behind the hill what awaited them was a river that had just opened up to let them ford it.

The drought that struck the Southern Colonies that summer was not all bad. So Pélagie in times to come never tired of telling those of the other carts ready to listen. For if the Savannah hadn't almost run dry, how'd they ever have got the oxen across, eh? And the load of exiles they were carting home? . . . Got to give thanks to God for heat like cold; for drought like rain, whatever you say. So *Benedicamus Domino!*

"Well, we could sure do without this heat and drought, whatever you say."

And Célina yanked the boot off a clubfoot as hard as a mare's hoof.

It was the first time the cripple had exposed her infirmity to the general view, and she cursed and grumbled to cover her shame. Not even a heap of rocks, not even the least little bush to hide one's intimacies behind . . . Soon have to do one's business right out in the sun, under the oxen's noses, arse in public . . . And then when you go and squat down on a tuft of cactus, why, you forget you ever wanted to go . . . But they're moving, them cactus . . . What's up? . . . Could it be the wind? . . .

"Porcupines! Three, four . . . a family of porcupines!"

And the whole cart took off across the fields armed with sticks and clubs. Two hours later, wiping chins drooling with broiled porcupine grease, they listened to Bélonie tell the story of Port-Royal. And it was right there in the middle of Port-Royal, between Poutrincourt, Biencourt, and Sieur Menou d'Aulnay that who should turn up but the young Cormier, son of one of the deported Acadians. He had come to greet Pélagie in the name of a nearby settlement of compatriots who were dragging out a miserable existence in a misbegotten place they'd christened Beaufort. They were Cormiers, Héberts, Girouards, formerly from Beauséjour . . .

"How's that again?"

Well, it came stumbling out, but it all came out just the same, the fifteen years of comings and goings and wanderings and attempts to catch their breaths, of playing at hide-and-go-seek with planters who refused them even a bit of land to scratch a hole in and drove them from furrow to furrow till finally they dropped from exhaustion into the pit of a quarry all pricked round with brambles, which the refugees called Beaufort in memory of Fort Beaufort of the good old days. He told them all that, this messenger from their relations did.

"That's to say you'd be Cormiers from the Pierre-à-Pierre-à-Pierrot branch, perhaps?"

Think of that!

And Hup! Into the cart and off again!

Next day they reached Beaufort and the first of their relatives since Hope Island. Héberts, Douérons, Chiassons, Girouards, Cormiers . . . Could it be true? Praise the Lord, it was true. As true as Célina was standing there, trying to shut up Bélonie who hadn't got out of Port-Royal yet, poor man.

"These folks here are from Beauséjour or thereabouts, old boy, not from Port-Royal."

. . . It's not his fault, he's muddled up.

"From Beauséjour and from Beaubassin, Bélonie, from Beaubassin."

. . . Pay no heed to the old chin-wagger.

Beaubassin? Did Catoune remember Beaubassin now? She came up to the Girouards and began to sniff them. In fifteen years your head may fail you, but not your nose.

"Anybody here among you recall a little slip of a thing from Beaubassin called Catoune?"

All the Girouards looked over at old Charles-à-Charles; if anyone knew, it was him. And Pélagie repeated for Charles-à-Charles: "A creature called Catoune, a foundling, thrown into the schooners, she surely hailed from Beaubassin."

The old man screwed up his cheeks, his forehead, his nose, folding his whole face in round his eyes.

"Caton, that was my poor mother's pet name," said Charles-à-Charles.

Try delving that one back! At least three generations separated Caton from La Catoune. At least. And Pélagie saw that Catoune would never climb back up her family tree.

"Try a mite harder, *grand-père*," said his daughter-in-law. "Time was you were a good delver."

Time was. But back then, Jeanne Aucoin Girouère, everyone was a root-delver. And they delved and cleared the land, too, those good sleek lands between Beaubassin and Tintamarre. Like the ancestor who had delved the basin of Les Mines; the way his sire had Port-Royal.

Jeanne Aucoin shrugged a shoulder and came over to Pélagie. He was dwindling, poor thing. And the more he sunk his feet into the earth, the more ancestors he dug up every day.

There he was all the way back to Port-Royal on a day like today. At that rate he'll soon have no place to go but back to the old country, France.

And Jeanne Aucoin couldn't help confiding to Pélagie Le-Blanc, called the Cart:

"He's loved life so much, old Charles-à-Charles, that before he dies he wants to try to swallow down the life of his whole line in one gulp."

Pélagie felt a lump in her throat hearing her northern neighbor talk this way. And suddenly, without a second thought, and with a wave of her arms that traced loops in the sky that are probably quivering there still:

"Climb aboard!" she says. "Come on back home."

Jean LeBlanc was the first to feel the buffet of her declaration like a northeasterly squall. A single cart, six oxen, a family, plus three Acadie-bound passengers, and his Pélagie of a mother was taking on more?

"Where are we going to bed them down?" he huffed.

"At Beauséjour and Beaubassin, my boy."

And meantime, who lives the longest will see the most.

"Maybe we won't live to see it," says the son, kicking at the shafts.

And turning his temper on his brothers:

"Unyoke the oxen, you slackers Charlécoco. The poor beasts

deserve a day or two in the fields to chew over their fate in peace before they start toiling on again."

Pélagie made a sign to her guests to pay no attention to her son's outburst—a hothead like his late father . . .

"How's that? Your man's passed on?"

All their news was fifteen years out of date at this encounter of Grand-Pré, Beauséjour and Beaubassin in South Carolina. And for days they exchanged their dead and their births and their wanderings and misadventures and even, in secret, their dreams.

"If only you could find a wagon of some kind, and then everyone would take turns walking more often, that's all."

"There's a continent left to cross, Pélagie. I don't know if you know that."

Yes, François-à-Pierre, son of Pierre-à-Pierre-à-Pierrot, hero of Beauséjour and the Great Disruption, she knew it. But she took it in just one day at a time.

"Nothing says we have to empty the whole cup at a gulp."

No, nothing. And François-à-Pierre filled a pipe and passed it round to Bélonie, to Jean, to the twins—who choked generously on the same puff—to all the males in Beaufort huddled that night in the Cormiers' hut, a smiling hut that said to the cart, as in old times, "Make yourselves at home."

And so it was decided that the Cormiers and the Girouards would hook up a wagon to Pélagie's cart and leave for the north too.

"Who do they take themselves for anyways?" said Célina who nevertheless had been, with Jean, the first to protest against this collective departure. "How come one cart's not good enough for the likes of them Héberts, Chiassons, and Douérons? Do they need the whole hold of handsome Lawrence's *Nightingale* to stretch their legs in?"

"Hee! . . ."

"Don't mind the old chin-wagger there," she ended, addressing everyone to unload her bad humor on Bélonie. "At any rate, from here on we'll have two old fogeys to pester us with their phantom cart."

And "Ha!" she went, right under old Charles Girouard's nose, who pretended to pretend not to notice. As if at a certain age you passed the age for pretending.

Not everyone, however, could get into the same cart, Célina, at least not into the same one all at the same time. Some would have to accept a sacrifice. Anyway, the Chiassons and the Douérons were shepherds for a rich American breeder who had thousands of sheep, and they managed to get enough to eat almost every day. As for the Héberts . . .

"What about the Héberts? . . ."

"They've buried half their folks here at Beaufort; maybe the other half has a mind to stay behind to see their graves are flowered on All Saints' Day."

Célina fell silent. And Pélagie was able to complete the count of Beauséjours and Beaubassins who hereafter would be hooked to her cart. A few men, a few more women and—Dear God!— children, for the first time children in Pélagie's cart. Madeleine and Catoune's cheeks shone for it; Charlécoco grumbled a bit for form; then everything settled down.

Almost everything. For there remained the question of Charles-à-Charles.

"Look, father, Bélonie's older than you and there he is as limber as a sapling."

"He's a fir, Bélonie is, he keeps his needles winter and summer. Me, I'm the birch family and my bark's beginning to peel."

But Jeanne Aucoin wasn't going to give in like that. Not this woman who had saved at least a third of the Girouards in the Great Disruption, as much by cunning as by courage. She had used her wiles on Winslow, the second-in-command, and on the soldiers splitting families up indiscriminately. She had used her cunning with the greedy sea that had twice capsized the ship's boat between the schooner and the shore. And each time Jeanne Aucoin, Girouard's woman, had paid her tribute to Destiny.

Destiny! It was old Charles-à-Charles who had lots to say to that rascal. Was he never going to lay his cards on the table? One day, either for or against, but declare himself at last? From the very beginning, from the first sound of the stones cracking in the fire at Fort Beauséjour or in the *aboiteaux* of Memramcook,

Destiny had been hounding the remnants of that earth-soiled, bedraggled people from shore to shore and from island to continent. How much longer was it going to last, this game of hide-and-go-seek?

"Heel . . ."

Charles-à-Charles saw Old Bélonie bring his stool over beside his. And the two ancestors looked each other over without a word. The others left them to confess themselves in peace.

No Bélonie in generations to come would have dared recount this conversation taking place soul-to-soul between two patriarchs playing blindman's buff with Life and Death. Though one day old Louis told me he had his own notion about it, and to judge what it might have been you just had to look at the result.

It came the next day. Charles-à-Charles instructed his daughter-in-law to make ready: Everyone was going back home. Jeanne Aucoin applauded this decision, but with the back of her hand only. She knew the Girouards better than her own father and mother, and she tried to guess with her weasel's nose from which side the contrary winds would begin to blow. She spoke to Pélagie who was drying her lioness's mane in the sun and who had already ordered Charlécoco to put the old man's stool in the cart.

"He wants to see his home again," says Jeanne Aucoin, "but will death tarry so long and so far?"

Pélagie grasped the shoulders of the mistress of Beaufort and laughed aloud to hear her courage ring.

"Death is Bélonie's affair; he drags it after him in that phantom cart of his. But Charles-à-Charles is riding in my cart, and I'll not quit, Jeanne Aucoin, till it falls into pieces the day I need planks to set up a cross on my grave."

Madeleine, Pélagie's daughter, joined in her mother's laughter, and Jeanne Aucoin went back to her hut comforted. Once again she had snatched a Girouard from the claws of Destiny. Once again she had mustered a crooked grin in the face of adversity . . . So—*Alouette, gentille alouette, alouette, je te plumerai* . . .

"Bring out the Jew's harps. We'll play a last farewell to Beaufort. Tomorrow at daybreak we set our course for Acadie-in-the-North."

At daybreak next day they found Charles-à-Charles, who had passed away in the night.

It was a hard blow for Jeanne Aucoin, for all the Girouards and for the rest of Beaufort. It was as if someone had killed old Charles-à-Charles.

"He put himself down," protested Célina the healer, who hadn't even had the leisure to practice her skills, but who knew all about natural death.

No, Célina, didn't put himself down, simply died. To let yourself go to your death isn't killing yourself, not quite. Charles-à-Charles had understood that to reach their home, his kin no longer needed him, to reach home what they needed more was that he . . .

"Shut up, father!"

If there was a person on earth, outside Bélonie, who knew how to speak to the dead, it was Jeanne Aucoin who carried with her in Pélagie's cart more of the dead than the living.

"You shouldn't have done that, Charles-à-Charles, you shouldn't have let yourself go. We could have cared for your legs and fixed up your bowels with yarrow. We could have."

During Jeanne Aucoin's reprimands to the late Charles, Pélagie looked straight and hard into the eyes of Old Bélonie, who hadn't said a word all morning long, not even a "Heel" not even a crease at the corner of his lips. But when she cast her eye on the shroud, she was forced to admit it was Bélonie's smile that played over the face of the corpse. A mite more and the "Heel" itself would have come straight out of Charles-à-Charles's mouth.

. . . Well, well, said Pélagie to herself, a lot of good it did offering to take him along in my cart. A fat lot of good!

And to settle her liver she went off to the fields to check on the oxen.

They were about to depart for the north after the late Charles-à-

Charles had been buried, when one of the Douérons took Jeanne
Aucoin aside, who then came over to speak to Pélagie. The palaver lasted for some time but without raised arms or voices.
Célina would have dearly liked to know why all this whispering
of lacy words instead of shouts of "Hue!" and "Dia!" and at the
very moment that the destiny of her people, in which it seemed
to her she had the right to play a part, was once more on the
move.

A part she would play, despite herself, the old gossip, but in
the destiny of the remains of another settlement, hiding in an almost inaccessible region of Carolina a little further south. In secret, a deserter had reached Beaufort by night and had begged
Antoine Douéron to plead with Pélagie the cause of the survivors of Port-Royal. Pélagie hadn't understood at first why these
deported Acadians were still in hiding after fifteen years, like
savages or wanted men. But little by little the light dawned on
this Port-Royal of South Carolina.

. . . They had come from Port-Royal in the north—Bourgeois,
Thibodeaus, and Légers known as La Rozette—all herded aboard
the *Black Face*, bound for the Caribbee Isles. But in 1755 the islands, and especially the Bahamas, still harbored the memory of
the dreadful golden age of piracy. And for months of heaving
seas the poor deportees down in the hold had fed on the worst
fantasies imaginable, each night dreading attack by Captain
Kidd or Blackbeard, king of pirates. Some claimed Blackbeard
was dead; others feared not. Anyway, dead or alive, if you saw
the demon, you fled. All the ships of the line in the golden days,
even pirate ships, would swear that on dark Caribbean nights
Blackbeard's head appeared all alight, his hair braiding itself,
curling and uncurling before your horrified eyes, and that from
his mouth came tumbling hellish yells in Satan's own tongue.
Such was the vision reported by three-masters and ships that
plied the southern coasts in the first half of the century. And in
1755 the deported Acadians on board the *Black Face* woke with
a start at every seagull's cry and each creak of the mast.

Then one day they were brought up on deck for a gulp of salt
air . . .

Young Thibodeau swallowed a gulp of air himself before telling Pélagie the rest, a gulp of air that gurgled in his gullet like a groan he'd been hoarding up since childhood. He'd been ten at the time of the Incident and only half aware. But all those pirate stories had heated his brain during his months in the hold, and perhaps sharpened his sight too, who knows? What he knew for sure and certain was that with his own eyes he had seen Blackbeard's head floating on the waves off the Pennsylvania coast, a head that right there on the open sea had brazenly gone on spitting fire.

That very day the prisoners of the *Black Face* had sworn on the heads of their forefathers never to set foot on the southern isles but to flee the schooner at the first occasion. They missed their first chance in Virginia, where the ship landed to lay on supplies, but succeeded the second time in Carolina.

"You mean to say whole families have been living there for fifteen years hiding in the briars and bulrushes of the swamps?"

"Not whole, but what's left of them."

Pélagie couldn't believe it.

"But even handsome Lawrence must have given up the ghost and his liver and lights by now. Would it still be Blackbeard you're fleeing from?"

The deserter didn't answer for fear of overstepping his mission, but he turned on Pélagie's face a pair of large sea-blue eyes, eyes that at ten had seen the head of the most monstrous of pirates heave up out of the waves.

Pélagie collected all her breath and called her son Jean, Jeanne Aucoin, the Cormiers, the Girouards, everyone, to come near.

"I reckon I ought to be part of everybody too, no?"

. . . Come on, Célina. Come over all of you.

It was delicate. A real troublesome case of conscience for Pélagie. This time there would have to be general consent. Just like the times of the people's assemblies in Grand-Pré, presided over by an elected patriarch, with the head of every family taking part in decisions. A self-governing people, though they didn't tell anyone else. Today, the head of the LeBlancs was herself, Péla-

gie. But from now on, other clans were grafted onto her own.
They would have to be taken into account, and everyone would
have to be asked to drop his bean in the hat.

François Cormier told Pélagie she had too many scruples, that
the cart was her own chattels, her fief by right of inheritance.

"Not by right of heritage, oh no, bought in hard cash from a
carter by trade who made me no gift of it."

It was her fief at all events, and consequently it was her right
to take on whoever she wanted.

Whoever she wanted . . . But did they have any idea, any of
them, what stuff these deserters were made of, buried for fifteen
years in the depths of the swamps? Just think of it, all of you,
think of this bunch still hiding from Blackbeard or Captain
Kidd! I ask you! And what's more, this Port-Royal was to the
south of them, remember that, and that meant turning around
and retracing their steps again, think of that.

At that, the occupants of the carts stared at the huts of Beaufort. Turn down south again? They'd been going up for months,
thanks to great whacks of the whip on the flanks of the oxen and
great shouts of "Dia!" Were they never, once and for all, to quit
this cursed southern exile and head back home? Pélagie passed
the heads in review and waited. Waited for a puff, a breath of
wind, a movement of air in one direction or the other. And just
as she was about to give up, it was Célina, believe it or not, who
brought in reinforcements.

"I'll go and fire up them oxen myself if they're too slack to
stick their front feet in the tracks of their back ones. If there's a
Port-Royal in the south I'll go and hunt it out, this Port-Royal,
and bring it home, hell or high water. That's what I say."

She needed to reassert her presence in the midst of the cart,
the healer did, ever since the dying had been tactless enough to
die without her professional ministrations. She would make up
for it with the oxen, and with those famished, frazzled, fright-
ened creatures run to earth in a so-called Port-Royal, who were
surely more dead than alive after half a generation in the wilderness. Giddap there, you slouchers, we're heading south! Somebody needs a witch down there.

Pélagie couldn't hold back the chuckle that tickled her gullet. After all, she said to herself, maybe the cripple's got more feelings than she lets on.

Maybe. But if the cripple had been able to guess the kind of wild game that awaited them there in the south, she'd have held her feelings in check. You can take Louis's word for it, Louis son of Bélonie, son of Louis, son of Bélonie, right back to the first-of-the-name who had witnessed in person the explosion to follow.

So there were Légers and Thibodeaus and Bourgeois . . .

That crowd!

. . . all stout artisans and peasants from Port-Royal in Acadie whom the English schooners had snatched away with the others on the morning of the Great Disruption. And more than the others they had suffered a misfortune they would drag after them all their lives long, these survivors from the *Black Face*. It was a Léger known as La Rozette who told the storyteller Bélonie and the crew of the cart the fate of the ship that had been their prison.

. . . In a harbor in Carolina at the mouth of the Coosawhatchie . . .

"The what?"

. . . the Coosawhatchie, a kind of river that winds inland flooding the marshes and making them uninhabitable. At the mouth of the river the schooner had landed.

"That's good."

. . . The first thing the captain did was check the prisoners' shackles, for they had already tried to escape in Virginia, he remembered that, and they weren't to be trusted, these Acadians who knew the ways of the sea, no, you couldn't trust them.

"He was right there."

. . . then for one night he let ashore his crew of grumblers inclined to mutiny. And as for the captain, he took the precaution of locking himself in the fo'c'sle cabin to down his grog in peace.

"The pig!"

. . . What he didn't know was that the Thibodeaus, from fa-

ther to son, were the most solid, skillful blacksmiths in the whole
of Acadie.

"Ah ha!"

. . . Yes indeed, from the first of the line that came from the
Seigneury of Aulnay, those Thibodeaus had passed on the
smith's trade like one passes on a silver goblet, from heir to heir.
Well then, if you think a blacksmith who's spent his life breaking
iron shoes for horses and oxen wouldn't know how, in one night,
to break the irons of his brothers and countrymen, prisoners of
the English . . .

"Aaaah!"

"And we got the women and children up out of the hold first.
Then, before leaving the deck, we struck two stones together and
set fire to a bit of cord that ran into the powder magazine right
under the fo'c'sle."

" . . . "

The storyteller fell silent too. For the rest of the story had a
hard time passing his gullet. He stammered out splinters of images that had stuck in all of their memories during the long years
in the marshes . . . images of a ship cracking up, then bursting
into flames, then spitting barrels of fire into the masts . . . and
then this image: a living torch, a captain running across the broken deck, holding in his hands the head of Blackbeard, blazing
like a brazier . . .

" . . . "

When the cart could catch their breath again, they let the last
flames die down in the eyes of the storyteller, who then rushed
on with the rest: a price put on the Acadians' heads; their names
posted in every town and village in Carolina; the manhunt up
and down the length of the river, for months . . . for years.

It was high time, thought Pélagie, that this southern Port-
Royal should return to the north and turn the page of exile.

3

A chest now! What next?

Wait a minute, let's not exaggerate. Silver goblets, linen sheets, and a chest? I ask you! Were they going to lug a hardwood chest filled with the scraps of 1755 all the way back to Port-Royal and Grand-Pré? Célina stuck her oar in:

"I left all my pots and pans behind, the whole kit. I'm leaving the south with a full heart but with empty pockets, except for my missal. So that means, ditch it."

Not likely! The Bourgeois hadn't managed to camouflage their chest in the hold of an English schooner for months, then unload it by night, that famous night! then carry it from boat to skiff to raft, right into the middle of the marsh, just to end up leaving it as a legacy to those slackers who didn't even have the courage to take on the journey back.

. . . The flabby-assed who? Who weren't going back? Which of the Bourgeois were staying behind?

"All the more reason. If nobody's staying behind, we aren't leaving that chest to no one at all."

The chest was a family heirloom that would go with the Bourgeois up hill and down dale, till death did them part.

"That's just it—down! I left my best eiderdown in the land of exile. So when it comes to your chests . . ."

Pacifique and Jeanne Bourgeois plumped down on the chest and refused to speak another word. And the chest left for the north with this people on the march.

They had been marching north, rolling their cart and its caravan over all the stones in America for months, when one morning little Frédéric Cormier woke up, his forehead hot and his belly in pain. He was no mother's darling either, why even yesterday he had climbed into a wild cherry tree, the scamp, and had shaken every branch. Madeleine, Catoune, Charlécoco, and the young recruits from Port-Royal and Beaufort had celebrated the feast of Saint-Jean with chokecherry juice and had crowned Pélagie's Jean and the two Jeannes with dunce caps.

> *Et j'ai du grain de mil*
> *et j'ai du grain de paille*
> *et j'ai de l'oranger*
> *et j'ai du tri*
> *et j'ai du tricoli*
> *et j'ai des allumettes*
> *et j'ai des ananas*
> *j'ai de beaux, j'ai de beaux*
> *j'ai de beaux oiseaux . . .*

"Ah, what lovely youngsters they are!" Jeanne Aucoin had burst out with a laugh, pinching her man's arm.

Alban Girouard wasn't, in fact, quite her man, at least not quite according to the laws and rites of the sacraments. Her true man, Alexandre, had perished in the Disruption, and his widow hadn't wished to abandon to its misery a family she had married into before God and his Church. So eventually she had taken as

legitimate husband her own brother-in-law, a legitimacy of cir-
cumstance that meant she was deprived of both dispensation and
the sacraments. The important thing, as Jeanne Aucoin put it,
was to give Charles-à-Charles a descendance in the male line
and not let the name of Girouard—which backward cousins still
pronounced Giroué—be snuffed out. So that's what Jeanne Aucoin did and she hadn't much to complain of, for taken all in all
Alban Girouard . . .

And this time she pinched her man's thigh.

At the child's first moan Célina had taken off across the fields.
The little chap wasn't suffering from smallpox or epilepsy, or
mumps. It was the belly.

"Too many cherries last night, just like I said, and chokecherries into the bargain. Ah! these kids today! In my time . . ."

But what use of talking about her time to the birds in the
trees! What use talking at all? Nobody in this new age believed
in anything anymore. Why take that good-looking Jeanne, for instance. No sooner widowed of her man than she beds down with
her own brother-in-law, without the blessing or dispensation of
the Church.

Is that Christian, that?

And what about those Blanchards and Roys from Hope Island
who went and had their children's wedding blessed by a Protes-
tant pastor! Did you ever see the like? And yet they were honest
folk, all of them, who in the old days only agreed to take the
oath of allegiance to the King of England on condition they keep
their religion.

"And what's the use of a deportation, in the name of the faith,
if you go get baptized by Luther or Calvin?"

My cousin, Louis-à-Bélonie, gave me to understand he'd have
had plenty to say to Célina on that score, but . . .

. . . At any rate that wouldn't have stopped Célina from grous-
ing or from going on collecting her plants to plaster on the belly
of the sick child.

And he got sicker and sicker, little Frédéric. Catoune and
Madeleine went wild over it and hung round the Beaufort clan,
who just waited in silence. The healer had a wide reputation;

she'd already cured throat goiter and even congestion of the lungs.

"And when Pierre-à-Télésphore almost passed on from shortness of breath . . ."

"Here's Célina!"

No, it wasn't Célina but a stranger coming out of the bushes at the edge of the woods, covered in an old cape and shod in moccasins, bareheaded like a madwoman or a witch . . . more like a witch. Don't budge anyone, she's shouting something, listen and shut up . . .

"That's not English anyway."

"What would you know about it?"

She came closer, waving her arms.

"Friend or foe . . ." and the rest was lost in the cries of the crows flying in circles round their heads.

Pélagie stepped forward.

"Who are you?"

A Scotswoman who lived far back in the hills, bone-setter and fortune-teller by trade, who also from time to time served as guide through these forests infested by brigands who by night attacked the caravans from Carolina or Virginia.

François Cormier explained to the stranger that they were neither Virginians nor from Carolina but Acadians deported south by accident, now peaceably going back home.

. . . As peacefully as you please, but if someone knew what to expect of the outlaws, it was surely one who bound their wounds in her shack at the edge of the wood.

"In times of trouble," said she, "no one bothers to check out the intentions or circumcisions of passersby. Go round the forest."

A painful cry escaped the belly of the little Cormier. The Scotswoman cocked an eyebrow and drew nearer.

Marie Cormier, his mother, hastened to explain that it was the cherries, only the cherries, chokecherries they were, it would pass, a little colic, and besides, Célina was coming back soon with senna and yarrow and you'll see . . . it's nothing . . . is it? . . .

The stranger and bone-setter turned from mother to child. She

concentrated, babbled some words from her Scottish mountains
and began to search the bushes, feeling along the ground.

Suddenly Marie Cormier's eyes grew round and she perked up
her ears . . . Stop that noise, stop it, those cartwheels creaking,
stop them, the child is sick . . . stop that noise of axles turning
. . . No, Marie, the cart's not moving, you're hearing things, no
one is moving . . . Yes, yes, I hear them, be quiet, I hear the
axles, the whip . . . stop them! . . . Oh where is Célina? For the
love of God, Célina! . . . Stop the cart! . . . But where is it?
Over there, over there, no to the left, very close, very close . . .
Stop!

When Célina came back weighted down under her bundle of
herbs, the child was dead and the healer dropped her plants
back to the ground.

"It's no easy thing," she said, "to know senna and wood tea in
another's country; it's high time we got back home."

And the whole cartload knelt on the Carolina earth and sent
up a litany for the dead.

All of a sudden Célina noticed the stranger standing apart and
registered with alarm:

"Where's she sprang up from, that one?"

But already the Scotswoman had drawn the child's father off
to the field and was showing him the place to dig. In times of ep-
idemic you mustn't wait to bury the dead.

. . . Even without a ceremony?

For fifteen years they'd been burying their dead without ceremony and they weren't used to it yet. And each time, they took
up the same litany:

"Are we to bury him without sacraments?"

"Is there still no one to bless his tomb at least?"

"Not a priest or a man of God to pave his way to paradise?"

"Even the dead have lost their rights. Even the dead are without Church or country."

Marie Cormier moaned, staring at the cart standing immobile
by the oxen. It stood quiet, this one did, no longer creaking its
axles. But hadn't it moved at all during the child's agony? It was
the other, Bélonie's cart, that had snatched one more child from

life. And instinctively she turned toward the old man and looked
him full in the face.

Pélagie saw her movement and stepped in.

"Come on," she said, "come loosen your legs a bit, Bélonie.
You're not trotting around enough nowadays."

And taking the old man by the arm she led him to the top of
the field. When they were alone, the two of them, Pélagie let fall
from her heart:

"So! Your faithful companion of man is taking after children
now, your Harvester, your Grim Reaper?"

Bélonie nodded and didn't reply. She might have known,
though, this Pélagie, widow of the Great Disruption, that life
spares neither man nor nation, and to grow one has to leave
one's childhood skin behind.

Pélagie gritted her teeth.

"No, Bélonie, no parables. That's not the childhood of our
people lying there in the wild hay; it's little Frédéric who only
yesterday was climbing trees and eating chokeberries and singing *J'ai du grain de mil* and turning his blue eyes on the line of
the horizon seeking a land he will never know. That's what the
Reaper took and tossed into the back of her filthy cart!"

And lowering her voice she added hoarsely:

"Does it please you to hear the creak of the wheels of that
damned cart of yours?"

Bélonie would have had lots to say on that score. Did Pélagie
know, at least, where the cart came from and the face of its
driver? Could she imagine for a single instant what kind of a
world this world would be without the coming and going of that
Wagon of Death, which of all the scales that weighed the rights
of men and nations from the beginning of time was the only just
and equitable instrument? One day it would pick up hangman
Lawrence and his dogs Winslow, Murray, and Monckton, even
though they'd believed, one night of September 1755, that with
the last flames of the church of Saint-Charles at Grand-Pré the
breath of a people had been extinguished. Without the cart
creaking up to the great as to the small, to the gates of the

wealthy as to the gates of the needy, who would restore the balance and prevent the world from swinging wild?

Pélagie would have none of it:

"And you think death doesn't set him swinging wild, the one she takes under her wing?"

. . . Sooner or later one tires of life.

"A child of eight hasn't had time yet to taste disgust; life hasn't had time to sour him yet."

Bélonie turned round to make sure his cart wasn't too far behind. For fifteen years it had followed him with all his kin aboard, three generations swept up in a single wave off Île Royale. And among them a child of eight like Frédéric, and another scarcely born, still wailing in swaddling bands, a child who bore the name of the forefather, Bélonie.

"And can you take that?" says Pélagie. "Do you find that just?"

. . . Just? And what is just? Grubbing your childhood away in a land of exile perhaps, slave and beggar, forgetting the land of one's fathers, one's roots cut off at the knee? What is just? For the four thousand years that the world has been humping its sack, how many generations stretch between Adam, Abraham, Moses, and the first of the Bélonies, issue of a certain Jacques-à-Antoine who sailed from France in the middle of the last century? And all those had been lost, gone down with parents and cousins and kindred, leaving the world to others, who would be lost in turn. That's what it was, the fate of the world, a sharing between living and dead, but by many more dead than living. Why not accept it and grant each his place?

"The place for the dead is in the ground. I won't have them dragging along with the living."

. . . The place for the dead is in the memory of the living, Pélagie. That's why you're heading back home.

"I'm headed home for those who are left, for our children and those who will spring from our children's children. And one day, in our ancestors' land, a Pélagie will say to one of your Bélonie descendants . . ."

Pélagie choked on the last word, for as to descendants it seems that Bélonie . . .

Pélagie-the-Grouch served up the whole sentence a century later to Bélonie's descendant:

"So it seems you sprang from the wrong cart, eh?"

"Hee!" . . .

Pélagie heard from afar the high-pitched voice of Célina and the grumbling of the men. It sounded very much like squabbling around the cart; it was time to put a halt to it.

"What's this charivari? Have you no respect for the dead now?"

Quite the contrary, it was out of respect for the dead that they were attacking the Bourgeois who were still being mulish about their chest and refused to give it up for the mortal remains of the child.

"They'd rather see the little chap go all naked into the grave, the gutless bunch."

Pélagie recognized Célina's guts in that way of foisting the blame on others. Come on now, come on! What next?

But it was a good-for-nothing Girouard who cut in next, accusing the Bourgeois of loading Pélagie's cart with the wherewithal to rebuild Jerusalem.

The Bourgeois got the wind up:

"And since when did Jerusalem fall apart?"

"Just listen to that! Just listen! They'd even refuse the dead a winding sheet."

"And why our chest? Why not your bread-bin, you Giroués?"

"On account of because we don't have no bread-bin, whilst you've got a chest."

"You've got other stuff. And you're hanging on to it."

Alban-à-Charles-à-Charles sneered:

"You can't very well bury a kid in a piss-pot."

Whoa! Pélagie judged that was enough blasphemy for the day of a funeral and brought the butt of her whip between the Bourgeois and the others.

"That'll do!"

. . . Didn't they have enough to do to reconquer a country and a home without already beginning to haggle over the furniture? And was it a commode they were squabbling over now or a cupboard?

A chest, was it? And so what? If the Giroués or even Célina needed a chest all that bad, all they had to do was carve themselves one out of a bird's-eye maple with a plane or a pocket knife like the Bourgeois had and say no more about it. And as for burying the child in it, out of the question; the Cormiers themselves were against it. Could you see that? Under the parents' own eyes shoving the little Frédéric into the corner of a chest they had trailed with them all the way from Port-Royal in the south? Besides, they weren't beggars, the Cormiers weren't, they'd never coveted their neighbors' goods. So let Célina and the Girouards take a lesson from that.

They took their lesson, grumbling a couple of hours for form and to save face, and finally simmering down. And then they were able to bury the child to the strains of nothing more than the *Dies irae*.

. . . No, not just to the *Dies irae* but to a chant improvised by Catoune, too; a chant that blended words and melodies the like of which the cart had never heard before. A recitative of nothing but meaningless words but one that soothed the soul of bruised and amputated Acadie. Attentive to Catoune's song, Pélagie seemed to understand and even accept the fate of this people called upon to sow the whole coast of America with its living seed.

It was Jeanne Aucoin who first caught sight of the Bastarache gang. They approached, the whole tribe of them, hauling a two-wheeled cart heaped up with straw pallets, callithumpian clothes, and a collection of kitchen utensils as battered as their hats. They were bohemian refugees who had crept out of the nearby forest where the Scots sorceress had gone to dig them out. She had often seen them between the trees, camping like gypsies, living off the hunt, from petty larcenies and whatever

the wind blew in. Ten more years and the Bastaraches would
have returned to the savage state, like bears or wildcats.

"Like our forefathers the Basques," said one of them, François-à-Philippe, with a flourish, "we've centuries of closeness to
the woods and seas. That's why that plundering wind that fell on
our ship couldn't drown us. We've sea legs from father to son
and we know how to fool the waves and skip hale and hearty
through the teeth of the hurricane."

And then Jeanne Aucoin informed them of the misfortune that
had just struck the Cormier family, and the Bastaraches in their
fashion joined the lamentations of the cart: on the violin.

A violin! Would you believe it! The only one to come through
the Great Disruption. A violin in pure white ash, more than a
century old and passed down in heritage to the Basques from
their ancestors of Fort Lajoie on Île Saint-Jean.

A fine island it was, all in red clay, its edges torn into creeks
and bays as if the whales from bygone times had bitten big
mouthfuls out of its coastline. Whales that even today made free
to come and piss their fountainlike jets right up to the shore.
Like the porpoises, for that matter, and walrus and sea cows.
And for the folk of the cart the Basques delved back their ancestral line of sailors and walrus hunters who for centuries had provided Europe with ivory.

"Just go dig up the skeletons of sea cows in the shallows of the
isles and you'll see for yourselves they've no horns on their
chins."

In the shallows of the Îles de la Madeleine, as of Île Saint-
Jean, the animals used to beach themselves to calve. Today these
shallows were sea cow cemeteries. The Basques alone had almost exterminated them. So after that they'd gone back home to
the old country, all except one named Joannes Bastarache,
known as the Basque, who settled on the mainland in a bay
called Shediac.

"And weren't you dug out and deported by the English
schooners with the rest?"

"Deported, yes, twice," admitted François-à-Philippe-à-Juan,
"but not destroyed. It's no easy thing to wipe out a race of ad-

venturers used to the way the ice shifts with the tide. We learned in time to skip from one island to the next, to cross the straits, to keep our heads out of water and thumb our noses at the barbarians who tried to drown us, and play peek-a-boo with them!"

And with a belly laugh the Basque added:

"You can't cut off the breath of him who keeps it inside; nay, and you can't get the life away from him who hugs it close."

The Bastaraches saw the Cormiers hang their heads and hastened to take up their funeral air on the violin.

The Scotswoman raised her nose and sniffed. With a gesture she cut short the violin and ordered the whole of the cart, large and small, to stand round the wooden cross.

"Say nothing," she warned. "Act like nothing was up."

But the sorceress couldn't mask the grave from the eyes of the planter inspecting his fields.

"What is it?"

What were they doing there, the marauders? And that hole in the ground, in his field? All the country around was his. Who had dared dig here? Who dared bury their carrion in his land?

The Cormiers huddled together. But Pélagie and the Bastaraches stood their ground. And the Scotswoman declared to the planter in English that they had just buried an eight-year-old child.

The planter squinted a little but held firm. No one had a right to his fields, living or dead.

Pélagie stepped up to within a foot of the master of the cotton fields. They had buried a little boy called Frédéric under the eyes of his mother and family, a child who had died in a day from inflammation of the bowels . . .

"It's not catching," put in Célina.

. . . He was no longer a danger to anyone, poor thing, and they could neither abandon him to the crows and vultures, nor carry him in the cart of the living. They were going to leave him there in the place God had struck him down, the planter could fix his price.

And fix it he did, the skinflint, after closely examining the cart and its caravan. And to pay that planter, who had surprised them digging in his fallow fields, for six feet of ground, the Cormiers had to give up the last souvenir they had brought from Fort Beauséjour: the cartridge pouch that had belonged to none other than ancestor Pierre-à-Pierre-à-Pierrot, hero of 1755.

"We won't forget your weedy fields!" broke out Célina the Clubfoot, shaking a scrawny fist under the nose of the planter booted to the knee.

The Cormier clan, at any rate, would never forget.

"Some day," one of their kids swore between his teeth, "I'll come back for grandfather's cartridges. But maybe I'll leave one of them in the ground in the cotton planter's fields."

Pélagie looked with tenderness and compassion at the young Cormier. Poor child! If the heroes of Beauséjour hadn't been able to defend a people ten times as numerous as their attackers, how could a single cartridge in the heart of English America give Acadie back its soul?

As a country it had become more and more absurd after the surrender of Louisbourg and the defeat of the Plains of Abraham. It was dead, poor thing, buried with a low mass and struck from the map of the world. Well may you dance up there in the north round the embers of a country that had blazed to the sky one September morn. Yes, dance and sing and recite the dirge of the dead between six candles and the crucifix.

But during that joyous funeral feast for Acadie-in-the-North, joyfully toasted by Lawrence and Wilson and Monckton and King George in all his joyous majesty, the tatters of Acadie-in-the-South were moving upward; hangdog, snorting, sweating, puffing from both nostrils, moving up across an America that didn't even hear the creak of the axles of the cart.

4

PROPERTY OF THE PUBLIC LIBRARY ST. MARYS, ONT.

The day after little Frédéric's burial when the convoy was on the point of starting out again on its march north, diminished by one child but swelled by the whole Bastarache tribe, the Scottish sorceress in place of adieu gave Pélagie a large basket of provisions she had stolen from the brigands bivouacked in the woods. And when the cart went to open the basket at their first camp, what did they find but Pierre-à-Pierre-à-Pierrot's cartridge pouch lying between the cabbages and the potatoes.

"Hey, hey! What a good fortune-teller! Never try to tell me all the angels are in heaven."

"Angels, you say? To my way of thinking it's a funny sort of sorceress who's given to this kind of sorcery. As for me, I wouldn't be surprised one day to find the master of the cotton fields stretched out stone cold across our route."

. . . But she was a sorceress for sure just the same, a reader of the left hand who predicted to Maxime Bastarache and to Jean, Pélagie's son, the two proudest young blades of the troop, that

dangerous and gallant adventures awaited them both. And from
that day forward the two young males went around sniffing the
wind like dogs in heat . . . François-à-Philippe slapped his
thighs in amusement at his son's friskiness and even came to
Pélagie to propose a small detour to the right, toward the sea,
just to give a little fun to the hightailed youths.

Pélagie gave a start and Célina clapped her hands to her head.
What sort of debauchery had the convoy let itself in for now?
Were these Basques looking for a country, or a promenade
across the land of America, part holiday and part carnival? What
with their violin and their folderols . . . But Pélagie had to
admit with the shade of a grin that since the Basques had come
the violin had drowned out the creaking of the cart. And Mother
Pélagie cast a sly look in the direction of Old Bélonie. She had
opted for life, that was firm. Well, with life you could also count
on love and the generations below.

. . . Yes, Bélonie, life was also *la joie de vivre*.

Heel . . . What will you come up with next? If you think all
those sentiments belong in the same basket! If there's a man in
this world could speak to you about life it was certainly one
who'd carried it around under his skin for well nigh a century.
He was born in 1680 or thereabouts, Bélonie son of Jacques, descendant of Antoine, day laborer in Paris under Louis XIII. The
old chin-wagging, storytelling chronicler hadn't forgotten a
word of the family history of his ancestors or his descendants.
He could roll you out the whole lineage without dropping a
stitch. He could crochet you in a trice the history of a people
who went from France to Acadie passing through exile, one little
generation of exile, one wee little generation, Pélagie, nothing to
get overheated about. Go on up, go on back up north, but don't
get so agitated, and don't go kicking so hard against Destiny,
who'll always get the upper hand anyway.

Look!

And Pélagie lifted her eyes from the edge of the brook spilling
over the stones and saw her son Jeannot and handsome Maxime
Basque wrestling.

"Jean!" she shouted at the top of her lungs.

And she rushed over to the fighters.

Once again François-à-Philippe came over to speak to Pélagie. And Célina and Jeanne Aucoin too. Everyone had his version. Maxime had started it, that much was sure and certain. Alban had seen him, and Jeanne Aucoin had spread the word. But there's never smoke without fire, and the Basque hadn't got so steamed up in the head and tripes over nothing.

"And what if someone did that to you?"

"Let him try!"

"Seems you're not quite the spring chicken you used to be."

"Oh! There's them here has their tongue hung up too close to their palate, I'd say. Ought to rest it a little."

"And there's others who've got no tongue whatsoever, but a serpent lurking in there behind their throat-dangler."

"And I've heard say that certain folks I know of, one day a thunderclap fell on their backs and turned into stone and got lodged 'twixt their gullet and their gut in place of a heart."

"Old bag!"

"Big gawk!"

"Church mouse!"

"You step on my toes and you'll hear about it!"

"To step on your toes, you'd need a foot at the end of your leg, not a hoof."

Pélagie stepped straight into the middle of the circle and with one toss of her head reduced everyone to silence.

"The first one who opens his mouth will have to deal with me," says she. "You, Célina, shut up and speak out: Who started this and about what?"

Célina clenched her lips and was silent.

Very well. Then we'll begin with the Bourgeois. But the old maid cut short the first word to come out of a Bourgeois mouth and in a single breath supplied all the details of the fight. This account was contradicted on the spot by the Bourgeois, upheld by the Girouards, countered by the Thibodeaus, and confirmed by the Bastaraches who didn't believe a word of it because they hadn't even understood the question. Meantime, Jean and Max-

ime, forgotten and left to themselves, had quietly started up
fighting again just to make a clean breast of it.

Because their hearts were still so troubled, poor things, they
hadn't understood the sense of the Scotswoman's prophecy. So
for weeks they had been combing the four horizons expecting
the promised beauty to appear, while all the time the beauty had
been sitting right within the confines of the cart. And as luck
would have it, the two love-struck boys first noticed her at exactly the same moment.

Jeanne Aucoin went so far as to maintain that alone, and without the spur of rivalry, neither would have fallen head over heels
in love with La Catoune, and that in the circumstances jealousy
had antedated love. It must be said that on this subject Jeanne
Aucoin la Girouère was better informed than anyone else in the
cart.

In a manner of speaking.

However that may be, from that day on Pélagie had a new
thorn in her side. The world of the cart and its carts was really
too narrow to hold two such high-hackled young moose. She
consulted the Bastarache clan.

"Should head for the sea," repeated François-à-Philippe-à-
Juan.

The sea! How could he think of it! They'd already lost months
in detours and forced halts. How much longer before Grand-
Pré? Already two deaths, and the voyage had hardly begun.

"Speak to your boy, François-à-Philippe Basque. I'll see to
mine."

So they spoke to the two fired-up youths, each on their own
side of the oxen.

During the skirmish no one had seriously thought about La
Catoune. Since her birth the poor girl had defended herself as
best she could without counting much on others. Except on Pélagie. And once again it was on Pélagie that she turned her two
wide-staring eyes.

And Pélagie understood.

La Catoune was one of the war-wounded, her soul bloodied
with memories stuck to the skin of a childhood tossed in the

holds of the English ships, and as one of the war-wounded she
had a right to indemnity. She, Pélagie, would stand her guar-
antee.

But she had a hard time of it, for the young suitors didn't seem
ready to understand such language. Catoune was so beautiful, so
white, so immaculate. The fluttering hairs that strayed from her
cap sent lightning flashes into the southern wind, which set their
hearts and thighs atremble. And again they locked horns like
young bulls.

One of the Bourgeois drew Pélagie aside. He whispered. She
leaned closer. He muttered a little louder. She checked and
started.

"Never on your life!"

"And yet . . ."

"I said never. And I won't hear another word."

The Bourgeois shied off, went "Hmph!" said no more.

And Pélagie saved Catoune.

What a business! It would take a Bourgeois! A Bourgeois who
hadn't consented to surrender a chest, a souvenir from home, but
who had just calmly proposed to Pélagie to drop young Catoune
overboard, Catoune the last twig of the race. Could you believe
it!

And Pélagie spit in disgust.

. . . Yes, to be sure, she was the fifth wheel on the coach, Catoune was, and then what? Who in the cart would dare claim to
be the first? Or the second? Mother Pélagie had left Hope Island
with only her family, plus a couple of rejects of countrymen to
deliver back home. Since then, Georgia and South Carolina had
each day tossed her way other bits of family flotsam, each expecting to be returned home: the cripples, the aged, the whiners,
the loudmouths, the hunted, and the abandoned. Who'd be so
bold as to sort all that out and deal everyone his share? A people
isn't an infantry regiment. It doesn't know how to keep step.

"And I'd like to know the scalawag could tell me who's to be
first to pass from one cart to the next . . ."

Once again Bélonie cracked his candid, beyond-the-tomb grin.

Pélagie saw that for the common good it was best to avoid this particular dead end, so to sidetrack Old Bélonie,

"Tell us one of your joyful tales," she proposed.

So for a joyful tale Bélonie launched into the story of the White Whale.

Célina grumbled that she knew lots more joyful stories than that, but it wasn't up to her, a mere midwife, to get mixed up in what didn't concern her, so the old chin-wagger was free to tell the tale of Adam and Eve if he had a mind to, or the shipwreck of Noah's Ark, or the story of the giantess's labor that brought into the world, besides her baby giant, a string of six teams of draft oxen and a cartload of fodder in the year of our Lord . . .

"Hush! He's about to begin."

Célina held her tongue but finished her sentence just the same with a concerted shake of her head that showered exactly what she thought on Bélonie and the rest of humanity.

After which Bélonie took the time to clear the rust from his throat, to draw his stool to the fire that Pélagie's Jean was tending, to ask the company's permission to begin, and to enter into his trance:

> Now here's a tale that came
> Straight from my family tree
> From forbears lost in time
> Until they came to me.
> If you think it isn't so
> Just sit thee down and see.

And everyone stared at Bélonie who stared at the horizon.

. . . There once was a poor peasant who had nothing in the world but a white hen who laid him an egg every day. One evening, being very hungry, he began to hem and haw and tell himself that maybe he should eat the hen without further ado.

"Poor me," says he to himself, "if I eat the hen, then what shall I eat tomorrow?"

So once again he contented himself to eat his egg. But in his

haste to swallow the egg, didn't he strike his tooth on a yolk that
was harder than most. That surprised him, and he spit it out.
And instead of a yolk, if you please, he found a golden ring.

So here's our peasant amazed, overjoyed, and already counting
his fortune made.

"Tomorrow for sure," says he, "I'll go to the king and we'll see
what I can make of it."

That same evening, happy as a lark, with the ring clutched in
his fist, he goes out to feed the hen.

"Look," he says, "look what was buried in the heart of your
egg."

But so saying he drops the golden ring and no sooner done
than the hen gobbles it up with the millet.

"Wretch!" he howls, "give me back my golden ring."

And he jumps on the hen to wring its neck. But the chicken
squawks and flies into the woods carrying off her master's fortune.

"There's only one thing left to do," says the peasant. "I'll set
off in quest of my hen."

So he starts off into the woods. He walks for three days and
three nights till finally he meets a white fox sitting on his tail and
licking his chops.

"Now here's someone who can maybe tell me where my hen
is," says he.

But that very instant the fox lets out a burp and white feathers
drift up into the wind.

"Devil!" he shouts. "Give me back my hen who swallowed my
golden ring."

And he jumps on the fox to wring its neck. But with a laugh
the cunning fox takes off into the forest.

"Well then, I'll set off in quest of the fox," says he.

And he plunges into the thick of the forest. He walks for three
days and three nights till finally he comes on a white bear sitting
on his haunches and rubbing his paunch.

"I'll inquire of this fellow if he hasn't seen the fox," says he.

But that very instant the bear lets out a fart and wisps of
white fur drift up into the wind.

"Rascal!" he roars. "Give me back my fox who ate my hen who swallowed my golden ring."

And he jumps on the bear to wring its neck. But with never a word the bear climbs into a tree and from branch to branch escapes into the forest.

"So now I'll set off in quest of the bear," says the peasant.

And he gropes between the trees, feeling his way. He walks for three days and three nights. And one morning he arrives at the edge of the sea. And there he sees a white whale yawning in the sun with its jaws wide open.

"Maybe the whale has seen the bear," he says. "I'll inquire."

But that very instant the whale pisses a jet of water out of its nostrils that falls down full of long white hairs.

"Vile beast!" he bawls. "Give me back my bear who devoured my fox who ate my hen who swallowed my golden ring!"

And he was just about to jump on the whale to wring its neck when he changed his mind, because of the fact, as he noticed, that a whale doesn't have any neck. So then the peasant sat down on a rock and began to hem and haw.

. . . And he hemmed and he hawed, and he hawed and he hemmed . . .

Pélagie cocks an eye. She has just counted over the cart. Catoune is missing. She gets up quickly. Célina and Jeanne Aucoin see her move, both at the same time. Then the rivals, Jean and Maxime.

"What's going on?"

One by one all the heads pull out of the tale, leaving storyteller Bélonie to slow down his phrases, brake, then cast three or four points of suspension out into the waiting air, before lowering his eyes to his audience who are already busily dashing hither and thither.

"She was right there at the fireside."

"Who saw her last?"

"What could have got into her?"

"Let's start up a search party."

"Ca — tou — ne!"

No more Catoune, disappeared, took off like the hen, the fox, and the white bear.

The sea!

Catoune must have made for the sea. She must have heard the suggestion made by François-à-Philippe-à-Juan.

Pélagie roused the oxen and the carts.

"If we leave right now maybe we'll have a chance to catch her."

The Bourgeois and the Girouards, however, came round to remind her that it was practically night and that there were children and cripples aboard.

Feeling herself in the line of fire, Célina took Pélagie's side once again.

"If anyone here is ascared of the hobbity-goblins, they just have to pull their bonnets down over their eyes and they won't see nothing. I'll lead the march myself."

The men snickered, the women shook their heads, and everybody made ready for a night departure.

"Everyone stick to the carts," Pélagie called. "We've enough on our hands hunting one in the dark."

In the end it was Jean and Maxime who took the lead, from time to time answering Pélagie's "Hue-Ho!" that rang out to them in the night.

And so it was that after three days Pélagie's cart entered Charleston.

Charleston was already a populous, bustling town in those days, and it had seen many others. The haunt of pirates, adventurers, hucksters, and false prophets, it had seen half Carolina and part of Virginia come ashore at its port. The strident streets of this town a century and a half old would hardly have noticed a caravan of deported Acadians looking for a lost child.

Yet take notice it did.

It was market day in Charleston when Pélagie drove her cart through—slave market day. Blacks, mainly blacks, a few mulattos, and here and there a poor white putting himself up for sale for a bowlful of corn. In their fifteen years in the Southern

Colonies, Pélagie and her crew had never seen a real slave market and their eyes were agog.

"What is it?" inquired Madeleine.

"It's nothing, don't look, nobody look," said Pélagie, her eyes fixed on the platform and its file of blacks, young, old, sickly, scrawny, strong.

"Come on, let's go."

But nobody moved, as if the oxen themselves were transfixed, unable to lift the weight of their iron shoes. The parade continued: women, men, children, linked by chains, their great white eyes staring above the Charleston crowd that was cooing like pigeons in a public square.

"Like a flock of chickens, you mean."

And Jean gave a hearty kick at a tower of empty crates that came tumbling down around his ears.

Now you could see the aged dragging themselves up on the platform to the muted murmur of onlooking Charleston, noses in the air.

"Make your price!"

"One guinea!"

"This man has muscles and two strong legs!"

"Two pence!"

Two sous for a man? It was time to sneak away. Those merchants could sell anything, anyone. Let no one fall into their clutches. Let's go.

But they didn't have time. The cart had barely shifted its shafts when it was nailed to the spot. There on the platform mounting after the aged blacks was a young white, hair fluttering in the wind.

"Catoune!"

The cry sprang in a single breath from all the throats of this little fragment of Acadie that Destiny this day had led to the sea.

Catoune, Catoune the little savage, the orphan, the waif of the north, had strayed into the midst of a continent that had confounded her with animals and put her up for sale in the market. The whole of Acadie stood there with open mouths and terrified eyes.

Suddenly the wheels began to groan and the racks to shudder in the wind. It was Pélagie who had seized the reins and was whipping the oxen. The caravan of carts drove into the crowd, heedless of the pyramids of pineapples and cauliflower and ears of corn, without respect for the counters of spices and oriental silks. All Charleston was no more than a platform, a stage across which the slaves of America paraded, amongst them Catoune.

"Hue-Ho, the oxen! Hue-Ho!"

Taken by surprise, old Charleston didn't catch up to the carts until two or three blocks farther on, just about in front of the prison. And the prison swallowed them up in a mouthful. But the crew was complete, Catoune included.

At least there was that to it.

Better than that. In the hurly-burly they had even acquired a Negro.

A what?

Why, yes, don't you see? Look here! Catoune had her two wrists chained to a stake, and in his haste and ardor Jean hadn't taken the time to free her but had carried off both together. It was only in prison, laying his burden down on the rotten straw, that he rubbed his eyes and saw that the stake was one of the Negro slaves from the platform.

The Basques' peal of laughter was so contagious soon the whole jail was shaking with it. The poor exiles had acquired a slave in the skirmish! The laughter finally simmered down, however: they were in a pretty pickle, decidedly . . .

Yet Pélagie, Madeleine, Jean, and Maxime had taken a scaffold by storm to wrest away a Catoune.

. . . And after all, a prison, for survivors of deportation, dispersion, and exile . . .

"An exile's no honeymoon!"

It was Bélonie, Pélagie-the-Grouch's contemporary, who repeated the phrase a century later precisely when Acadie, fresh out of the woods, had just begun merrymaking again. But Pélagie-the-Grouch didn't like hearing her lineage spoken of in such terms and flatly refused her ancestors the right to joking or feasting, even in retrospect.

Poor grouchy descendant of her ancestors! If only she'd known! If only she'd been able to slip through the shabby prison walls which that night held huddled together the scraps of the Cormier, Girouard, Bourgeois, Thibodeau, Léger, and Basque families. And the LeBlancs, Oh the LeBlancs! Her own branch. If only she'd been able to step back into history and relive with her ancestors that night of carnival in prison!

And a strange night it was, truth to tell, as if the cart had just been waiting for chains to shake loose and allow itself at last its first night of revelry.

. . . Well, not quite, not quite. But just the same! A night of festivities right in the middle of the Charleston jail!

They'd begun by asking the Thibodeaus, who had smithery in their family and consequently in their blood, to break the chains that bound the prisoners to the floor and Catoune to her Negro. Then the Basques, more sorcerers than gypsies, drew out of their secret pockets . . . Louis-à-Bélonie hadn't dared call them their codpieces . . . drew out of their pockets then, two or three hidden phials, which Célina used to brew up an elixir the like of which is never mentioned except in the blackest of books. An elixir that produced such an effect on the jailers that you could hear them gurgling in their gullets all through the prison. That's what they say.

. . . Gurgling or not, they'd have still come, two by two, to stick their heads through the bars to listen to that sobbing violin. It's even said that they listened right through to the end of Bélonie's tale of the White Whale, which he finished for the benefit of the cart and which, the elixir helping, the jailers seemed to understand in its own tongue.

It had strange powers that Basque phial doctored up by Célina, for Bélonie himself, so it seems, found a new ending to his whale story that night . . . so it seems.

. . . So it seems indeed, for instead of slaying the whale to free the bear, slaying the bear to free the fox, slaying the fox to free the hen, slaying the hen to get back his golden ring, which took back its shape as the yolk of an egg and thus went on feeding the man for the rest of his days, instead of that, the hero—who was only a peasant—ushered his astonished audience right into the jaws of the whale, through the arcades of the palate, down the tunnel of the esophagus to the bottom of the stomach, and from there to the depths of the entrails, gurgling and stinking . . .

Ugh!

. . . right down to the heart of the bowels twisted in a mysterious labyrinth, and there at the end of it all lay the golden ring!

He'd lost nothing from his old Gaulois sack, this Bélonie hadn't, issue of Jacques, issue of Antoine, issue of a Paris in the times of Gothic drollery and songs. And even armed with muskets and harquebuses, those jailers were no match for the Basques' violin, Célina's elixir, and Bélonie's fantastic tale. So when the golden ring was reached, they threw the main gates wide open, after passing the people of the cart through the stinking corridors and labyrinths of the Charleston prison.

In the next century, when the cart's descendants seated in a half-moon round Pélagie-the-Grouch's hearth recalled this chapter of their history, Bélonie, father of Louis, father of Bélonie, father of Louis-à-Bélonie, fourth-of-the-name, packed into a single phrase all the joyful and fantastical philosophy of his race, sending a stream of pipe juice into the hearth:

"And that's how we're still alive today, we exiles, on account of because we consented to come out of exile and come on back home through the arse end of a whale."

Hee! . . .

PROPERTY OF THE
PUBLIC LIBRARY
ST. MARYS, ONT.

5

And that's how this new version of the White Whale came to be added to the stock of tales of old Acadie and was passed on by Bélonies around the hearth from forbear to father to offspring. Yes, offspring. Have confidence in life and you will soon see by what miracle, in a country like mine, offspring can even spring up from a race snuffed out, from a line swallowed up in a single wave far out at sea off Île Royale. It's true what the Basque said: You can't cut off the breath of him who keeps it inside.

So the caravan of exiles led by the oxen crossed the town on the tips of their hooves while Charleston slept on in its feathers and good conscience.

The seal At last.

And Pélagie, who for almost two years now had held the reins of the cart twisted round her closed fists, opened wide her palms to the dew of the breaking day. Even the oxen, shaking their yokes and horns, tried to gallop to the beat of the song that rose in a low swell from the survivors of the night . . . *Et j'ai du*

*grain de mil, et j'ai du grain de paille, et j'ai de l'oranger, et j'ai
du tri, et j'ai du tricoli . . . j'ai du tricoli . . .* What's that?

. . . It's Bélonie staring at the horizon . . . a bad sign.

"What's he gawking at now, the old chin-wagger? We got out,
old boy, out of prison, the whole gang, with a Negro thrown in,
and we're just going to soak our feet in the salt water a bit to
cheer them up," Célina crooned to reassure the old chap.

To reassure Old Bélonie! Just who did she take herself for this
morning, the mere midwife? Healer all right, even witch or fortune-teller, if you will. But to reassure Bélonie, harnessed for
seventeen years to his phantom cart, chatting away to his deceased ancestors as freely as to his traveling companions? Come
on now, Célina!

All of a sudden he lifts an arm and points to the horizon in a
gesture almost forgotten, from the time he would read the waves
and the weather for the sake of the fishermen setting out to sea.
He's babbling something, it's barely a babble, but he's saying
something . . . to someone . . . Come on, Old Bélonie . . . say it,
tell Célina and the cart.

"The phantom ship!"

He's said it. And the cart and its carts and the oxen, the whole
troop stand rooted to the spot. The phantom ship! Everyone
knows it. For centuries that condemned vessel has been passed
on, forever burning at sea, now in the north, now in the east,
eternally expiating a crime lost in the night of time but one that
heaven and earth refuse to pardon. And burn it will and rekindle
and burn again till the end of the world. He'd already said so,
had Bélonie: The greatest punishment is not death, oh no! But
death without rest, eternal wandering between heaven and
earth, perpetual dying, and ever dying again.

. . . Lucky are those who can die once and for all!

The miserable fate of this pirate ship, steered by the devil in
person, is to sail between life and death until the expiation of its
incommensurable sentence. And each of its appearances is followed next day by a tempest at sea—that's why the phantom ship
is also known as bad weather fire.

The carts shudder before this living brazier shooting its light-

nings to the skies and driving onward from the break of day.
The hull afire, the sails afire, the seaboys, the sailors, the quartermaster flaming in the sun before the dazzled eyes of the deportees, who thought they had left all phantom ships behind in
Acadie. Then one by one the fires in the sails go out and they
swell in the morning breeze . . . Dear God! It's coming into port,
it's tacking as if to land, stop it, for the love of Heaven! . . . And
now they clearly see the phantom crew on deck, their hands
black with ash and their faces lit up by the last of the dying
flames, a crew of seaboys, mates, and quartermasters, enormous,
transparent . . .

God!

. . . All splendid and transfigured, filled out with flesh between skeleton and skin like living men, returning spirits so perfectly returned that their ship must have sunk keel up in the
clouds somewhere in the land of forgetfulness.

Once more Bélonie opens his mouth:

"The English four-master that went down with all hands in
the Great Disruption."

Célina throws herself on her knees, dragging Cormiers, Thibodeaus, Bourgeois, Girouards, and even the Basques after her.
Only Bélonie remains calm and only Pélagie remains standing
with the oxen.

Suddenly the captain appears, immense on the quarterdeck.
The rising sun picks out a hat and neckpiece in the style of Louis
XV, and the northbound Acadians stare at this apparition out of
their past and hold their breaths.

Upright at the heads of her impassive oxen, Pélagie with her
bold gaze and all her hardy soul confronts this phantom who
deigns cast her a wink from home in this land of exile. She will
neither show fear nor take flight, let the dead be advised. She
who without hesitation had seized an absurd and tottering future
in her own two hands is not one to falter before a past reincarnated in a captain and his ship sunk on the high seas a generation ago. Let him speak, this herald of heaven or hell. Let him
speak his piece.

The captain's brow unfurrows, and his cheeks crack in a broad, old-style laugh the like of which Pélagie hasn't heard for an age. Whereupon the arms of the dazed woman cross over her heart, to keep it warm and to keep it from bounding out of its cage: That laugh comes from the past all right, but not from beyond the gravel And from the breast of this widow of Acadie that for so many years has harbored an open wound is torn a cry that even the dead might hear:

"He's alivel"

One after another the carts groan in surprise to the call of the sea horn at the top of the rigging hallooing them all a good day from northern seas.

Alivel Captain Broussard, Broussard-called-Beausoleil, master of an English four-master rechristened *Grand'Goule* and a full crew of survivors . . . Aye, Bélonie, survivors, survivors from midocean snatched from the furious sea and their pitiless jailers by none other than Beausoleil, another deported Acadian.

And Beausoleil-Broussard himself, alive in body and soul, jumps to the quai at Pélagie's feet and presents his ship to the cart.

One after another the sailors leap ashore and shake the shoulders of their countrymen, neighbors and cousins: a Bourg . . .

"Salutl"

. . . a Belliveau, a Léger . . .

"Cousinl"

. . . a Gautreau . . .

"Old cockl"

. . . a Cyr, a Gaudet, a Robichaud, a LeBlanc . . .

"And yet anotherl Great God, did you ever see the like of it now!"

The cart chokes with emotion and wipes its axles dry. In God's truth these are the most moving and joyous espousals between sea and dry land in all the memory of Acadie.

Most moving for Pélagie at any rate and for Broussard-called-Beausoleil, captains on land and on sea who had thus reached across the years and recognized each other.

. . . My cousin and contemporary Louis-à-Bélonie used to say

time and again that our countrymen could recognize one another
without ever having met before by certain small signs: a hoarse-
ness in the voice, the smell of salt under the skin, the hollow
blue eyes that look inside as well as out, and last but not least
the laugh that comes from so far away it seems to have tumbled
down from some seventh heaven.

At least according to my contemporary Louis-à-Bélonie-à-
Louis.

It was thus they recognized each other, Beausoleil and Pélagie. And with them their double crew. A meeting of ocean and
continent after seventeen years. Pélagie stroked her throat and
wiped her eyes. Had her skin lost the whiteness of winters at
Grand-Pré? And her lips their confident smile in the face of the
nor'wester? And her look its vision that swept beyond the horizon of the French Bay and the basin of Les Mines seeking new
lands to conquer? That morning Pélagie breathed with all her
might and roughened her voice to prevent it betraying the shiver
that tickled her throat and the small of her back.

"Break out the jugs and demijohns! Unpack the kettles and
add plenty of juice to the stew!"

She must haved imagined it only needed the clink of spoons
on the pots to bring everyone back to earth. But the spoons
mocked Pélagie and took up the beat of the song, making the
mugs sing . . . *Et j'ai du grain de mil, et j'ai du grain de paille*
. . . make room for the guests . . . *et j'ai de l'oranger, et j'ai du
tri, et j'ai du tricoli* . . . some pap there for Old Bélonie . . . *j'ai
des allumettes, et j'ai des ananas* . . . eat up, Bélonie, it's a party
the cart's throwing, eat your pap.

What can you be thinking of? Do you think Bélonie has the
stomach for pap on a day like today? For once heaven had sent
him some real ghosts, right there within reach, a whole schooner-
ful of the departed, enough to fill his cart to the brim. For once
Death stood before him in full flesh and blood, and only to make
a fool of him. The phantom vessel had dumped in his lap a
bunch of impostors, charlatans, false-defuncts, all talking non-
sense, tricksters and swindlers. And Bélonie seemed to get visibly older. Whatever you might say, his own deceased never car-

ried on like a lot of fake human beings, lending their voices to men or their gestures to life; his own deceased knew the meaning of self-respect and respect for death.

"But they're alive, Bélonie, their schooner didn't go down at sea."

. . . Alive! What next! A shipwrecked schooner that didn't even know how to sink decently!

And Old Bélonie, past master in the ways of dying, turned his back on the slim, trim schooner that hadn't even known how to face its own death.

Slim and trim? That four-master, the only one to have plied the coasts of the French Bay in prosperous days? She carried twenty-four sails and had been the envy of every French and Acadian mariner sailing between Nova Scotia and Newfoundland. But she had flown the flag of England in those days and was called the *Pembroke*. And as fate would have it, Bélonie, when the deportees were split up, it was into this same proud ship that they cast a bold young sailor named Broussard.

Aye, Bélonie!

He wasn't thirty years old the day the Great Disruption deported his people south; but of those thirty years, he'd lived more than half at sea and he knew the ocean better than his own backyard. The Broussards from father to son had sported with whales and mocked the waves and the nor'easter. They had all drunk more than one gulp at the big cup, as they say, and from that they had all kept a coating of salt in their gullets that made their voices grave and rough.

"And a thirst passed along from father to son."

But they'd always bobbed back to the surface, the Broussards had, as if the sea herself feared to swallow a race bold enough to unknot her watery roots and veins in the depths of the deep. Chroniclers of the time concluded that no Beausoleil would ever disappear under the waves but that they'd spend their eternity under sail far out to sea where the giant seaweed moors the horizon to the setting sun. That's what the chroniclers understood by "lost at sea."

"After that, little wonder a captain bobs up again after twenty years."

"Tell on, Beausoleil, tell on."

And Beausoleil-Broussard took up the story of his adventure from the place where he lay in the hold of the *Pembroke*, carried off into exile with the rest of his race . . . It was a hold so well-rounded in its hull, its sides so well-balanced, one that handled so well in high seas that the young mariner was surprised to find himself navigating the *Pembroke* every night, steering her over the shoals and between the reefs and in the very heart of the hellish cyclone that drove the waves seventy feet high. So much so, that on a night the old men in the hold felt in their bones and noses a storm approaching, the doughty youth bet his companions in misery that even disabled this four-master could ride out a hurricane. Yes, he bet that.

"You're crazy. With an English foot soldier at the helm?"

"Nay, with Beausoleil at the helm."

"Ah! . . ."

"But for our misfortune and Acadie's, Beausoleil is in the hold."

Ah, but he was a bold lad, this Joseph Broussard-called-Beausoleil, not yet in his thirtieth year. That very night he climbed up on deck, slipped along to the fo'c'sle and, nobody knew how, disabled the schooner. She began to veer dangerously eastward toward the tornado, right into the throat of the waves to the cries of her improvised crew, formed by the fortunes of war of English infantry from Nova Scotia and Massachusetts. A crew so completely overwhelmed and terrified they were already lowering ship's boats into the sea. Abandon ship! Leaving the *Pembroke* and its unfortunate cargo to the whims of Destiny.

Benevolent Destiny!

For it was at this very moment that our gallant hero steps up to the desperate captain and offers him the services of a knowledge and practice of the sea ten generations in the making.

"I can save the ship," says he, "if you turn her over to me."

He was careful, you see, not to commit himself to saving the crew. A man's word is his word, and Beausoleil's people had already paid dear enough for the word they gave the King of England who, over a controversial clause in the oath of allegiance, had packed them all off to sea without standing on ceremony.

. . . And without ceremony the new commandant packed a few recalcitrant soldiers over the side and took over the helm, which he made haste to repair before the storm broke loose.

". . . ?"

By his own special magic.

The Bastaraches and Girouards, who also had thirty-two quarters of seamen in their blood, would have liked to know how. Just think, repairing a tiller on the high seas in the teeth of the beast . . .

But with a broad laugh spreading over his sun-filled face, all Beausoleil did was tap the bone of his thigh with the back of his hand, addressing the next to Pélagie from the edge of his eye:

"If things are bad enough," says he, "a man can find a tiller and even a mainmast in there."

And Pélagie felt her own thigh shiver.

So many emotions in a single day! After all those dry-hearted years, Pélagie let the sea wind flatter her cheeks and the skin of her soul. And without even thinking to restrain herself, she chuckled and giggled and whispered, even to her oxen whose tender, complicit eyes grew wide in wonder.

Hadn't life stopped for everyone for the past half-generation? While she, Pélagie, had grubbed in the earth to dig out roots and rotten seed, while rib by rib she had built the frame for the cart that was to carry them back home, all this time a schooner was carting remnants of her people from the coasts of New England to the shores of New France! Did you ever hear the like!

And all the carts laughed and bawled copiously to hear it.

. . . You mean to say the Melansons of Rivière-aux-Canards didn't stay down south? And the Bernards, the Bordages, and the Arsenaults? You don't say! They all went up to Gaspésie? And their idea was to settle there? And the Pellerins, what happened to the Pellerins? You'll never make me believe they shared a passage with the Robichauds, why they weren't even on speaking terms at the time. Good Lord! And the Vigneaults, any news of the Vigneaults after all these years? What's that? They went to Îles de la Madeleine and others to Saint-Pierre and Miquelon? And some of the Gaudets and Doucets and Belliveaus took off through the woods for Quebec? Why, the country would be flooded with deportees!

The carts choked on so much news yet couldn't hear enough and wanted to know about everyone all at once. So they jostled the Marins and the Martins about the fate of the Mazerolles who had washed up in the Dupuis line, married into the family of the Lapierres known as Laroche. You don't mean to tell me . . . Everything, Célina, you'll be told everything, even about the alliance between the Allains and the Therriots, even about the third marriage of Joseph Guégen, so-called Seigneur of Cocagne, now accumulating a nice fat little fortune in furs.

You don't mean to say so!

"And Abbé LeLoutre?"

"Ah, that one!"

. . . Quiet now, leave religion out of it.

"His religion didn't stop him from betraying us all."

"Not betraying us, Antoine, defending us."

"You call that being well defended?"

. . . Let the priests alone.

"Priest or no, he's a crook. If it wasn't for him and his rebel Indians, the English would have left us in peace and we'd still be planting our turnips in the basin of Les Mines."

"If it wasn't for him, we'd have forgotten we were French."

"But because of him our descendants may forget they were ever Acadians."

The Girouards, Thibodeaus, and Bourgeois were well away, tearing Abbé LeLoutre into shreds, a rending of reputation that History hasn't been able to mend to this day.

For Louis-à-Bélonie tells that in the time of Pélagie-the-Grouch at the end of the last century they were inclined to gloss a good deal—they wasted a lot of spit, is the way he puts it—on the fidelity or felony of this double-, triple-, or multiple-agent. The only conclusion the Bélonies ever reached about the equivocal character of this man of God was that it would have been better for everyone to let sleeping bears lie. And without the tempestuous deeds of Abbé LeLoutre the bear might have gone on sleeping a lot longer, in London as in Chebucto, which little by little they were beginning to call Halifax.

At least according to the Bélonies.

"Back then, it was only in Boston that things were really boiling."

It appears that in Boston they had good reason to have it in for the French, who were running surprise expeditions against the New England coast from time to time. Frenchmen from France and New France they were, but Bostonians didn't distinguish them from the Acadians, dumped off in their towns by the English ships, hands and feet bound. So the deported Acadians paid for the others' raids.

"If you can avoid it, don't pass through Boston with your carts," Beausoleil counseled them.

Just then Catoune slipped away from the group and ran to the *Grand'Goule*. Her cat's eyes had seen a sail move on the foremast. Someone on deck had climbed up among the yards and was trying to make off with the ship. And Catoune scampered up the catwalk and jumped to the deck.

The Negro was first to notice her and, with eyes as round as if he'd been freed from his chains a second time, he too ran up the gangway. Jean and Maxime scrambled aboard after him. And soon everyone from this scene of reunion at the foot of the *Grand'Goule* was milling around to the great confusion of the oxen.

"Good God! Now what's happening?"

Pacifique Bourgeois didn't like more to happen than was absolutely indispensable in an expedition of this kind, an expedition into which he had been launched much against his will and which he would gladly have exchanged for a good old-fashioned featherbed.

"Ca—tou—ne!"

. . . If the little bitch went on running away, neither Pacifique nor any of the Carolinian deportees could ever be sure of seeing their sleek lands in Port-Royal Valley again.

"Come back, Catoune!"

. . . For that matter, it seemed quite likely Pélagie herself
didn't know what route she intended her oxen to take; and as for
the oxen, they'd never make it, Pacifique was certain of that, and
if necessary he'd take it up with the Thibodeaus and the Cormiers, though not with those whining, flabby-assed Giroués . . .

"What's she found?"

She had found the giant P'tite Goule! P'tite Goule was a giant
of the same breed as Gargan and Gargantua who had roamed
over the old country in bygone days, flattening mountains in
their path, sinking lakes in the prints of their sabots, dangling
their legs astride the ridgepoles of churches and pissing a welcome on the crowd below.

Yes, P'tite Goule came from that kind of line, according to
Pierre-à-Pitre, known as the Fool, who had been his companion
since the time of the whale rescue.

The cart had to draw a deep breath to follow Pierre-the-Fool's
tale, for he tumbled his stories together mixing giants and cacha-
lots telling how he and P'tite Goule had escaped from the English with the help of a whale who had tossed them up on the
deck of Captain Beausoleil's four-master.

"How's that?"

Why sure, that's what happened, believe it or not. A cachalot
cruising around one Sunday afternoon in the dead of winter off
the Maine islands had a brush with a schooner transporting Acadians south in its hold, including our two inseparable barnyard
heroes—that's to say the dwarf and the giant, those notorious
goose and chicken thieves. Now these heroes, P'tite Goule and
your humble servant, continued the Fool, they'd never cared
much for life in the hold, so they jumped out, right under the
captain's nose, onto the floating ocean ice and made their way to
a whale who carried them off on its back.

Célina blinked both eyes, Pacifique Bourgeois went "Hmph!"
and all the rest listened avidly.

. . . You have no idea, nobody here, what fun it is to gallop
over the sea straight into the wind, drinking the froth from the
snout of the beast, awash in the spray of its jet, diving, now over,
now under the waves, whistling, singing, defying the sun—al-

ways according to Pierre-à-Pitre the Fool—one day to land on a
four-master's deck, snatched from the high seas by a hungry
schooner that swallows you up in its *grand'goule*, its mighty
maw. You can't imagine . . .

"I can't imagine telling such stories to children."

Quiet, Célina. Neither children nor adults could ever get
enough of the Fool's fantastic tales. Despite their own rich stock
of adventures, making up an oral legacy that would fill many a
Sunday afternoon for generations to come, these deportees on
their way home at the century's end still thirstily gulped down
the marvelous stories of others. Whether they'd seen with their
own eyes the head of Blackbeard floating off the coast of Maryland, or had just escaped themselves from the Charleston prison
through the arse end of a whale, they gleefully gobbled up the
narratives the Fool made up as he went along.

For here is the lasting difference between the two greatest
Acadian storytellers of the journey home: Whereas for almost a
hundred years Bélonie faithfully passed down to his line a repertory of tales and legends from the time of the Great Rains,
Pierre-à-Pitre, the people's fool, went spilling into this repertory
such versions, variations, improvisations, and elucubrations of his
own fabrication that it isn't easy today to know what's authentically old.

. . . At any rate, said Pélagie-III-called-the-Grouch a century
later, the only story that counts in all that is the one of the cart
that brought its people back home.

No, not a people, not yet, Pélagie-the-Grouch. At the time of
this first meeting between sea and dry land the troop was only
scraps of relations and neighbors. The LeBlancs of Grand-Pré,
the Cormiers and Girouards of Beauséjour and Beaubassin, bits
of Port-Royal . . . But this day the schooner had dropped in
their laps good scrapings from Rivière-aux-Canards and Beausoleil as well.

"And of Terre-Rouge."

Yes, and Terre-Rouge, also known as The Bend because of the
way the river angled, that very river where the giant P'tite Goule
had landed on earth in primeval times. And his gigantic child-

hood was passed somewhere in the mists of the Petitcodiac that ran through the red clay marshes of Tintamarre and Memramcook.

"And where did his family come from?"

Just try to find out! P'tite Goule wasn't a talker. That's where he got his nickname, for *petite-gueule* is the opposite of *grande-gueule*, or blabbermouth.

"No way. P'tite Goule is cabin boy of the *Grand'Goule*, that's where his name comes from. Just ask the captain there, he always gives you the truth."

The captain looked at his fool of a second cabin boy and smiled. If he started to straighten out every truth Pierre-à-Pitre ran away with, it wouldn't take a day to destroy the credibility of this taletelling-chinwagging-legpulling-trickplaying genius. Besides, it was such a splendid image, the one of the two sea riders astraddle a cachalot in the ice floes of the Great North. So Beausoleil settled for telling the carts the extraordinary exploits of the giant of Terre-Rouge who, when prisoner of the English, had with his own hands dug a tunnel that came out on the other side of the river in a free land.

For in those days they still spoke of French Acadie, or Free Acadie, lying to the north of Beauséjour and consequently opposite that other Acadia that had already fallen and was called Nova Scotia. By means of his tunnel through the clay, others say by fording the river, the giant had managed to bring across a good part of the Acadian families imprisoned by the English. The Gaudets and Belliveaus remember it to this day, according to my cousin Louis-à-Bélonie.

And that's why P'tite Goule, who had spent the flower of his youth underground, in a potato cellar or digging tunnels under the river, had got out of the habit of company and had taken to rolling himself up in a sail each time the schooner landed. But since he was eight feet tall, the foresail was barely long enough to make him a coat. And Catoune with her sharp eyes and keen nose had spotted him.

"That'll teach you, my fine giant," says the captain, "to act so shamefaced and hide away from everyone. Whenever you do, the smallest of God's angels will dig you out and bring you back to your crew."

And now that the crew of the *Grand'Goule* alias the *Pembroke* was at full strength, they could begin to recite, bead by bead, the chaplet of adventures lived out for twenty years by this new Robin Hood.

"Robin Hood of the Seas, that's it," one of the Bélonies was to exclaim later. "Beausoleil-Broussard was our Robin Hood of the Seas . . ."

Pélagie-the-Cart once more clasped her arms over her breast to stop her heart from bounding out on the deck of the *Grand'Goule*.

PROPERTY OF THE PUBLIC LIBRARY ST. MARYS, ONT.

6

Robin Hood of the Seas!

From the time the first colonists had arrived at Port-Royal, family lines had never been jumbled; criss-crossed if you will, but never jumbled. Ah, no! Cormiers married into Landrys married into Bourgs married into Arsenaults, in bonds so cleanly knotted that the least apprentice-delver could unknot them on his fingers, backward and forward, up and down the branches of the family tree.

But with the arrival of the Incident, for the first time Acadie faced a danger that threatened its very roots. Lineages were jostled and tumbled around, names were jumbled, family branches were strewn to the four winds. The previous wars had only pruned the tree; deportation threatened to uproot it.

The captain ruminated such thoughts every night as he transported his cargo of exiles up to Gaspésie. And it was precisely to retransplant the tree he had turned himself into Robin Hood of the Seas, attacking the English ships, liberating their prisoners, and delivering them to their homeland.

A homeland that the Dispersion was enlarging to fill every island and creek capable of hiding this dislocated people. For the *Grand'Goule* had begun to unload Arsenaults and Hachés known as Gallants on Île Saint-Jean; and Vigneaults in the Îles de la Madeleine; and Chiassons on Île Royale, known as Cape Breton; and Blanchards, Hachés, and Lanteignes on Île Miscou; and all round the Gaspé Peninsula entire branches of Richards and Arsenaults; and far inland, between the Miramichi and the Saint-Jean rivers, Godins, Poiriers, Gaudets, and Belliveaus.

Plus LeBlancs everywhere.

Everywhere? . . .

It was Célina, born with neither name nor ancestors who called Beausoleil into question. For the cripple had fallen into root-delving the way she'd become a midwife: by default. And now the old maid would trim the small wood off others' trunks with the same zeal as she rummaged in the bellies of her countrywomen and neighbors. And this way she quickly became a specialist in second beds. Straight-line delving is fine for illiterates; true skill begins in second beds. Without these more subtle distinctions, no one could lay claim to real delving, Célina would tell you. For example, the offshoot of a second marriage has a half-line that forks at the hip or thigh, and it's usually there the trouble begins. Take the case of Ernestine . . .

And growing bolder as she climbed the branches of the LeBlanc's family tree, Célina lay round her with axe and sickle clearing out everything right back to the trunk. Pélagie dove back into her memories, excited by the rasping voice of Célina delving into her in-laws without so much as scratching a single finger.

. . . Ernestine, stepsister-in-law by a second bed, as a very young girl had shown a curious disposition for adventure and anarchy, frequenting neither her own age nor her own rank but going around with her nose in the air as though she had aspirations. Pélagie couldn't very well see what Célina meant by that, since the stepsister-in-law could hardly aspire higher than the highest rank, which at that time was about the same level as the lowest. In a country where the younger stepsister-in-law in second wedlock marries the father of the sister of the first bed, you can't go telling me that people are very strong on form or respecting rank.

Contrariwise!

Even the ants have rank, even the bees. So when it comes to LeBlancs or Therrios . . . Rank is, above all, an attitude, a way of holding your head or arching your back. Don't ever believe that the fact of being descended from the very notary René LeBlanc who went off to Halifax one day to plead the cause of his people, or to come down from Pierre Therrio, the rich landowner of half the Chignectou Valley who left his progeny spread right across the country . . . don't you ever go and imagine that all the Therrio or LeBlanc descendance has a right to the same heritage and the same pretensions! And Célina savored the effect of her cruelty on the hearts of the Bourgeois who, according to her, were *parvenus* from the left hip via the wives of a Port-Royal bastard.

"A bastard who was none other than the true son of Seigneur Charles de la Tour, the first seigneur to land in this country."

"The same La Tour who left his descendance in a wigwam," Célina was quick to add to avenge her own Indian blood.

And she raised the bid on the Bourgeois's bastard past by delving a few more skinny and twisted branches.

"La Tours they were by the milk-tooth of the maternal granddam and had no relation to the real old founders' root."

Beausoleil smiled at Célina's distortions of history. Old or new roots didn't mean much in a country where everyone had come out together from Touraine or Poitou; where everyone had taken the same boat and landed on the same shore, at Port-Royal or the basin of Les Mines; and where everyone, except for a few who had fled to the woods, had been shipped to the south or the islands. The oldest roots were only five or six generations in Acadie, and yet they were the oldest European roots in North America.

"From here on it's in the future one must look for roots. And

it's my thinking that to count them all will need lengthy journey-
ings, far north and far south."

Beausoleil's prediction hit all of them at once. Without measuring the exact distance between north and south, just the same
the carts had a feeling that the veil of the horizon had been
pushed back.

"Is there any real mystery to it?" inquired Jeanne Aucoin who
was always trying to bring home Girouard branches carried
away by the plundering wind. "How far away do our kin reach,
Beausoleil?"

So then Robin Hood of the Seas told the story of Louisiana.

Louisiana, fancy that!

All the deported Acadians had heard tell of it: a French land
lying to the west of Carolina and Virginia, almost next door. A
country of liberty, sun, and watermelons.

"And bayous full of shrimp!"

Ah, but he knew a lot, this Beausoleil! He could name you the
nicknames of every ship landed at New Orleans, and number
you the families, and provide you their homeports and the details of their peregrinations and the perils of their adventures.

He made mouths water, Cormiers' and Girouards' alike, but
mostly Thibodeaus', with his story of exchanges of prisoners between English and French by a pact that sent a healthy handful
of Acadian colonists back to Poitou and Belle-Île-en-Mer.

Charles-à-Charles's son blinked his eyes.

"So that's how they got back to the old home!"

The Girouards had nostalgia in the blood the way others have
fear or anxiety. Even the bare idea of a return to the home before home tickled Alban Girouard's soul as if a hundred years
hadn't been enough to cure him of the past. How he envied the
few survivors of the *Duke William* shipwrecked in the Channel
who had managed to reach the continent in a leaky boat.

"They got back home," he repeated.

The Bourgeois looked askance at Alban-à-Charles-à-Charles.
Why take so much trouble to found a new land if after a hundred years you have to abandon it to wild animals and the English? The Bourgeois had dug and weeded and drained the

marshes all round the French Bay all during their long lineage
from Pacifique to Jacques to Jude to Jacques to Jacob, surgeon at
the Seigneury of Aulnay. Did you think they'd done all that for
someone else? Or that they'd go back to France as old folks to
relate their troubles to their forefathers' descendants? Pacifique
Bourgeois and his wife Jeanne sat firmly down on their chest
once again and swore they wouldn't open it till Acadie.

"You'd think all the gold in Peru was hidden in that chest,"
protested Jeanne Aucoin.

By way of reply to Jeanne Aucoin la Girouère, all that Jeanne
Trahan-called-the Bourgeoise did was wriggle the point of her ass
more squarely over the lid of the chest; and everyone rubbed
their hands at the prospect of a fine fight between the Jeannes.
And had it not been for the thoughtlessness of young Olivier
Thibodeau who led the carts back to Louisiana, they were surely
on the verge of seeing the two sharpest beaks in Acadie clash in
all their glory.

. . . But it's still a long way to Grand-Pré, mustn't despair,
there'll be other occasions.

Thibodeau's small fry, then, put Beausoleil back on the track
to Louisiana. The Thibodeaus had so often dreamed of Louisiana, that land that had stayed French at a time when all
America was falling, piece by piece, into the English lap.

"At the mouth of this Louisiana pond you wouldn't by chance
have seen a sluice big enough to let a small man with little baggage swim in?"

Young Olivier was dogged and his dream was solid stuff. Instinctively Beausoleil-Broussard liked hardheaded folk, and he
furnished details. When the deportees were disembarked at the
hazard of East Coast harbors, they got their Georgia, Carolina,
or Maryland straight in the face. But Louisiana they chose. From
the prisons of London, from Belle-Île, from the Antilles, and
even from Saint-Pierre and Miquelon they had outfitted
schooners and sailed for Louisiana. In fifteen years Louisiana
had welcomed more Acadians than French colonists or soldiers,
and the governor, hard pressed, had shoved them far up into the
bayous.

"There's even some spent ten years coming down the Missis-
sippi on rafts or in bark canoes. But at the end of the ten years
they could start up their line again."

Ten years, thought Pélagie, that's a big chunk out of the heritage of a lifetime.

Olivier persisted:

"Seems to me we can't be far from the frontier. If we took off
across the fields and woods . . ."

"And the mountains . . ."

"Better to come in by the front door, by sea. Louisiana's
within sailing reach of Virginia through the Gulf of Mexico."

The more the captain talked, the more the cart clan began to
squirm and slither into dreams and fantasies.

An Acadie-in-the-South, closer and warmer than the northern
one, maybe richer, certainly more welcoming in this day and
age. A Louisiana overflowing with Martins, Dugas, Babineaus,
Bastaraches and—think of it!—Bernards and Landrys so thick
there was barely room to bed them down.

"Landrys! You don't say!"

Landrys from the parish of Saint-Landry, if you please, already branding their cattle with their own mark to ensure respect; Martins who had given their name to Saint-Martinville;
Moutons talking to the governor, man to man . . .

"Sweet God in Heaven!"

. . . With priests to sing them mass, and laws to protect them,
and lands to feed them . . .

. . . But no graves to plant with flowers, thought Pélagie, and
no roots to delve.

"Winters are hard in the basin of Les Mines, Pélagie," Anatole-
à-Jude Thibodeau, the blacksmith, came whispering in her ear,
"and if I remember rightly . . ."

"And try to remember, too, the harvest season with the apple
trees so loaded the branches are cracking at the joints; and the
sugar season with the maple sap dripping in the cans; and the
season of the little wild strawberries . . . Have they got wild
strawberries and maple syrup in your Louisiana?" Pélagie asked,
fixing the captain straight in the eye.

And the captain laughed his salt-roughened, sea-windy laugh
. . . What a woman, this Pélagie! Capable single-handed of
bringing her people home. And of bringing them back against
the current. For the current ran south in those days, and Beausoleil had seen half his people slip into it and let themselves be
carried along to the Antilles or Louisiana. But now who had
crossed his path but this stiff-necked, proud-browed woman who
dared stand up to her people and, harnessed to her own cart, call
out:

"Is it the burning, feverish swamps that choke the bayous of
Louisiana that you're looking for? And is it the stale bread you'll
go begging at the doorstoops of the Creole plantations of New
Orleans? Have you forgotten the country we left behind up
there, eh?"

No, no one had forgotten, Pélagie could sleep in peace. A people who haven't forgotten France after a century of silence and
isolation are not, after seventeen years of exile, likely to forget
their dreams of Acadie. Like the salmon remembering their
spawning grounds they remembered, and, like the salmon, they
were ready to remount the current.

That day there was no more talk about Louisiana. Besides,
Louisiana dreams, like those of exploring Martinique and Guadeloupe, were interrupted by a new clash between the carts' two
lovesick colts.

"Isn't that finished yet?"

No, because not only did the carts cross shafts and horns with
one another but now the schooner too, yes the four-masted
schooner, too, had entered the lists.

Beausoleil rushed over. But it was Célina who was in the
thickest of the fray, waving her arms, charging head first in all di-
rections, yelling and swearing that she'd bring back peace to the
tribe even if she had to leave a leg behind doing so. It was this
choice of legacy that set everyone rocking with mirth and
deflected the course of the combat, for Célina's foot alone was a
prize to equal Blackbeard's head or Captain Kidd's treasure.

"We'll make pig's foot stew out of it," roared one of the
Basques, slapping his thighs.

"Well, you'd better soak it in vinegar first so it doesn't poison anyone."

"And if some Christian is unlucky enough to croak from eating it, we'll bury him under a cow flap so he doesn't stink too bad."

Things were turning sour; Pélagie and Beausoleil judged it was time to restore order. They separated the belligerents, isolated Célina, and began the inquiry. It was then that they discovered P'tite Goule, arms hanging like a couple of oars abandoned to the current, his face full of wonder and delight, defended tooth and nail by none other than Catoune. The poor giant was at a dead loss, not knowing how to protect his protectress without defending himself against his assailant, an assailant attacking his right and left flank at the same time, trying to make a breach in the wall behind which the giant was hiding none other than Pierre-à-Pitre.

"So that's it!"

That's who started it all, Pierre-à-Pitre Gautreau, the Fool. As if La Catoune didn't already have enough suitors, it was the Fool, out of sheer mindlessness, who had come over and pinched . . . he wouldn't say what. But Pierre-à-Pitre went around pinching everyone; it was a tic, like Saint Vitus's dance. So Jean and Maxime had got the wind up for nothing. Besides, he'd skipped away as fast as he'd darted in, the coward, taking refuge behind his giant.

But that's when the bubble had swelled. For the giant, who never defended himself against anyone smaller than himself, which left him totally defenseless, stood there without flinching and without understanding under a rain of blows from foot and horn dealt out by the Catoune's suitors. But La Catoune, as you might have known, wasn't going to tolerate any such ignominious scene, and she drew herself up to her full height before her giant, covering about the fifth part of him. And approach who dare!

The Basques and the Thibodeaus spat in their hands, Célina tore her hair, and Pélagie began to realize that the eldest son of her late husband was jamming the wheels of the cart every day that passed. And she turned her anguished face to Beausoleil.

The Bélonies from father to son faithfully reported the deeds and words of the homebound cart on its voyage at the end of this eighteenth century; but they were less ample when it came to the comings and goings of the schooner. To explain this, one might have suspected the reserve or discretion of Beausoleil or, on the Bélonies' side, some spite or perhaps umbrage. My cousin Louis doesn't believe either. According to him, Beausoleil's personality, on the contrary, must have strongly roused the curiosity of his forbear, perhaps even his sense of metaphysical anguish, which he called the cramps of mortality. For Old Bélonie observed this Robin Hood of the Seas closely, as if seeking the flaw in his behavior as one of the living, as if he hadn't given up the thought of tying the *Grand'Goule* to his Wagon of Death.

Still, it was Old Bélonie and he alone who passed on the saga of his people from father to son, and it is he who presented us with a Beausoleil so full of life.

Pélagie, it will be remembered, was the first to recognize him, and soon enough was to be first to carry him, day after day, under her skin. Ah yes! He was full of life all right, this Broussard-called-Beausoleil, captain of the *Grand'Goule*, hero of the seas, savior of his people; full of life and even quite frisky when the spirit moved him.

. . . And so, when Pélagie's fine eyes searched his, seeking aid and answer, Beausoleil sounded the look of this splendid Acadian creature to its depths. Yet the sailor who had plied his schooner between the isles of the south and the seas of the north since his earliest youth must often have heard the song of the sirens in the night, and this seigneur of the seas must have carried more than one load of disconsolate and grateful beauties in his four-master. But at the 'foot of the cart Bélonie saw with his seer's eyes an invisible fluid pass from the four masts to the four posts of the rack and passed it on to us by proxy.

A century later, seated before Pélagie-the-Grouch's hearth, a Bélonie was to say in an unguarded moment that Pélagie's line must have produced some pretty tempting morsels in its day but that time, alas, always tarnishes and dents the mold . . . It appears that The Grouch didn't let Bélonie finish, for she was still

ticklish on this subject after four generations. And she took it
upon herself, says my cousin Louis-called-the-Younger, to de-
scribe the splendors of her ancestor.

"Pélagie-the-Cart had tresses of gold. I hold that from my
mother who was none other than her direct granddaughter."

The Grouch had a weakness for direct descents and straight
lines, reserving them for her family and leaving others to make
their way into the world from their own fathers and mothers as
best they could. In that vein you could hear her go on endlessly
about first cousins from the same bed or right-angled side shoots,
creating her own mythology of families and relationships. It
must be said that the Bélonies didn't pay much attention to these
ramblings and kept on root-delving as they spun their tales or
tale-spinning as they delved, without worrying about such side
effects.

"Golden tresses and fairy fingers."

Fairy fingers was an expression brought over from the Old
Country that, to tell the whole truth, hadn't sent over the fairies
along with the expression. Which didn't prevent the new country
from keeping well up-to-date on stories and properties of fairies,
and of elves and dwarfs too, classing them in the same rank as
goblins, werewolves, witches, and will-o'-the-wisps, which, you
may rest assured, were perfectly real in Acadie.

. . . But one can't have everything.

"Golden tresses, fairy fingers, and many other advantages to
boot," The Grouch added smugly, taking care not to enter into
the presumed details that were already making mouths water
among the smoke-eating, spit-gurgling crew at the corner of the
hearth.

The advantages of a goodly size, first of all, Louis-the-Younger
informed me, and of a solid frame. But above all . . .

"The eyes!"

People of the sea have a propensity to blue, it's as old as the
world, and a tendency to look deep, as if they had never done
searching the horizon or the firmament. That can be seen in the
arch of the arcades—elsewhere called the eyebrows—and in the
sparkling of the pigments around the pupils. It can also be seen

in their high, richly veined cheekbones. But the people of our
own seas have, as well, the whole of their laughter in their eyes.
That's what distinguishes the eyes of northern from those of
southern seas.

So says my cousin of the north.

He doesn't say more. But regardless, I still had the time to
catch in a corner of my storyteller's sack the only physical description of the heroine of the cart that the chronicle provides.
And a woman with laughter in her eyes besides!

When Pélagie, despairing of her son's behavior, addressed herself to Beausoleil, she was abundantly gratified.

"I'll take you all aboard," the captain proposed.

"All?"

". . ."

The ten or twelve wheels creaked in unison. And the carts?
What would become of the cart and its caravan? And besides,
they were many too many; it didn't make sense. Not to mention
that half of them still had memories of the sea that continued to
haunt their nights.

"And didn't you say yesterday you had families to go and pick
up in Guadeloupe?"

The *Grand'Goule* was indeed headed for Guadeloupe, and
Charleston was only a stop to take on provisions. But after all,
Moutons, Breaus, and Comeaus were no more Acadian or no
more deported than this clan of Pélagie's on its road north.

"Our thanks to you, Joseph Beausoleil-Broussard, but we
won't take over anyone's turn, especially not our cousins' and our
brothers'. Go first and pick up those poor creatures in their
southern isles and take them home again."

And Pélagie wiped the thought of his offer from her cheeks.

Beausoleil found the courage to say the whole of it.

"They're not returning home, Pélagie. I'm sent to take them to
New Orleans."

Them too!

Well, so be it, let them settle in New Orleans if that was their
choice. She wouldn't oppose their free will.

"And if someone here's still dreaming of Louisiana, let him join the ship and resist his destiny no more."

Olivier Thibodeau was the first to smile and blink as if he had the sun in his eyes. But very soon his smile changed to a grimace. He must have seen again Blackbeard's head emerging from the water and the one that had appeared some months later, the head of the captain of the *Black Face*, spitting fire. Thibodeaus, Bourgeois, Cormiers, and Girouards, the whole troop stood around, now on one foot, now on the other, peering now at the sea and now at desires they nursed deep in their hearts.

Beausoleil made a new proposition:

"Wait for us on the coast. Leave us time to go and come from Guadeloupe and Louisiana and we'll meet again in Maryland."

Pélagie's nostrils flared, Beausoleil saw and quickly added:

"My four-and-twenty sails are more limber in the wind of the open sea than the twelve horns of your oxen by land. I'll overtake you before the moon has blinked twelve times."

These warm words went straight to the pit of Pélagie's stomach and she herself blinked a dozen times over.

Next day at dawn Pélagie and Beausoleil went walking at the Carolina sea's edge. Together they saw the shepherd's star vanish and silver droplets light up and sparkle at their feet. For a great while they said nothing and Bélonie, following some paces behind, could hardly hear their breathing. Finally, it was Pélagie who spoke:

"I have a kindness to ask of you, Beausoleil, before we each take off on our own tack."

Beausoleil stopped and Bélonie saw him bend his head.

"I have three boys and a girl left, plus a foundling child that heaven tossed into my apron lap the day of the disaster."

Beausoleil smiled and Pélagie drew strength to continue.

"The choice I make is commanded me by life. To my own children, issue of my womb, I can give no more, no more than life. But to Catoune I must restore that."

"Restore her life?"

"When I took her in, poor orphan of the Good Lord, she was crippled in belly and soul. Now she needs protecting, for she's coming on twenty and into her womanhood."

"If you trust her to me, I'll care for her, and I give you my oath no one will touch her."

"No, it's up to me to defend her. From now on she's my child. I ask you to take in your ship the two greatest dangers to Catoune: the young colts Maxime Basque and Jean, my son."

"But isn't Jean also your child?"

"You'll defend him in my place."

Beausoleil took a deep breath of salt air and enfolded Pélagie in a voice so rough she felt the pain of it to her backbone.

"And if I took the mother with the son? And all that's left of the family of Jean LeBlanc of Acadie?"

. . . He would have taken her just so, right then, and would have carried her off and lodged her like a queen on his quarter-deck, and together they would face the sea, the century, and History. Yes, she and he would reverse the tide of History.

"Pélagie, Pélagie-of-Grand-Pré, you well know that life never passes twice down the same furrow, no more than the keel of a schooner twice in the same wake. If we let the sea gulls carry off this hour we now hold in our hands, we risk seeing it depart forever. Why not accept the present life grants us both this very day. Don't we deserve some small part of respite and content-ment after a life of wandering far and wide?"

He took her shoulders in those hands that one day had broken the helm of a four-master. And, breathless, added:

"Will the day never come when we see a dove appear in the sky, Pélagie? A dove with an olive branch in its beak?"

A rough voice, hands of a helmsman, hollow sea-blue eyes that emptied into her soul twenty years of dreams and desires . . . Pélagie could hardly breathe. And Bélonie, overcome with con-fusion, tried to slip away without betraying himself. She strug-gled, she tried to defend herself, tried to save a family and a country that had seized her arm and dragged her against the current toward the river's source where the fish mount to spawn and die. But she lost her footing in his arms and let herself sink

toward deep waters on the quarterdeck of a four-master that
sped toward the sun . . . the sun, the south, the hollow of a
shoulder that smelt of salt, and one day, one's feet anchored
somewhere, in a new land, living at last, and free. A new land
and a free one . . .

Bélonie saw her suddenly pull herself up straight. That was
the very land her ancestors had chosen a century ago. That very
Acadie so virgin they had planted wild seeds and plants there.
Never, anywhere, would they find a land more vigorous or free.
Never a land more like the dreams of five generations of her
forefathers.

She lay her cheek in the palm of her captain's hand and
caressed his fingers.

"Go off now, Joseph Broussard-called-Beausoleil. Go off yet a
little while and fight the sea. Go and prevent the waves from
devouring a single one of yours and mine. There still remain
remnants of families scattered in foreign lands who must be
brought home. And don't grieve, sometimes the same ship passes
again in the same wake, and the gulls return to the same place."

She lifted her head and looked at him:

"What good to have an olive branch in its beak if we had no
land to plant it in?"

Beausoleil took the face of this woman in his hands as if it
were his compass.

"I'll catch up to you in Maryland, Pélagie-the-Cart, in the port
of Baltimore. And there I'll give you back your boy who meantime will have learned to drive oxen true north. And then, if the
gulls have returned . . ."

"Till Baltimore, Beausoleil."

"Pélagie, till Baltimore."

Bélonie came trotting back to the group that was milling around
the baggage and squirming with anxiety. It was hours since the
two of them had taken off. Had grave things been happening
they were fearful to tell? Pélagie wasn't given to secret ways,
and Beausoleil . . . It was Bélonie who restored peace, and with
it the instinct for self-preservation and renewed combat.

It had begun in a game of exchanges: I'll pass you my to-bacco, you give me your knife, I'll trade your boots for my hat, and my shirt for your basket . . . two bushels of wheat for a jug of cider . . . and your chest . . . not on your life!

"Whoa! You're not going to start that all over again!"

No, nothing at all was starting over. Sacred objects must be left alone, like priests and religion.

"Bah!"

"One day some half-wit's going to set fire to that chest of yours, by accident, and that'll be the last we'll hear of it."

"Yes, and the same day some scatterbrain just might give your half-wit a kick in the ass that'll send him flying round the moon, by accident."

But there were no accidents and everything was finally shared fairly, Beausoleil and Pélagie seeing that justice was done. The sharing of things first, then the sharing of men, to which Jean and Maxime gamely consented without fuss.

Before noon schooner and carts, rigged out like new, began tugging at their hawsers. Beausoleil, just about to step aboard, turned brusquely to Pélagie.

"Two men for two men," said he.

"What? . . ."

"My cabin boys for your carters."

His cabin boys, that meant the fool and the giant, his best men.

"You don't mean . . ."

Yes, of course. You didn't think he was simply going to leave this woman defenseless among three or four such prickly, touchy clans? He was leaving her a bodyguard: his most devoted crew members. A bit of himself in a way.

So Pierre-à-Pitre and P'tite Goule came back down the gang-way, their sacks on their shoulders.

"We'll take good care of them, Captain, don't worry about that."

But Célina said this just to say anything so the farewells wouldn't drag on unduly, never suspecting the importance of the pact she had just contracted. And she pushed the cabin boys in the back toward the carts.

Meanwhile, Jeanne Aucoin went around repeating from one group to another:

"Everything's ·fine, everything's fine. You've seen a schooner raise anchor before this, haven't you? Just be reasonable."

Reasonable, she says. As if that's all there was to it! As if reason were any use in times like these! It's not because you've said farewell more than once in a lifetime that you get used to it. No, Jeanne Aucoin. A person never gets used to deportations, heart rendings, open wounds. And in times like these a person never knows if his farewell may not be for good.

Brron! . . . It's the sea trumpet.

"Better keep to the woods. Follow the Indian trails!"

"Beware of reefs close to shore!"

"Spare the oxen!"

"Don't tarry! Come back soon!"

"Avoid strange camps! Watch out for bandits!"

"Sou'westers and woolen socks, don't catch cold, and don't go throwing yourselves into the teeth of the gale!"

"Always keep heading nor'nor'east!"

"Take care of yourself, Jeannot!"

Jeannot waved broadly to his mother and family, his eyes fixed on Catoune standing so tiny beside the giant. He wouldn't be gone long, not long, Catoune, he'd come back rich in adventures, rich with treasure . . .

"I'll bring back Captain Kidd's chest! . . ."

"Forget the chest," shouted Alban-à-Charles-à-Charles, "we've enough with one as it is!"

"Hee, hee! . . ."

An albatross hovered above Pélagie who threw wild words into the breeze to him and the bird carried them off to the *Grand'Goule*.

Pierre-à-Pitre danced around in everyone's road, poking here and prodding there and making a thousand faces to distract the carts from the sight of the ship, its mainsails swelling as it cast its moorings.

"Take care of yourselves!"

"Till Baltimore in Maryland!"

"Till Maryland! Take care! . . ."

And the northwest breeze pushed the schooner out to the open seas of the south.

An olive branch in its beak!

Oh God! . . .

And Pélagie buried her face in the breast of the giant with the whole of the sea in his eyes.

PROPERTY OF THE
PUBLIC LIBRARY
ST. MARYS, ONT.

7

What were they doing with all that stuff? The cabin boys exaggerated. But since yesterday the two of them had begun to feel for the first time what it was like to have two arms dangling useless at their sides. One knows what to do with one's limbs on the deck of a ship, on the poop, or down in the hold. The tough thing for the cabin boy of a cart is to find no moorings to slip, no sails to hoist to the top of the masts. So the sailors set about rigging out the carts: A plane, some nails, a bunch of gourds, a maple-sap tap, a trowel, a chaff-cutter, a dog collar, a scythe . . . Ah no! not that. They'd quite enough already with the old man dragging along his Wagon of Death after him, not even a sickle, thank you.

"That'll bring us bad luck. Get rid of it."

And Jeanne Aucoin spat three times on the horseshoe tied to the yoke of the lead oxen to exorcise them.

"Hey! Who's the vampire harnessed these animals up all wrong?"

"These animals" were the team called the Corporals who pulled more than their share and had been adopted out of natural sympathy by Jeanne Aucoin Girouère, a beast of burden herself, hauling a whole family after her since the hard times began. The Troopers, somewhat thinner and a team that didn't work well together, were used more and more now for the smaller carts and it was Jeanne la Bourgeoise who curried and cared for them. As for the Hussars, Pélagie's favorites, they followed the convoy at an ox pace ready to answer their master's call in times of difficulty. The Hussars were the reserves for mountains, marsh, or sandstorms.

"That's no reason to feed them on cornmeal," La Bourgeoise objected. She didn't appreciate favoritism.

Her own team, the Troopers, had taken charge of the family chest since Port-Royal-in-the-South without moaning or crabbing or sticking their snouts in the air, like some we know. And scrambling right under the horns of the Hussars and the Corporals she marched off to add two or three tassels of blue wool to the festoon that decorated the heads of her favorites.

It was thus, without consultation, that Pélagie and the two Jeannes had come to share out the affection and care of these draft oxen, who recognize their mistress by her clucking call. The Bourgeoise, for example, called her Troopers with a tic-tic that came from somewhere back of her wisdom teeth, she contorted her jaw so to make sure she was understood. And the oxen, who must have sensed the Bourgeois's proprietary nature, responded briskly to their master's call.

Jeanne Aucoin had a little more trouble with her Corporals, solid beasts, low-slung, undemanding but stubborn and slow-witted, poor things, not having sprung from the thigh of the Bethlehem ox like some we know who, because they were pulling the Bourgeois's chest, imagined they were hauling the Baby Jesus' manger. Hmph! So to call her Corporals, Jeanne Aucoin Girouère used a language suited to their degree of understanding, one that Acadian cowherds were to pass on for generations: tooee-tooee! tooee-tooee!

So you can begin to get a faint idea of the harmonious canon that sprang from the mouths of the two Jeannes calling their oxen simultaneously: tic-tic . . . tooee-tooee! . . . tic-tic! . . . tooee-tooee! . . .

Then, in the midst of this counterpoint, would rise up the voice of Célina, first lieutenant of her captain, who for want of oxen of her own had adopted Pélagie's Hussars. She joined in for the sake of not being left out, and simply to exercise the share of lungs that heaven had granted her. More than her share, thought some without seeming to, as if nature were trying to compensate. But Célina turned a deaf ear to such evil tongues and in her voice of root-delver and good fortune-teller buried the tic-tic! and the tooee-tooee! under a moo-oo-oo! that staggered all three teams of oxen.

Meantime the cabin boys continued to load the carts without heeding the recriminations of Célina and the two Jeannes, for from the first day they had decided to obey only Pélagie . . . A sickle, a jack, harrows, tin snips, what next? . . . a rake, a scraper, some wood shavings, what a mish-mash . . . They would take orders only from Pélagie who would keep them like a dowry in a cedar chest, one day to be returned to Beausoleil.

. . . She watched them without speaking. She was far away from the carts and the loading, far away in the north . . . far away in the past at the time of her marriage at fifteen to the man who had given her his children, then left her a widow in the heart of the torment. The widow of a man, of a family, of a people. Widow of all the Acadie she had tried to revive and re-build. It was madness to think of returning home alone. Was it any country for a single woman? Yet she still had all her hair and all her teeth, her breasts were firm, and the skin of her arms was barely wrinkled inside the elbow . . .

The elbow . . . The Bend! . . . Beausoleil's village lying just at the bend of the river on the banks of the Petitcodiac. All those names danced in her mind and beat against the wall of her forehead sending to her ears and throat the loveliest name of all: Beausoleil . . . Beausoleil . . . Broussard-called-Beausoleil! Names to lock away in her cedar chest.

. . . She had left her chest in Grand-Pré between the alcove

and the double cradle for the twins. A whole life had been left
behind, stored for a long winter. But spring would come back
with the wild geese, breaking the ice, opening the fields, bursting the buds on the oaks and the white birch. He'd be a man to
fell a tree with three swings of the axe, Broussard-called-
Beausoleil, and his shoulders would fill the horizon . . . his
shoulders . . . his shoulders . . . She hadn't rested her head on
someone's shoulder in seventeen years! That's a long piece of
life, seventeen years. How much more would she have to give?

"Hee! . . ."

Bélonie was there beside her, watching the carts, not speaking.
At last Pélagie tore her eyes from the south and turned to look
the north in the face. Mechanically, she glanced at the Hussars
and managed a feeble "Dia!" that set the oxen in motion. The
spare team, which usually followed the convoy, this time was
leading the front oxen. Bélonie's smile wrinkled his skull: On this
September day at the end of the century the world was running
backward sure enough, and at the first false step there was a
good chance it would reel right off its axis! Hold tight everyone!

Catoune rushed out in front of the cart. Don't go! Wait! In the
hustle and bustle of departure no one had thought of the Negro
they had saved from the slave market. He had hung back, leaning on the horizon, watching the convoy leave without saying a
word. Pélagie was ashamed and wiped her brow.

"What are you waiting for," she called harshly to hide her
emotion. "Can't you see we're leaving right now?"

His white eyes grew larger and he lowered them to his feet,
which remained nailed to the Charleston soil.

Pélagie got down from the cart and went over to the slave.

"You're free, Negro. But if it so happens you've no country,
we're on our way to find one up north, so climb in. And if you've
forgotten your name, from this out you can take over the name
of a man who perished without trace in the Great Disruption:
Théotiste Bourg."

The slave raised his eyes to Pélagie, then threw himself at her
feet.

Just how much of Pélagie's speech the Negro had grasped remained to be determined, and Célina took charge of this, having determined on her own that he understood everything . . . Just look at him, you can see for yourself. He jumped into the cart in one leap, I tell you. And with a pair of legs that could stand a little scrubbing, if I may say so, without offense. You don't have to go around filthy just because you're black. And he answered to his name, too, and the proof of it is . . . And to prove it, Célina stuck her beak under the slave's flattened nose and mouthed out: Thé—o—tisse!

"You see? What did I tell you!"

In fact, Célina would have said almost anything, even litanies of saints or rogation prayers, to distract Pélagie, whose soul seemed likely to break in two with each jolt of the cart. But the bone-setter stood ready with her collection of splints and ointments to dress her chief's wound. Pélagie might sigh and moan her fill, Célina would always be there doubling and redoubling her little attentions, with her clatter and chatter. To the point that the carts begged Bélonie to take up one of his favorite tales just to drown out the barnyard cackle.

The old man raised an eye to Pélagie, let out a Hee! then fell silent. He hadn't the heart for his phantom cart today, their souls were deep enough in mourning as it was. And without further ado he passed the stool to Pierre-à-Pitre.

This time it was Pélagie who turned to face him. She had seen it all, don't try to feign and pretend, Bélonie, she had guessed everything. She was miserable to her heart's core but she hadn't lost the thread of life unrolling before her. She would go on marching north at the head of her oxen even if she had to wear her heart in splints. Yes, Bélonie.

And so he would understand perfectly what her eyes said as they bored into his, she arched her back and lifted her head. No, no one among LeBlancs to come would ever say that Pélagie, even for an instant, had bitten the dust. She would march on without looking back, get that into your head, old chin-wagger.

But just as she went to take a deep breath to face the north again, a sob knotted her throat and a tear trickled down her nose. Bélonie quickly turned his head away, looking for a bit of ground he could place his foot on without crushing an ant. Let the Fool spin his tale, let him weave and invent and transpose if he must. Let him re-create the world from beginning to end, and turn it inside out, and . . . Poor Bélonie!

. . . Go on, Pierre-à-Pitre—that's what passing him the stool meant—amuse them if you've the heart for it. He, Bélonie, would never improvise like that, to the whim of the wind and the sway of the oxen. He held his tales from his father who had got them from his. You didn't go passing them around like chewing tobacco.

It must be said that Pierre-à-Pitre Gautreau, known as the Fool, had fewer scruples than Bélonie when it came to the storyteller's trance; let's say he was more accommodating to his public. He could spin you a tale as well by day as by night, at twilight or dawn, standing, fasting, eating, walking, jumping, farting . . .

"Shut up and spin."

He spun:

"It was in the time when animals could talk, just before the Great Rains."

. . . He means the Flood.

. . . Shh!

"My companion, the giant P'tite Goule, who was already alive then—it stands to reason on account of the fact that a year in a giant's life is as long as his guts, which are seventy times seven leagues long—well, this particular day the giant was lying in a bed of wild roses taking a nap with his mouth wide open. So as I was passing by I looked in and saw at a glance his eighteen rows of teeth. Not at one glance, no, on account of the fact I had to count and name them all: the upper teeth, the lower teeth, the front teeth, the molars, the grinders, the dog teeth, the palate teeth, the milk teeth, the eye teeth—which were cross-eyed I might add in passing—decayed teeth, impacted teeth, hollow teeth, wisdom teeth—completely empty those—saw teeth, sweet teeth, sharp teeth . . ."

This enumeration might have gone on a long time, since the

anatomy of a giant is limitless, but Pacifique Bourgeois, who had
an abscess devouring his cheek, realized he couldn't hang on a
minute longer. For days the poor man's tooth had been aching
and the long description of this gigantic dentition had done nothing to ease it. Arrived at the sharp teeth, he grasped his jaw and
groaned.

And that's when the war of the pinchers began.

At Pacifique's groan, and he wasn't one to groan over trifles,
up stepped the midwife-bone-mending-healer, Célina by name,
at the same time as the master smith.

Well now!

"And what's he doing here?"

"He's a blacksmith, that's what!"

And Marie-Marguerite Thibodeau thought it proper to add:

"In my country, the blacksmith's the man with the pinchers."

It was doubtless this reference to "her" country that got
Célina's arse in a tizzy. As if only the Thibodeaus had a right to
claim it as theirs! And Célina planted her fists on her hips and
stuck out her chops.

"Really?" she said.

"How come you say that, Célina? Would you have blacksmith's pinchers in that workbag of yours by any chance?"

Since Célina seemed to be getting the worst of it, Pierre-à-
Pitre the Fool, who loved to play tricks as much as tell tales and
fables, slipped up close to Célina and whispered two or three
words in her ear.

Célina seemed not to heed, but smiled a smile that at home we
call a grinch: a variation on "Aaah!" and "Heh! Heh!" that is
much more eloquent than your ordinary smile. So she grinched.

Did she or didn't she have any pinchers? That's what they
wanted to know. At last they discovered she didn't, but that she
could do without.

"What's the idea? Does the old witch think she can pull teeth
with her claws? That's black magic right out of *Grand Albert*."

The Bourgeoise was getting ready to add a string of choice
words when a new groan from her man cut short the sally. Better swallow the string back, they might need a healer yet. As for

the Thibodeaus, they didn't camouflage their scorn; they weren't
suffering from toothache. Marie-Marguerite summoned the cripple to get the pinchers out of her kit and show what she could
do.

The cripple swallowed the slight and went on grinching.
Then, taking in a great breath of air all round, as if marking out
her territory, she drew herself up, got down from the cart, and
tossed over her shoulder:

"I'll be over there at the foot of that wild plum if I'm needed."
And she made off for the tree so designated.

Marie-Marguerite and Jeanne Bourgeoise, thinking they had
the field to themselves, hailed the blacksmith.

"At least he's got pinchers."

. . . Pinchers: Oh yes, as for pinchers, they were pinchers all
right, no one could deny that. They were even such pinchers as
have rarely been seen applied to hoof of mare, and assuredly
never to the gums of a poor Christian suffering from an
abscessed tooth. And Anatole-à-Jude turned his long tongs
around and around in his hands.

"If the Bourgeois weren't such a close-beaked bunch," muttered Marie-Marguerite between her teeth, "it wouldn't be such
a job to stick a pair of pinchers in."

The Bourgeoise overheard and fired back:

"A pair for a giant's jaw, those are," said she, "but we Bourgeois don't live in the times of the Great Rains, and we don't
come down from Gargantua."

All this time the master smith was racking his brains and
measuring his pinchers against Pacifique Bourgeois's jaw. Then
on an impulse he decided to light up a fire and forge.

"What are you thinking of, Anatole-à-Jude?"

He went from thinking to doing just the same.

He lit his fire, tended it, blew on it, gathered the coals, and
began again. In the middle of a field it's no easy task to husband
the flame to heat the iron white hot.

"Go fetch me some wood chips and kindling, you young'uns."

Charlécoco, Madeleine, Catoune, the Cormiers, Thibodeaus,

and Basques, all led by the Fool, fed the flames while the giant blew.

"More! More!"

And they toted splinters of dry wood and huffed on the coals and puffed themselves out of breath. Quit squirming, Pacifique-à-Jacques, it's coming, the flame's turning blue.

"Him too, he's turning blue! Hurry up!"

Anatole-à-Jude hurried. But the blacksmith had run into a serious problem. Pinchers are used for pinching, but what was he going to pinch the pinchers with?

"Sweet Jesus!"

And all the tools and utensils were tried in turn.

"Not a hayfork, Charlécoco! A hayfork to hold pinchers with? Blockheads!"

. . . What a to-do!

"He'll never make it."

Yes, he'd make it. That's to say he managed to make the old pair of tin snips more or less into the shape of a set of tongs which more or less fit into the Bourgeois mouth. But what the blacksmith hadn't foreseen was that the tooth was impacted.

"Don't tell me!"

. . . It's true.

Just like him, wasn't it, the tooth impacted, its root completely crooked in the bone. Jeanne Trahan tried to explain that it was a sign of strength and virility, but for the moment they had other things to worry about than Pacifique-à-Jacques's virile instincts, and they made her shut up. You couldn't have found a pair of pinchers in the whole country to pull out a tooth like that. And the Thibodeaus looked at the Bourgeois, who looked at the Basques, who looked at the others, who returned the look to the blacksmith. There was no choice: he picked up the pinchers and jammed them into his patient's mouth. But at Pacifique's first howl, friend Anatole felt his own knees go weak and he ran to the edge of the path to flip his biscuit.

"He's going to puke! Clear the road!"

"Dear God in Heaven!"

The Thibodeau and Bourgeois clans clamped their heads in

their hands. It was just too much to ask of one man, to be smith
and tooth-puller the same day. You can't push a talent too far.
He had turned out a very fine pair of pinchers. There was always
that to it. And to save the honor of the clan, Marie-Marguerite
passed the pinchers to her son, Olivier, who passed them to Alban-à-Charles-à-Charles, who passed them to François-à-Pierre
Cormier, who passed them to François-à-Philippe Basque who
turned his head from right to left until it aimed straight at the
plum tree at the edge of the woods where, fresh as a bride, stood
none other than Célina.

She stepped out of her plum tree straight as a fence picket,
some would even have sworn under oath that she came on without limping, lordly, dignified, as proud as a girl who'd enjoyed
wealth and family all her life . . . which gives you some idea
. . . and then, casting a scornful eye on the new tongs still hot
from the fire, she reached under her cap and produced a long
hairpin, which she stuck into the coals of the forge. Next, on pretext of inspecting the patient's gum, she poured down his throat
half a flask of eau-de-vie of her own concoction, which immedi-
ately put Pacifique into a joyful mood. So joyful that he even forgot the quarrel about the chest.

"The chest? What chest? . . ."

A good sign. The tooth is ready. And Célina hails Pierre-à-
Pitre who steps up with a cork.

Marie-Marguerite and Jeanne Bourgeoise crane their necks.
But nobody dares say a word.

Now Célina takes up the blacksmith's pinchers . . .

. . . I told you so. She's going to use the pinchers . . .

. . . Be quiet.

. . . takes up the pinchers and uses them to remove from the
coals the hairpin, which by now is white hot. Then, under the astonished eyes of the Bourgeois and the Thibodeaus, she sticks it
into Pacifique Bourgeois's impacted tooth. It seems Célina's elixir
must have been stronger than her burning needle, for the victim
let his torturer burn the tooth to the root with no more reaction
than a spasm of the jaws that cut in two the cork that was meant
to keep his mouth open.

Once the operation was over, all that remained for the healer to do was to stuff the wound with a compress of figs and drain the abscess with a cataplasm of linseed applied to the throat.

"And from here on," she said to the circle around her, "let you all remember to put your left shoe on first when you get up in the morning."

". . . ?"

"Yes, that's right," my cousin Louis-the-Younger confided. "Put your left shoe on first to keep toothache away."

It was their belief and custom. And that explains why Célina, who was nevertheless so touchy about feet, especially the left one, felt free to mention it. Above all, it marks Célina's triumph that day over nature and over the forge, a victory that smoothed down her fur and unwrinkled the skin of her heart. She had succeeded in taking in all the carts' clans without letting out slack once, and shaking her head all the while as if to say, "Don't fail to let me know early next time you need me."

And all Acadie in the carts applauded their Célina. Poor Pacifique was half-dead from the experience, but the honor of the midwife-healer-bone-setter-and-henceforth-tooth-burner was safe. She gave the Thibodeaus back their pinchers without a word.

A few hours later she was discovered rejuvenating her cheeks with beetroot juice.

Where was Pélagie?

She hadn't attended the operation or shared in the jubilation over Pacifique's resurrextraction.

"Resurrextraction? What kind of language is that?"

Since their departure from Charleston, Pélagie had been absent long hours at a stretch, like a person with a pain to hide. Some talked of her son gone off to sea, while others . . .

"Couldn't you fix her up another little broth, Jeanne Aucoin?"

But even Jeanne Aucoin's broth lay heavy on her stomach. Grasp as she might at the least tuft, the least blade of grass, Pélagie felt herself sinking into the depths of her lethargy. In the blacksmith's flames she had felt her own heart flaming. Let it flame, let it flame and let that be an end to it. All the abscesses of all the Pacifiques in the world pulsing in her blood could hardly distract her from this pain more intolerable than fever.

"Hee! . . ."

She turned brusquely: Bélonie. You could hoist yourself up over everyone and everything, but not over Bélonie and his near one hundred years. Each of his "Hee's" was too heavy with meaning. They stared each other down, then it was she who dropped her eyes. But he hung on as if insisting. Pélagie tried to ignore him: The old chin-wagger had plenty of "Hee's" in reserve, and grinches to burn; he pulled a long face the way other folks stretch their legs; nothing to be alarmed about there.

"Hee! . . ."

All right, let's have it. What is it this time?

Then Bélonie got up and walked off, leading Pélagie to the edge of the wood where the Thibodeaus were holding a parley. And there she understood.

In less than two hours the Thibodeaus had confessed everything to Pélagie: the pull of the south, the dream of a new, unknown country; in short, Louisiana!

Louisiana!

So that was it! That's what had been gnawing at them so long, keeping them apart. Louisiana! And what about the others then? What about the rest of these carts that had been moving north for two years almost? And Acadie, what about Acadie? Had they been thinking about the land of their forefathers, the land they had quit that September morning and left fallow all this time?

. . . The Thibodeaus weren't abandoning their country, Pélagie, they were transplanting it in the south.

. . . In the south? But what's it got, this south, to bring on a change of heart like that? Haven't you had enough of the south after seventeen years of exile and black misery? Is it a death far from the graves of your ancestors you're seeking?

. . . No, no. Not death but another life with those cousins the Moutons, the Martins, and the Landrys who are founding new parishes along the bayous and already pasturing out their own cattle branded with their own mark. A plantation life, perhaps, on vast, rich, virgin lands . . .

"In the midst of strangers who'll sleep with your children and jabber in a tongue you can't understand."

"Not understand? Have you forgotten Pélagie of Grand-Pré, that the tongue they jabber in Louisiana is the same we brought out from France a century ago? And that in the century to come maybe it will be only there in Louisiana that we'll hear it spoken anywhere in the land of America?"

Pélagie swallowed this without replying. Anatole-à-Jude came quickly to her side and said gently:

"There's a fine lot of our own people settled there already. Be it in the north or in the south, it will always be Acadie, and we'll always be at home there."

"You'll be at home," replied Pélagie. "But then it's your choice."

Marie-Marguerite placed her hand on the arm of her cousin and companion.

"If you wanted, Pélagie, it would take only a single 'Dia!' to turn the oxen round to the south. And the whole family could enter Louisiana together by the front door."

Pélagie heard the words of her captain: "Better come in by the front door, by the sea."

"You'll be coming in the back door, by the woods and mountains, Marie-Marguerite. But no matter. Any gate is good that gets you home."

When the carts got the news with the first rays of the sun, beaks began to clatter again. Because of the mixed feelings. The Girouards, for example, like the Cormiers, had become very close to the Thibodeaus during the journey. Whereas more than once the Bourgeois had had to hide their scorn for these honest artisans who were very resourceful and not such a sorry lot as all that. As for the Basques, they generally got along well with everybody but were intimate with none; the blacksmith's departure mainly provided them an occasion to improvise farewells on the violin.

There remained Célina, Célina fresh from her victory that would have to be forgiven her. For already Jeanne Trahan was spreading the word that the Thibodeaus were having a hard time digesting yesterday's defeat and that . . .

Marie-Marguerite intercepted the word on the wing and winged it back in the Bourgeoise's face who nearly choked on it . . . A fine state of affairs when certain people, not too far off either, went around peddling calumnies at the very time they were just about to divide a people in two; a fine state of affairs when a family didn't have the right to decide its own future without the family next door sticking in its weasel nose and its wildcat claws! Well, it was high time to take off for Louisiana and start life over there; high time to leave those others all the room they needed to stretch out their legs in the cart, those niggardly, quibbling squabblers . . .

And Marie-Marguerite burst into sobs. In calling them pet names like that she suddenly realized that "those others" were the same who for more than a year had shared the bread of her table and the straw of her mattress: that these same crabby squabblers had squabbled with her and had crabbed round a fire that was hers also. From now on their life would be split, their homes would be rooted in lands a thousand leagues apart, and for generations perhaps . . . And in under an hour Marie-Marguerite's tears had reconciled all Acadie.

"You can send us pineapples by the *Grand'Goule*."

"Don't let the crocodiles snip your shanks in the bayous."

"I left a barnful of barley back at Les Mines. If you find it, make yourselves some soup."

"Don't eat shrimp in the dog days. And if you find any Cormiers down there . . ."

"We'll marry their daughters!"

"Heh, heh, heh!"

"Kiss the soil of Port-Royal for us and the shores of the French Bay."

"And give a good boot in the ass to any Lawrences and Moncktons you meet for a century or two."

The feasting and preparations lasted four days. Not that there was all that much to prepare, but . . .

"Give us another refrain, Basque, another rigadoon!"

Finally, however, they disengaged and parted, the Thibodeaus in a cartlet pulled by a single ox ceded them by Pélagie, one of the Troopers. Jeanne Bourgeoise had bawled all night claiming bias and unfair favoritism, which had the good effect of diverting both convoys from the wound that was driven into every heart. To the point where no one but Bélonie heard the adieus of Acadie-in-the-North to Acadie-in-the-South:

"Come back and see us in a couple of centuries, we'll still be there!"

And Pélagie watched this absurd and miserable little bit of the family move off to found a people down there in Louisiana.

Then suddenly in the midst of the general emotion Célina, who had just discovered a foreign object in the bottom of her apron pocket, brandished a fist toward the south, shouting:

"I'll never believe it! It's that handsome blacksmith who's left me his pair of pinchers!"

And the cart and its carts shook with laughter while the healer swallowed back her final snuffle.

PROPERTY OF THE PUBLIC LIBRARY ST. MARKS, ONT.

8

At the end of the last century Pélagie-the-Grouch used to insist to Bélonie's descendant that this story didn't hold water, that her ancestor Pélagie couldn't have strayed so far from her duty or so far from the straight line that led from south to north, from the Carolinas to Acadie.

"You won't get me to believe your stuff about Baltimore."

"But Baltimore was in the north, in the straight line."

"Not true north, north-northeast."

"Because according to your way of thinking you couldn't swing off course an inch? You had to cross the whole continent with your eyes shut, without reckoning on mountains and rivers, regardless of roads and paths? America wasn't a field of oats, Pélagie-the-Grouch."

She sat up with a jerk. They dared in this day and age to call her by her nickname, straight to her face!

Nickname? Everyone's got one.

Everyone's got one, well and good, but not everyone's got a

rascally, mean-minded one. Grouch! Who was the first mischief-maker to stick her with that name? Calixte-à-Pissevite was it? or Johnny Picoté?

Closer, Pélagie-the-Grouch, you'll have to look closer to home. Not that fine fellow the Hare-Lip, not her own brother-in-law? Still closer.

Pélagie-the-Grouch held her tongue. Closer than her husband's brother there was only her husband. And before venturing out on that ground, she'd have to explore the state of her heart to see how to behave in the event that she came up with any conclusive conclusions.

"You won't get me to believe that stuff," she repeated.

Not stuff, no, the straight truth. Driving her oxen north in the year 1772, Pélagie-the-Cart called out more Hue's than Dia's. And the oxen veered to the right.

"Toward Baltimore in Maryland."

"Had they already reached Maryland?"

Not just yet. First they had to cross North Carolina and later Virginia, and Virginia had plenty to tell this marching people.

A people is a big word to use for these shreds of families, pawing the ground and whipping the oxen, more and more often mired in the southern marshes. A big word, and yet . . .

For even the departure of the whole of the Thibodeau clan hadn't eased the cart's burden. No sooner had they gone than new families sprang up from the hayfields and the reed beds, Dear God! from the very stones of the roads, bestraddling the sideboards and throwing themselves on the necks of their friends and relations now climbing the continent. From the four horizons of North Carolina out sprang Héberts, Boudreaus, Robichauds-called-Robin, Landrys—Great God in Heaven! the same who were tied by legitimate bonds to the very family of Pélagie of Grand-Pré.

"Don't tell me!"

"My Lord! Is it possible?"

"And Jean?"

"And Pierre?"

"And that fine big gander Charles-Auguste?"

. . . No, Charles-Auguste had perished, struck down by English musket fire just as he was making for the woods, *pater noster qui est in coelis* . . . he's laid to rest there, an Indian assures me that he buried him himself at the mouth of the Rivière-aux-Canards, and since no family was present, he mumbled his own brand of prayers in his own tongue, Micmac it was, Christian prayers just the same, poor Charles-Auguste . . . But his son now, here's the youngest of his boys, look at that for a prize specimen, nearly of age and his eyes fixed homeward.

The prize specimen Charles-Auguste, Junior, a nervous, prancing youth, in reality had his eyes fixed on Madeleine, by your leave Mother Landry, for his homeland memories went way back to when he was three, memories of months of seasickness followed by a landing in North Carolina, his skin clinging to his bones and his bones emptied of marrow.

"Still, we were luckier than the Thériots and the Chauvins in Virginia."

". . . ?"

It was Célina who wanted to know everything, from top to bottom, about the fate of the Virginia deportees, Célina with no kin of her own inquiring endlessly about the missing ones.

"When we pass through, we'll pick up what's left of your Chauvins and Thériots. What's a cart more or less? Our oxen aren't fussy."

Agnès Dugas known as Landry, wife and mother of Charles-Auguste's line, felt the time had come to enlighten the cripple and her relations about the fate of the Virginia Acadians.

"There's none left," she said.

"What's that you say?"

"I say what is. The Virginia lot were pushed back to the sea; then thrown into prisons in London; then exchanged for English prisoners and sent to France; and finally lodged, at the King's expense, in Belle-Île-en-Mer in Brittany, and others on lands in Poitu around Poitiers and Archigny. That's what I heard from one Jean-Aubin Mignault, who held it from a certain Marin Petitpas, who traveled a lot, as his name clearly indicates."

But the most terrifying story told by Agnès Dugas Landry,

called the Magpie, wife of the Gander, she saved for the hour when the carts oil their axles, that's to say twilight. So it was to the sound of creaking wheels that she began, without preamble and without asking permission, to tell her tale.

"Cap-de-Sable, now, the following spring . . ."

"Following what?"

. . . I ask you!

". . . The spring following the autumn of 1755, at Cap-de-Sable, as I say, that handsome Lawrence—may the devil take his soul!—sent one of his majors to inquire after the Acadians settled there."

"At Cap-de-Sable?"

"You've got it. A Major Prebble, then, turned up with a troop of soldiers who didn't notice, the brutes, that all the men were out at sea and the women and children quaking alone by the hearths. A nice mess they made of it, them soldiers: set fire to the houses, slaughtered the cattle, shipped off the whole race. When the fishermen came to come home, each to his own, nothing left: no house, no animals, no wife, no heirs, no little nipper in the cradle. There's some went mad on the spot, others threw themselves into their boats to chase after the schooners, already far out at sea. They didn't catch a thing. And the survivors of the deportees of Cap-de-Sable still drag out their days in Carolina as I speak to you now. It seems they still sit up waiting for their fathers' return. Think of that!"

They would wait for years, those survivors of Cap-de-Sable, a whole lifetime; but according to my cousin Louis-à-Bélonie, they could wait an eternity and it still wouldn't be long enough. And when I asked what he meant . . .

"It wouldn't be long enough to reassemble the families," he explained, "or to make them forget. I've heard say that the massacre at Cap-de-Sable was the last shameful act the English could swallow, because six generations of storytellers and root-delvers vowed to pass on the true story from forbear to father to offspring, which means that Major Prebble's descendants will have to stay clear of Cap-de-Sable for a long time to come."

"Think of that," echoed Jeanne Aucoin.

And all the carts stopped oiling their wheels.

"Anyways," said Charlécoco, "there's no oil left."

"No more oil! That's the last straw!"

You can do without most everything in a cart, but not without the cart just the same. And with the cart you need wheels and well-oiled axles.

"Well, we can't just spit on the hubs."

"Or pump off a little elbow grease."

Célina turned to the Fool. He'd have to scratch his genius again. Come on, inventor of the tooth-burning pin, invent, discover, imagine something or other. Oil's a thing you find somewhere in nature, in plants, in the earth . . .

"We could kill a pig and melt down the lard."

"We need that kind of grease more on our own skinny bones than on your cart wheels."

"Come on, Pierre-à-Pitre, word-juggler, juggle."

But the Fool had time neither to show his genius nor his juggling, for the Negro was there before him.

The Negro? Yes, indeed! The Negro, the Charleston slave, the famous Théotiste, who refused to the end to take the name, out of respect for Théotiste Bourg, Pélagie's father, one of the Grand-Pré notables, no, he couldn't, he was a slave, black of skin and origin, wrested out of chains, brought up from a cargo hold . . .

"And what about us, didn't we pass through the cargo holds?"

It wasn't the same, not the same at all. He was black in a white land; then, too, he owed his liberty to Pélagie. He could accept life, thanks, thanks very much, but his liberty, that he cast at the feet of his masters, masters who in two years now had neither whipped him nor deprived him of food, who had even hidden him from the slave traders throughout the whole length of Carolina and Virginia. He would gladly have drawn oil from his own bones, if bones gave oil.

Instead he took it from garter snakes.

"Yuck!"

Why yes, Jeanne Trahan, why not! A garter snake is one of

God's creatures like the rest. It's got to have some use. So they used it for oiling the carts' axles.

The Negro grabbed a dozen snakes one after another and held them wriggling between his fingers; then he rolled them carefully around the axles. Don't wriggle, little fellow. The giant did the rest, lifting each twelve-spoked wheel at arm's length.

"Well, that way I've one worry less," declared Pélagie. "It so happens there's no shortage of snakes in America."

And turning to the Bourgeoise she added:

"And then pass the basin to them that needs it."

Little did Pélagie know how much to the point she spoke. That night they needed more basins than the carts could supply. It was François-à-Pierre Cormier who hastened over to ask for Célina: Marie was about to give birth before term.

"Great God!"

"Is it the sight of the snakes brought it on?"

"If only the little one's not marked by it . . ."

"Shut up. What kind of talk is that now!"

"Go fetch me sheets and lots of water. Light a big fire, Charlécoco."

And change this, and turn that round, and get that out of my road.

What a turmoil! Yet she'd seen plenty of others, this midwife who had brought half of the basin of Les Mines into the world. Why so excited all of a sudden?

This time it was Pélagie who smiled at Old Bélonie and his phantom cart. The midwife was giving a child back to the Cormiers, a new Frédéric to replace the other. Life had spare parts in reserve and knew how to renew itself from within.

Bélonie felt his nose out of joint. And how, according to Pélagie, did this dialectic between life and death explain Célina's fidgets?

Pélagie remained silent. It was true. Célina was seized by a sort of agitation like a vicarious joy. Yes, she had brought plenty of children into the world, but none before had been drawn out of her own heart, pushed forth by her own muscles. How's

that? . . . But what had got into the cripple today? Did she
think to deliver a child out of her own barren belly? Célina was
sweating and swooning at once, and when finally she got the
new Frédéric's head out from between his mother's thighs, she
spread her own legs wide to pull better. A cramp invaded her
body, a cramp held back for thirty years, thirty years of her life
as a neglected woman.

Because? . . .

Because something had happened. A look, a tenderness, a sign
of complicity, and that had sufficed. Perhaps she was madly in
love? No, Alban, it wasn't a passion. Except that . . . Affection,
surely, at any rate. There was that to it. And in the heart of this
cripple who had been left on the shelf since she'd come into the
world, the first gallantry shown her in fifty years made her head
spin. Head, tripes, and feet. Yes, she was dancing, Bélonie's
word for it, dancing on her clubfoot yet!

Did he have such great charms, then, this fool Pierre-à-Pitre
Gautreau? Anyway he had great . . .

"Not in front of the children, François-à-Philippe Basque!"

Above all he had veins and arteries full of blood, and under
his pate a well of resourcefulness and creativity; and a skin sensi-
tive to the slightest breeze; and a perpetual need to pinch and
prod other people's skins. And whereas no man, no matter how
frisky, would have dared tickle or prod Célina, he, Pierre-à-Pitre,
had become so bold he'd run his hand round the nape of her
neck and down the rake of her spine without getting massacred,
and some even claim . . .

Nothing whatsoever. That's enough of that. You're not going
to start making up stories about Célina's virtue after fifty years
of blather and gossip about her deformities. Enough! Let everyone look to his own onions.

Célina's onions, at this Virginia stage of the adventure,
consisted in bringing a new little Frédéric into the world. A little
Frédéric who had been groping all night in the dark to see the
light of day, and finally, at dawn, when he at last got out of
limbo, declared himself a girl.

"Not possible!"

Now who was it that for months had been announcing a boy?
Who'd taken it upon themselves to step in and teach God his
business? They'd wanted so badly to turn the tables on Death
and avenge the little Frédéric left in South Carolina, they hadn't
for a second imagined heaven might fail in its duty and miss the
rendezvous.

"What do you mean, miss the rendezvous?" snapped the midwife feeling herself somehow guilty of not having finished the
job. "Since when did heaven promise nothing but boys? And
why make boys in times of peace? Or even if there was a war
on? Eh?"

And all the men thought Célina was going to declare war on
the spot, just to clear her conscience.

"Who here leads the oxen?" she added, tapping the ground
with her clubfoot.

All heads, male and female, turned toward Pélagie. If Acadie
hadn't perished body and soul in the Great Disruption, it was
thanks to women. And Célina spat on the ground to show what
men could do.

Which didn't prevent little Frédéric from being a girl, a girl
they'd have to begin by giving a name to.

"What a to-do!"

Someone proposed Frédérica—not Frédérique—but no, in 1773
no one would have thought of confusing the sexes to that point
—or what about Marie after her mother, or Madeleine-Mar-
guerite-Marie-Anne-Jeanne, or Jeanne-Anne-Marie-Marguerite-
Madeleine-Marie? In old-time Acadie they didn't range outside
those set names. A name was passed on like a heritage: family
names for boys; given names for girls. To start a fresh line required a great event. Finally, it was the father who had the pre-
sentiment the time was ripe. For the little girl just born was
above all her brother's heir; she had inherited the life of her
brother left behind in Carolina. And here was Frédéric reincarnated now in Virginia.

"So how would it be if we called her Virginie?" ventured François-à-Pierre-à-Pierre-à-Pierrot.

Virginie! This Virginie Cormier would be heir to a land, a land of passage, a halting place on their way. And later she would be a living memory of the Virginia stage of their journey.

"But there's not a single Virginie in her whole line or her whole connection, assuredly."

"A line's got to begin somewhere. From here on we'll grant the name of Virginie to the last-born Cormier in every generation to come. And it will become a family name like Madeleine, Jeanne or Marie-Marguerite."

So they baptized the first Virginie with due form and ceremony: with water, salt, christening robes, credo, paternosters, and the violin. The three-stringed violin. For these same three poor strings had sounded with all the airs of France and Acadie since the violin left the islands. And don't go thinking it's as easy as all that to find a violin string in a foreign land, in the woods and back pastures of Virginia at the beginning of the troubles. Besides, since the departure of the Thibodeaus for Louisiana, they had lacked tools and craftsmen.

They were to lack a good many things that year, it seems. But they found a crucifix.

It was the Allains' crucifix. Neither the LeBlancs nor the Girouards nor the Bastaraches had seen the shadow of a cross since the shores of the French Bay, of a real Christ on the Cross, that is, nailed at the three corners, in pewter or silver, no, not since Port-Royal or Grand-Pré. So you can imagine the commotion when the Allains of North Carolina turned up, came puffing and panting after the carts in Virginia—wait up for them for the love of God!—and tossed into the lap of the caravan an authentic crucifix saved from the catastrophe.

"Not saved from the church in flames, you don't mean it!"

"From the same flaming church in flames."

Jean-Baptiste Allain had taken it down himself from the Stations of the Cross of Saint-Charles of Grand-Pré, believe it or not. Of fourteen Stations, thirteen had perished in the flames. But one was left, saved by none other than Jean-Baptiste in person who proved it by showing around the marks of the fire on the palms of his hands, the same hands that had taken the cross down from the flaming wall.

Beautiful big scars that he'd kept in the palms of his hands like the stigmata of Christ on the Cross. And he circulated them under the eyes of the carts so they would remember till the end of time. Others had managed to save old men or children from the Great Disruption, or to save their own lives. He, Jean-Baptiste Allain, had saved his Lord Jesus Christ. His heroic and pious act would count for him in paradise.

Pélagie silenced the Bastaraches and the Groués who were preparing to put their word in. After all, the Allains had as much right as anyone to a place in paradise, and in the meantime an equal right to join in the journey home.

"From here on, the cross will have its place at the head of the caravan to show the road and fend off demons."

And turning to Bélonie:

"But first we're going to rebaptize Virginie in the sign of the True Cross, the one from Grand-Pré, as a pledge of fidelity to our ancestors' religion. And it's Bélonie who's going to officiate."

Bélonie? . . .

Indeed, Bélonie the patriarch who for the moment would forget his Wagon of Death and preside over the rites of life. It was Pélagie who pushed him into it with taunts of:

"A life for a life, Bélonie."

"Heel . . ."

. . . Did she think she'd bring back home less of the dead than the living? Did she really think her wooden cart would reach her front gate before his, the one that had never ceased creaking its wheels after them since Georgia?

And yet life was springing up anew in the carts, Bélonie. Despite the defections, despite the deaths, life was coming out on top. Look at Catoune, the child snatched from perdition, today her breasts are round and she's rocking the newborn babe as if it were her own; look at that fine young gander Charles-Auguste's son who's turning around Madeleine, who's pretending to try to pretend she doesn't notice; look at the Fool Pierre-à-Pitre who's got Célina giggling . . . Cut that out, you big nincompoop!

What shocking behavior! . . . Hee-Hee! . . . look at the Negro
wrested from his chains who's fuller of life every day and already speaking our tongue, almost rolling his r's, and who, by my
faith, has turned a shade whiter, sure as I'm standing here; and
look at the giant, P'tite Goule, the faithful cabin boy who blushes
hours on end kneeling at Catoune's feet.

"And always squinting east, the giant is, too."

It was true. The giant hadn't forgotten. The Fool was a scatterbrain, a genius but a giddy creature, while the giant, despite
his devotion to Catoune and Pélagie, still smelled the salt in the
air each time an onshore wind blew inland. And then he would
turn his large, nearly empty eyes on Pélagie and stare at her
wordlessly.

They had been wordless both of them for more than a year.
Baltimore! Baltimore! Was this Maryland so far then? In a year
you age twelve months. And a woman going on thirty-nine, soon
forty, has no time to lose. Time won't wait; time spares no one
. . . It's the cruelest tyrant, after Death. . . . Out there on the
sea he'd be bronzing in the sun. His voice would have dropped a
note or two in his throat. A man's year on the open sea swells the
nostrils and hardens the muscles. But a woman's year, whipped
by the winds . . . Would he notice the lines that had crept up
her neck and invaded her temples and blemished her forearms?
And how much longer would her breasts stay firm? My God!
Hurry on! Northward. On, on, to the north, to the north-
northeast.

And Pélagie-the-Cart, who for fifteen years had aimed fixedly
south to north, now began more and more to veer to the northeast. "Hue! Hue!" she would call to her oxen. And the oxen, each
day a little harder of hearing, would no longer obey the first
command. But P'tite Goule with a flick of the back of his giant's
hand more cutting than a leather whiplash would bring the Hussars and the Corporals around the right way, to the high-pitched
protests of Jeanne Aucoin and Célina whose affection for the
beasts had never faltered.

As for Jeanne la Bourgeoise, better not lay a finger on the single Trooper she had left.

A finger! They were even talking of eating it.

"No!!!"

And Jeanne's cry echoed throughout the whole of Virginia.

"In that case," interjected François-à-Pierre, who now had an extra mouth to feed in his family, "we'll have to go work in the fields."

In the fields? What was he thinking of? Fifteen families already, as many carts and wagons, oxen, mules, old men, cripples, and newborn babes, and François Cormier was talking about haymaking?

. . . No, not hay, corn, Indian corn, maize, call it what you will. Let all hands, all arms strong and long enough, come work in the fields this harvest time in exchange for part of the crop.

"Even in the south the winters are long, especially in a south creeping up toward the north."

Pélagie cast her eyes east, then lowered them to her people of the carts. Virginia that had refused shelter to her countrymen fifteen years ago would be forced to feed them today.

"Unyoke, Charlécoco. We'll take to the fields to lay in stores. Because it's good to put aside some of the best for the worst."

And the whole of homebound Acadie, who were used to expressing themselves in half words, understood that there might be worse days coming when they would need their best reserves. So that's how, for the time being, the Bourgeoise saved her favorite.

A few months later, leaving Virginia, the Acadians turned around for a last time to look at this land that in 1755 had pushed the deportees back to the sea. And Alban-à-Charles-à-Charles, lifting the little Virginie up at arm's length, said to the whole of this land he now left behind:

"You weren't able to stop this seed from springing up out of your roots, regardless."

And the carts took the road to the east, straight east, there where the sun rises.

PROPERTY OF THE
PUBLIC LIBRARY
ST. MARYS, ONT.

9

Hold on, Pélagie! Pélagie, hold on! Better take time to try the lie of the wind.

Huh!

The wind! North, northeast, southeast, southwest, no force in nature could halt Pélagie's march to the sea. She whipped the oxen to the quick; she pestered those flabby-assed cart boys, Charlécoco who couldn't get the yokes adjusted properly; she shouted, yelled, let fly a string of Hues! Dias! Hue-Hos! and Giddaps! . . . You could scarcely recognize her.

And Bélonie shook his head, tut, tut! . . . trying to catch the breath that leaked out of his nostrils, hissing . . . ssss . . . ssss . . . Hold on, Pélagie!

"This going to last much longer, this trot of yours?"

Pélagie stopped short and looked Jeanne Aucoin in the eye. How's that? This woman who had righted an overturned boat in the icy waters of the French Bay, had revived the drowning, had collected their scattered belongings and saved half her Giroué in-laws, who stood there today as straight and tall as a stand of beech, she, the Jeanne Aucoin of the great moments, was she all of a sudden afraid of breathing in a gulp of salt air?

"What's frightening or worrying you? We all came out of the sea, every last one. And from time to time we need to flush out our lungs and tubes with it."

"By my way of thinking, we're going to flush them to death if we don't slow down some," Alban-à-Charles-à-Charles countered.

But from the first day Pélagie had seen that the Girouards were slackers and she set small store in their backchat: old men and children in the carts, the healthy on foot, no more need be said.

However, the Bourgeois came over in turn to talk to her. But the Bourgeois, why the Bourgeois had been talking through their hats since Carolina, everyone knew that. Whiners and busybodies they were. Like the Allains, for that matter, and the Babineaus, who since Maryland had been trying to carve themselves out a place in the carts without undue effort.

Whoa, Pélagie, now you're exaggerating.

And all at once here come the Cormiers, you could hardly call them groaners, not the Cormiers who had already buried a child and an ancestor, who had lost all they had and borne the weight of exile without raising their voices, now the Cormiers too came to complain to Pélagie. Little Virginie was suffering from colic and cholera—the small cholera, that acts like the trots—we couldn't afford another death, Pélagie, not this little Virginie, first of her line, who was to pass her name on to all Cormiers to come.

This time Pélagie stopped the oxen. A child is a child. And it was for children she had struggled all these years and shouldered the yoke and headed north.

"Célina!"

And Célina redoubled her attentions to Virginie who lay cradled in Catoune's untiring arms. Day and night Catoune watched over Virginie as over the child that she, the mutilated victim of the holds, would never have. Catoune and Virginie, those two innocents snatched from the leer of Destiny and the black mares of the phantom cart, yes, Bélonie, even if it meant leaving half one's heart behind into the bargain.

So Pélagie ordered a rest to replenish strength and stores.

It was about time. They lacked everything; and what they still had was going to rack and ruin: the mattresses spilled their straw from gaping holes; the oxen threw their worn, twisted shoes in the stones of the road; gums ravaged by scurvy bled profusely and Célina, seconded by her faithful Fool, couldn't stop the hemorrhaging. It was high time to rest the carts, men and beasts.

Poor Pélagie! How could she rest her heart, galloping toward the sea, almost racing out of her body? No rest for Pélagie in this land of Virginia, or in Maryland before they reached the port of Baltimore. And she sent her twin sons to left and right to gather news of the capital. Was it still far? How many leagues? What season did the ships come in? And the four-masters? Had they seen a four-master? . . . The twins came back loaded with information as rare and various as the price of tea, the changes of the moon, the return of the wild geese, the first signs of rebellion among the colonists around Boston, the poor codfishing season, the arrival of a cargo of oriental silks, the founding of an academy of music somewhere in the north in a town whose name they forgot. Then Pélagie flew into a rage and sent out her best reserves, the fool and the giant. The giant to break trail and defend the expedition and the fool to wheedle information out of those tight-lipped colonists who saw informers everywhere. Till one day:

"Baltimore's a wee bit further south. We've come up too far."

A bombshell! A cannonball right in the middle of the circle of campers around the fire. And the fire went pssst! and began to splutter.

"I'll never believe it! I can't believe we're going to turn back now."

Just fancy that! Such protests from the mouths of none other than the Bourgeois and Girouards in unison, the same who had made the cart turn back to Port-Royal-in-the-South three years before. It just goes to show you, eh?

. . . No, Pélagie, not the Girouards, you're rambling, you know very well they were settled at Beaufort . . .

Pélagie answered neither Bélonie's remark nor the others' grumblings. If they'd doubled back once before, they could do it again. Nobody, but nobody, do you hear, would oblige her to carry on north when her own son, and the Basques' own son, and a whole four-master were there waiting for them close by in Baltimore.

Of course, a four-master, above all a four-master, and its captain, were waiting for them there in the port, that was clear as day. Fifteen families against one captain, that's what she was putting in the balance, this Pélagie; three years against a day, no one was taken in there. A handsome fellow, this Beausoleil, and a fine man, too, no doubt, but . . .

"Who saved your kin at the risk of his own life."

. . . Yes, a brave man, no one denied that, but . . .

"And who, this very hour, is still ferrying what remains of your families over the Atlantic."

. . . On that score the Bourgeois, the Allains, the Giroués all agreed, but . . .

"And who was it, if not he, who with his own two hands broke the helm of an English ship full of prisoners and seized the ship to bring you home again?"

. . . It was Beausoleil, we know, Pélagie, but . . .

"But what, you mule-headed bunch? Has nobody here got any guts left? No memories left in the pit of their stomachs?"

"What we have left is mainly children," François-à-Pierre-à-Pierre came over to say. "And what's left for them is to survive into the future. And that means we mustn't endanger it, Pélagie LeBlanc."

She, endanger the future of their children? She, Pélagie-called-the-Cart! But who had got them out of their miserable Georgia and Carolina in the first place? And who had provided the draft oxen and the mastercart to trace the ruts for the rest of the carts and wagons? Eh? And even today when the colonies were begining to rise up one after another to wage war against the Empire, at this very hour when the land of America was beginning to tremble under the hooves of the battle chargers, at this same hour who, in her cupped hands, held the compass whose needle pointed north? Hadn't she earned a single day of life, of life for herself, this Pélagie, after a whole existence given over to saving others?

She wiped her brow and glanced round at the still-furrowed foreheads. Every line was a wound and each spark that filtered between the lashes a cry to the heavens. They had shouldered their share of trouble, every last one, without for all that renouncing their share of hope. Today their hope aimed north, and it was none other than Pélagie who had lit that fire in their hearts.

. . . The Bourgeois hoped to find their old lands spread out over a third of Port-Royal Valley where thousands of apple trees left untended might any day go wild; the Cormiers dreamt of the walls of Fort Beauséjour, that had sheltered the last days of an Acadie surprised in a heavy slumber; the Girouards thought of the dead they had not had the time or the right to bury; the Basques saw again those vast shores opening on an ocean dotted with unexplored islands; the Allains, Boudreaus, Babineaus, and Landrys all had their eyes riveted on this promised land that might still conceal the missing half of their families who had disappeared in the disaster.

Pélagie pressed her temples with her hands. And what about her? Did you think she'd forgotten this lost paradise buried in the depths of her entrails and loins half her life long? Toward what goal had she set her cart and oxen if not to this Acadie-in-the-North? An Acadie where she had left more than all these whiners put together, make no mistake about that, you band of slobbering crybabies. But of course she wanted to rediscover her Acadie just as it was before, with grain in the garret, cider in the cellar, animals in the stable, a fire in the hearth, and love in the belly. Her children were growing up . . . just look at Madeleine over there, born in the Disruption but now making up to the son of that fine gander, Charles-Auguste . . . her children would set-

tle there, they would rebuild the country around her, but she
Pélagie, whose veins had not dried up yet, who still had marrow
in her bones and juice in her voice, what would she do in a
Acadie that had turned her away from happiness?

"Dia!" she yelled to the oxen. "I'll take you north, but not be
fore I've taken news of our brothers in Baltimore."

And before the Allains, Landrys, Giroués, Cormiers, and eve
the Bourgeois had time to grouch, they had already turned hal
circle and taken the road south behind Pélagie's cart.

"Baltimore! My God, is it possible!"

Indeed, and a fine town it was too, almost welcoming, by m
faith, with its English and its Irish Catholics . . . the Allain
couldn't get over it, Catholics, do you hear that! And a whit
church in the middle of town with its doors wide open to the ex
iles the next Sunday morning, the first consecrated Roma
church they'd seen since the shores of the French Bay. And th
men took off their shoes before stepping into the nave.

"And that's not all."

No not at all, for a few leagues from there, on the outskirts o
Baltimore, was a whole village of Acadians that went by th
name of French Town, do you hear that! With a priest, Abb
Robin, who sang them Latin in their own tongue. The Jeanne
the Marie-Annes, and the Marguerites sniveled for joy whil
their men thwacked each other on the backs to loud shouts of
"*Salut,* old trunk of a Robichaud from Rivière-des-Canards
Salut, François-à-Pierre-à-Pierre-à-Pierrot!" Such a reunion a
they'd dreamed of since Georgia. Not just isolated branche
holed up precariously along the seaboard, but entire village
transplanted in Maryland soil: Newton, Marlborough, Belisle
and, hold tight everyone, Annapolis! "That mean anything t
you? Annapolis!"

Yes, indeed, that meant plenty to these men and women, na
tives of Port-Royal.

Pélagie grew gloomy:

"Let's hope they don't change the name of Grand-Pré before
set foot there again."

"Which is why," replied Pacifique, "we don't want to tarry too long on the way."

Pélagie planted a long hard look in the middle of his forehead.

"For that matter, we're well enough off here amongst our own people. Even the foreigners in Maryland treat us like brothers. We could well use the time to rest our bones a bit."

That was Célina's feeling too, and Charles-Auguste's and Madeleine's, and all of the young folk in general, and the giant in particular, the feeling of all the carefree lovers who had found happiness in the carts. Acadie could wait, the present hour was so sweet, the springtime so gentle. Baltimore overflowed with flowers and birds perfuming the air with words of love. It was almost indecent.

. . . Take that Célina, for instance, just look at her . . .

If Célina had only known, her own thoughts about Jeanne Aucoin were exactly like those Jeanne Aucoin entertained about her. For La Girouère, who made no secret of pinching the underarm of her second-bed Alban, and even his underthigh, remained completely astonished at the least giggle the gallant ticklings of Pierre-the-Fool solicited from her companion Célina.

"It just goes to show you," said Pélagie to herself, for from her first day in Baltimore she had felt beseiged by spring from the nape of her neck to the nick of her ankles.

It just went to show that no one quite understood what had hit the carts in this spring of 1774, overcome as they were by their own metamorphoses, or too preoccupied with trying to keep their hearts in place. Maryland was the first truly hospitable halt in four years, and the deportees drew a long breath of it to keep in reserve. For bad times to come, they told themselves.

Except for Pélagie. Pélagie believed she could see her bad times drawing to an end. The very appearance of the four-master in port would carry off her nightmares forever. And every morning she would go down to the harbor to ask for news from Atlantic shipping there.

"A four-master, *Grand'Goule* by name, with a golden-haired figurehead."

"I seen her six months ago in the Bermudas repairing her foresail. Seems last November's hurricane didn't spare her."

"If my eyes didn't deceive me, in January she dropped anchor at the mouth of the Savannah, the saucy bitch. Seems she ran afoul of a pirate ship off the Florida coast. But I heard say the pirate took to his heels and made for the open sea."

. . . French ships that spoke her tongue.

"Must have had a hell of a captain at the helm and a devil of a look on her, that *Grand'Goule* of yours, to scare off a pirate."

. . . A hell of a captain indeed. And Pélagie hugged her arms to her breast. Then the next day she came back to the port for more news.

"February was a tough month, ma'am. The worst in twenty years afloat on the northern seas."

"He says the month of February was a massacre, the worst he's seen in twenty years sailing the Great Northern Sea. So you shouldn't be surprised, my little lady, if your gallant captain's laid up in drydock somewhere in the southern isles. Meantime, I've a hold full of tars and one able quartermaster who'd be right glad to look after anyone that needs some consoling."

Next day Pélagie got her giant to accompany her, and her informers, French, Dutch and English, treated her with respect.

"*Hola! que hembra guapisima!*"

"*Bom dia, senhora!*"

"*Déu vos guard!*"

. . . Spaniards, Portuguese, Catalans . . . Baltimore was the crossroads of the world. Only one flag was missing. And Pélagie saw her people's feet beginning to twitch and the oxen beginning to paw the ground. Spring was swallowed up in summer, a summer as torrid as winter had been dirty and wet. And the Bourgeois, then after them the Allains, began to complain of not being able to support the southern heat.

"You put up with the fevers and dog days of those rotten southern swamps for fifteen years and now you've got the nerve to boggle and snort in this blessed land of the Virgin Mary?"

"The Virgin Mary? Where'd she go dig that up?"

Célina cut them short:

"And Maryland, what's that signify, according to you?"

For Célina didn't like to see them lay the blame on Pélagie and stepped up to throw the weight of her knowledge of delving into the debate. Once accustomed to clearing the brush out of family trees, it's an easy step to geography, and without drawing breath she could root-delve water courses, mountains, valleys, and place names. So, for the Bourgeois, Giroués, Allains, and other nigglers, she delved through the brush to the root of Maryland, which took its name from the "land"—like you say in French, *le pays*—of the Virgin Mary.

All that right off by heart on her fingertips.

The Bourgeois and the other nigglers stood there open-mouthed, and Célina strode off smiling, satisfied to have gained a day or two in Baltimore for Pélagie.

At last, however, they ran through Baltimore's charms. But mainly ran through the creative and inventive powers of Pierre-à-Pitre, who had managed to distract the carts from their compass bearing till August. But one day the north took over, and Pierre-à-Pitre sagged to the ground between Pélagie and Célina and threw in the sponge. He had tried everything, the Fool had, everything: He had mislaid the Negro in the jumble of slave huts on the outskirts of town and made the carts hunt for him for three whole days; he had practically poisoned the Trooper and the two Corporals by hiding wild mustard under their hay; had made the giant dismantle a bridge that led to the road north; got Catoune to run away; then Madeleine; then the son of that fine gander Charles-Auguste; then ran away himself. All this drove the carts to tearing their hair and hurling insults and to accusations that it was all being done on purpose.

Of course it was on purpose. It was even on purpose that Pierre-à-Pitre, at the limit of his invention, ended up behind bars. But that time the Fool had to pay more than he'd counted on, and if it hadn't been for the intervention of Abbé Robin in person, the poor devil might have spent the rest of his days tressing straw in the Baltimore prison, all for the sake of his loyalty to his masters Beausoleil and Pélagie, and for Célina's fine eyes.

"Célina's fine eyes! Ouch!"

And the carts rocked with laughter.

"Why not her fine legs while you're at it?"

The Fool laughed along with the rest, always being of the best disposition in the world. In fact, he was doubtless focusing neither on her legs, nor on her eyes, but on something somewhere in between that might be located just as well under her skin as under her skirts. He was a strange creature, this cabin boy, incomplete, unfinished, who after twenty years was still looking for his mother and must have found a vague smell of her lingering around Célina.

And the prison?

The prison was for theft. Think of the boldness of it: A deportee, an outlaw, who had left his base and was trying to get home down a back alley, a sailor from a ship guilty of mutiny and hijacking, and some would have said piracy, a wanted man, neither more nor less, and in broad daylight going out and stealing Indian silks off an open counter. It had to be on purpose!

"Hee! Hee!"

This time Bélonie himself laughed aloud. Not smiled or grinched but frankly laughed. And this got everyone to share the mirth. The whole thing had been done in such a clever, droll way that even the Bourgeois could appreciate the craftiness of it and even the Allains winked at the sin.

Everything had begun one morning of harsh sunlight that right down to the shadows of the folds brought out the threadbare spots in their well-scrubbed clothes. Scrubbed in stony stream beds for four years, then patched, darned, mended with ground ivy, and yellowed in the crude southern light. That morning Pélagie had cast a woeful eye on her shift and petticoat agonizing in the sun. And Pierre-à-Pitre had seen her.

She raised her head and, seeing the Fool, forced a laugh:

"Nothing much left to do with such castoffs," she said. "This winter I'll card them out to make blankets."

Her laugh sounded brave, but it rang hollow. It gave the Fool a pain in the stomach.

"We're scarcely presentable to strangers anymore," she added, looking out to sea. "But it's no easy matter to pound and comb flax in a cart."

The same day Pierre-à-Pitre decided to carry out his master stroke in the Baltimore market. He'd have to hurry to get the women well dressed before the *Grand'Goule* came into port. Pélagie was certainly worth a few widths of cotton. Better still, silk. Indian silks for Pélagie, Madeleine, Catoune, and Célina. And linen caps and lace handkerchiefs and bibbed aprons and fine wool shawls and soft leather shoes and striped bodices and petticoats and . . . and . . . And Pierre-the-Fool embarked on the most daring and ingenious acrobatics of his life. Acrobatics for legs, fingers, and wits. Especially wits.

"You mean? . . ."

Just so, magic. Not black magic, no sorcery, not a bit of it. Pierre-à-Pitre Gautreau was a native of his native land, son of an artisan in the basin of Les Mines, baptized with holy water and confirmed with the sacred cream. None of his kin had ever leaned toward evil ways or sipped at a cauldron of snake and toad juice. Pierre-à-Pitre's magic came not from the devil but from knowledge mixed with skill and nimblewittedness, nothing more. On the word of a Bélonie-à-Bélonie-à-Bélonie.

So he made his way to the marketplace and set up his stand. In a manner of speaking. In reality, he perched himself on an upturned barrel and started his spiel. He announced that he knew the secret of turning hemp fiber into linen thread, and linen thread into silk; of changing an egg into a rabbit and a rabbit into a pig; of changing tin into silver and silver into gold.

Humph! We'll see about that.

Then, just to test publicly how well his fingers functioned, he proceeded to perform five or six conjuror's tricks which drew an "Aaah!" from his audience that rapidly ran through the other stalls. In his fingers, chickens grew rabbits' ears and hopped off on four legs into the crowd; ducks began to converse with magpies in their tongue; calves sang and pigs turned somersaults; a donkey farted out the tune of *Comin' through the rye*. And to top it off, he flipped a tuppence in the air, which fell back a doubloon into the open palm of the governor's wife's lady-in-waiting.

Aaaaah!

In a trice the governor's wife pocketed the gold piece and sent her lady-in-waiting to the magician with a muslin scarf, which he sent back to her in silk.

That was the signal!

All the women in the Baltimore market tore off their collars, their bonnets, their aprons, their skirts, their petticoats, their bodices, their sabots, their laced boots, their garters, and besieged the upturned barrel. It was the first and only grand public striptease to be recorded in the annals of the town of Baltimore. Shoes, hats, and *déshabillés* flew in the air revealing underthings never before revealed even to husbands in the intimacy of alcoves. The Fool cast the spell, and the Marys of Maryland let themselves be bewitched. They tore the hair and skirts from one another, shouting and yelling and trampling their old clothes underfoot as if they never again intended to wear homespun or cotton. They had just discovered the court of miracles where a wizard could change pumpkins into golden coaches and Cinderellas into princesses.

But at the stroke of twelve noon . . .

The Cinderellas hadn't reckoned on the twelve strokes of the Baltimore town clock, which brought the guard into the market and the wives back to their senses. The Fool hadn't thought of it either. He was caught red-handed performing magic in a public place without a permit. In this eighteenth-century Baltimore, the Roman Catholics were Jansenist and the Protestants Puritan. And more than any acts of magic or petty larceny, it was the near nudity of respectable mothers and wives that shocked their sisters who had stayed by the fire. They all came running to contemplate the scandal, and then to lead their husbands back home.

The ladies of Baltimore, beginning with the governor's wife, took some time, it seems, to recover from the shock: first from the shock of having displayed the details of their underclothing to their cronies and rivals, much more than to the shopkeepers and soldiers of the town, who hadn't had time in the shindy to appreciate much; but above all from the shock of discovering next day that they'd inherited their neighbor's apron or bodice, who in turn had come out of the fray coiffed in someone else's bonnet. What a free-for-all! And the worst was, though they did manage to recover some lengths and shreds of country cloth or local woolens, they soon perceived that the silks, laces, and cashmeres had all disappeared. The governor's wife never recuperated her scarf. Or the doubloon that had fallen by magic into the palm of her lady-in-waiting.

So those are the reasons why Pierre-à-Pitre-the-Fool had a taste of the Baltimore prison. And without the intervention of Abbé Robin on behalf of a Church that had good reason to reprimand the goodwives of the town for disrobing in public before the very eyes of children still innocent of such things . . .

"Humph! . . ."

. . . goodwives who were required, after confession, to recite their paternosters . . . forgive us our trespasses as we forgive those whose trespass against us . . . without Abbé Robin, I say, without that chaplain of the Acadian tribe in French Town, why Pierre-the-Fool might never have given his native land a single heir.

"Anyways, it's not so sure he did leave any heirs."

It's not sure he did, not sure he didn't. What we do know for sure and certain is that he got out of prison some weeks later, having lost a few of his feathers but none of his spunk.

Now as to the role Célina played in setting the prisoner free . . .

"The midwife had a way with deliveries, didn't she?"

"Delivering pregnant women, not scatterbrained idiots."

That remains to be seen.

Some claim that not all the arguments Abbé Robin used with the governor were to be found in the Church Fathers, to wit, that a good dose of his argumentation gave off a strong odor of an elixir not entirely unknown to the people of the carts. But the carts kept that to themselves, and the rumor had no circulation in the grand old town of Baltimore.

That was the last that grand old Baltimore saw of its silks and cashmeres, for the wives and damsels of the carts took care to lay them away in the chest.

"Not in The Chest!"

"I said: in the chest."

"Well, I'll be! . . ."

Yes, the chest, the Bourgeois chest, more precious than a tabernacle, more secret than a state treasury, a museum piece if ever there was one in Acadie. One evening at dusk it opened its lid, with a creaking of hinges, to stealthily swallow up Pierre-à-Pitre's booty. Then it closed so swiftly on Célina's nose that she almost lost her wart under the lid.

"Sure as sin there's gold and pearls in there," she said over her shoulder, turning her back on the whole Bourgeois clan, who decidedly weren't ever going to trust anyone.

And to make a clean breast of it once and for all, she added:

"I never could understand, myself, how the rich came to take shelter in the cart of the poor."

There was that smell of vinegar again. They'd been inactive too many months, and Baltimore was beginning to pall. Hospitable or not, Maryland was only a stopover; the oxen should be reshod. And the Bourgeois, this time encouraged by the Allains, the Babineaus, and soon after the Landrys, began to ogle Pennsylvania.

Pélagie shivered. How much longer could she keep them tied up in this her life's port, these worrisome impatient grumblers who obstinately refused to understand? And how much longer would the contrary winds and waves run implacably against her, she who had already sacrificed so much to the sea?

"You wouldn't have seen the *Grand'Goule* standing out to sea, a four-master with a golden-haired figurehead at the prow? You wouldn't have seen her somewhere at sea?"

"Last spring she was headed full-sail nor'east off Carolina; but I fear the currents or maybe pursuit ships drove her back down south."

"A four-master, a four-master flying no flag, with a French-speaking crew, and a captain . . . a captain . . ."

" . . . "

"A schooner here says it saw a four-master stealing along the coast looking like it was seeking a landfall."

Pélagie leaned on her giant who squirmed for joy. And they spread the word. In a jiffy the whole caravan of carts swung into motion and rolled drunkenly down to the quai.

"There she is!"

"Four masts!"

"Will you quit pushing, you're going to shove us all into the drink."

"Hold your breath everyone, she's rounding the cape."

Pupils contracted, scanned the waves, then dilated, and it was all over. Not the *Grand'Goule*, no, a Dutch vessel with four masts and a dragon at the prow. The devil take Holland and England and Spain and every foreign fleet, all but a single vessel flying the flag of Acadie with golden hair on its figurehead. The Great Northern Sea could swallow up all their ships in one gulp, so long as it brought safe into Baltimore harbor the *Grand'Goule*, its crew, and its captain.

But the Great Northern Sea turned a deaf ear and went on cradling on its billows the fleets of every maritime empire of the age without a thought for the last remaining ship of a colony long since struck from the map. Had the sea claimed for its own this outlaw vessel with no home port, this living survivor of the Great Disruption? Each time the *Grand'Goule* came to port she hoisted a phantom flag, an impostor's flag. The four-master belonged to no one but the ocean and her own frail crew. And even the carts didn't dare ask about her too often.

"I fear, Pélagie, we must soon return to reason."

Reason? She hadn't much reason left, though it had guided and saved her for a lifetime. Barely a gleam of it. But Alban-à-Charles-à-Charles and François-à-Pierre-à-Pierre-à-Pierrot fastened on that gleam. The clans were restless to be off, and the oxen were scraping the ground with their hooves. Everyone felt the itch of the north, from the tops of their heads to the soles of their feet. The carts were on the verge of rebellion and mutiny. Mustn't push them too far, Pélagie.

Not push them? Some had been marching now for two, three, the first members of the cart for four years. Yet it was they who sulked the least, except for the twins Charlécoco who'd picked up the habit in their mother's womb.

"Poor little things, they must have felt cramped in there, two to one belly."

Jeanne Aucoin saw her chance and jumped on it.

"The wee ones have grown up a piece these twenty years past and they must be getting homesick for the land they left, scarcely out of the crib. Where are you fixing to lodge them, these sons of yours, Pélagie?"

Pélagie blinked.

"Let's hope there's enough of Grand-Pré left to make a bed quilt with," she said.

And summoning up what was left of the breath simmering in her lungs, she exhaled a great:

"Hue-Ho the oxen! North is up that way!"

PROPERTY OF THE PUBLIC LIBRARY ST. MARYS, ONT.

10

It must have put a kink into Old Bélonie's habits and ways of
thinking when once and once only he deviated from the path of
the cart and set out to sea. Let's get it straight, though. This
story of the miseries and glories of the *Grand'Goule* in that terrible year 1774, Bélonie must have picked up himself from the
mouth of his offspring and heir, who knew a lot more than his
ancestor about this sea chapter. Or maybe this page of the
chronicle simply skipped a Bélonie and came straight from the
mouth of the second of the name, that Bélonie, son of Thaddée
who had witnessed more of the open sea than dry land, as we
will soon have occasion to show.

The storytellers and chroniclers of the line had two centuries
to debate this question. And let my cousin, Louis-the-Younger,
tell you, there wasn't a single generation of Bélonies would let
slip such a fine opportunity to have their say with the following
generation. Bélonie III, for example, the one who sat by Pélagie-
the-Grouch's hearth in the last century, stubbornly persisted in

trying to convince his pig-headed son, Louis-the-Droll, that in the previous century his ancestor, Old Bélonie, had never heard out Captain Beausoleil's maritime narratives to the end.

But the son protested:

"Hold on! Whoa, now! Just who do you take him for, this ancestor of ours?"

"I take him for what he was, a loony whose mind was off the track. But a loony who was perhaps the only one in those wishy-washy times to have had a track that led somewhere."

"A track that led to his phantom cart hauled by six black horses."

"Where we'll all end up some day or other, sure as I'm alive. But he, at least, was ready for it."

"Don't you think, Pa, that a lifetime's a mighty long time to get ready for death?"

"That depends who and how long he's been living."

But here The Grouch put in:

"If there's any slackers around who're tired out living their life, let them leave it for others to live, on account of because I know folks, I do, who wouldn't sulk at the chance, as it so happens."

She rifled that out in a single breath, The Grouch did, that straight-line, first-bed descendant of the cart. For she'd inherited at least one virtue from her ancestor first-of-the-name: loyalty to life. Nobody, do you hear, nobody was going to dampen her fire. Let them get that wedged square in their noggins.

That night of storytelling they had plenty to get square in their noggins, stories to set your hair on end . . . If Pélagie and her carts had known, during their long wait in Baltimore, what was happening out at sea and along the coast, a coast the *Grand'Goule* had tried to approach ten times over . . . But the carts only learned a year or two later of the four-master's saga, which future storytellers passed on in tales now frightening, now marvelous, now droll.

In 1774 England's American colonies were in the throes of liberty and independence, some even frankly boiling up in rebellion. Imagine, then, the situation, on land or sea, of an outlaw

crew in open warfare with an Empire that had been hunting
them down for twenty years and now, suddenly, was arming itself to fight a continent. Poor *Grand'Goule,* sandwiched in between an Empire and a continent! She pitched and heaved handsomely in the Great Northern Sea, let me tell you, that schooner
of Beausoleil-Broussard's, so handsomely that more than once
she plunged into a swell that threatened to swallow her up. The
Baltimore sailors were right: It took a hell of a captain to save
the *Grand'Goule* from a sea like that. A sea armed to the teeth.
And as if war weren't enough, even the elements conspired to
drive the waters wild. It should also be said that Broussard-
called-Beausoleil never cut any corners on his ocean adventures
and never spared his ship.

. . . It's almost as if he got a kick out of taunting destiny.

"Go on! As if destiny needed that."

. . . At any rate, Beausoleil never shrank from risk, peril, or
the twists of fate. And more than once fate tweaked his nose.
Why, just take that business about the ship of ice.

"The what?"

. . . A ship of ice, no lie, scudding along off the Newfoundland banks with a full crew of ice: captain, quartermaster,
sailors, cabin boys, all transparent, all ice . . .

"The haunted ship!"

That's what they thought at first. The phantom ship. But the
phantom ship burns at sea, you won't catch it changing its ways.
Whereas this one was sailing along like the happiest ship afloat,
all encased in a block of ice, its crew congealed in sleet where
they stood, furling the sails or coiling the hawsers at the foot of
the masts. You could still see the smiles or the dreamy expres-
sions on the faces of the passengers; this was no ship out of hell.
She must have been hit by an iceberg, then let herself slip into
the long sleep of polar seas. Little by little, at the mercy of wind
and wave, she'd drifted further south, had begun to thaw out
gently and, who knows, one day might even awaken, come back
to life a century or two out of date.

"Just listen to that! What a story! You should be ashamed."

Yet even The Grouch drooled and shuddered at stories like

this, which the hearth could no more do without than soup on the table. And every storyteller raised the ante with his own sea visions and apparitions . . . phantom vessels, pirate ships, enchanted boats, burning ships, bad-weather-fire . . . there wasn't a fisherman would yield an inch to his fellow seamen. One had seen the Indian Maiden cloaked in her mantle of flames staring at a ship that bore, full sail, straight down upon her and that next day would burn, bewitched, at sea; another had seen with his very own eyes the little gray headless man who guards the treasure Captain Kidd left buried in the sand somewhere along the coast; one fisherman described a ghost ship three leagues long pushed by sails that tickled the clouds and steered by a helmsman with birds' nests in his beard; Bélonie, for his part, only dealt in the authentically true; for example, the story of the bells of Grand-Pré church which he himself had heard ringing on the high seas in the middle of a hurricane, believe it or not.

"What's that you say?"

It wasn't worth the trouble asking every tall-tale-teller to repeat his gimcrack inventions. But when it came to Bélonie, son of Bélonie-à-Thaddée-à-Bélonie, even The Grouch couldn't help jabbing out:

"What's that you say?"

He was saying, and he wasn't the first, that in the Baie des Chaleurs, south of Gaspé, on the eve of a storm you can still hear the bells of Grand-Pré ringing. A ship by name the *Tourmente* was supposed to be carrying them to Gaspé and she made the mistake, it seems, of trying to make off with the bells instead of delivering them safe and sound, for the next day she perished at sea, the brute. And they say that since that day the bells of Grand-Pré still ring in the tempest to warn would-be pirates to keep their hands off the treasures of Acadie.

"The treasures of Acadie? Ouch!"

"Well? And what do you call the LeBlanc fortune? What about that?"

"You can hear it ringing in the tempest, too!"

"Ah, you toad! So now we're even denying the LeBlancs their fortune, eh? Yet all the ancestors told of it and they all swore

Jean LeBlanc left a treasure hidden somewhere to be passed on to all his descendants."

"But they didn't add, did they, that the same Jean LeBlanc never left any descendants?"

"In that case we're all his heirs."

"Ah! Now you're going too far, Pélagie."

"Seems there's some here regret not having their little quarter of LeBlanc."

But what everyone regretted most that particular night was not being able to hear what Bélonie II might have said, the Bélonie who had died some thirty years before and was the last witness who could have thrown some light on the mystery of the hidden treasure, which at that date hadn't been quite unearthed yet. Still, one day the LeBlanc fortune is bound to resurface, and my cousin Louis hopes to be alive then so he can tell me the end of the story.

Meanwhile, they agreed on one thing that night around the hearth: to let Bélonie go on and finish the story of Beausoleil's adventures with the English patrols.

As long as they let the sleeping bear lie . . . But here they were in the spring of 1774 rudely yanking him out of his hibernation with cannon and musket fire. Just as well not to stand between the gun and the target in times like these. Easier said than done, though. For where do you slip a four-master when the two sides of the narrows are aiming their cannon across the gap at each other?

. . . Not that easy.

So the *Grand'Goule* was forced to quit the coast and to try taking on provisions from friendly ships on the open sea. They began by bartering island rum for supplies, but the rum ran out, and little by little they had to strip the *Grand'Goule* of companionways, shrouds, the ship's boats, davits, pulleys, the compass, the lead, the sheets . . .

"Before we get her stripped right down, maybe we should consider polishing up her cannon," suggested Jean, Pélagie's son.

Which, according to the chronicles of the time, led the

Grand'Goule into piracy against enemy ships, but only those, so they say, that sailed under the flag of the Mother England.

Well and good.

Except that England was that proud Albion, mistress of the seas, whose ships were strewn across the Atlantic like others sow a field of wheat. The poor *Grand'Goule* hoisted her twenty-four sails on her four masts in vain; in vain she scraped her hull and swabbed her decks and piled up her cannonballs, she was the only vessel sailing under that flag, like buccaneers and pirates. And everyone fired on her.

One day when trying to slip between Dutch schooners and Spanish galleons off the Florida coast, she ran across an English four-master that was her spit and image: two ships launched from the same yards, the same day. Their two figureheads saluted each other like two sisters astonished and delighted to meet again far from their home port after a quarter of a century, yet prudent and circumspect just the same. Each scanned the other without further signal, fearing to show colors to a possible enemy. A certain enemy, in fact, for neither the *Grand'Goule* nor her twin flew a flag of any kind.

"How's that? An English ship with no flag?"

Just wait . . .

An English vessel, indeed, like the *Grand'Goule,* but captured and taken over by rebel Virginians. Imagine it, these two insurgent ships meeting without knowing each other, in midocean, sniffing each other out, taking each other's measure, on the verge of mutual provocation yet drawn by a mysterious fraternal feeling, two ships that, in the end, at the same instant, broke out flags proclaiming peace and neutrality. Blood brothers they were, from the same Liverpool shipyard, destined to share the same tribulations, the same struggle, and the same glory in the chronicles of their respective countries, each having brought off an exploit few ships could boast of at the end of the eighteenth century: to have lodged a stone right in the brow of all-powerful Albion, mistress of the seas, like David defying Goliath. The twin four-masters had both, a quarter century apart, thumbed their noses at the British fleet.

. . . And shit to His British Majesty!

But His British Majesty didn't take kindly to the insult and struck back. And so began the real battle between the giant Goliath and these two puny Davids swinging their slings against a whole fleet. Cannonballs broke the masts, tore the sails, shattered the quarterdecks and smashed the hatches . . . Ah, the poor sea beasts! And still neither captain of either four-master would lower the flag, as if they were fighting for a country.

"It wasn't for a country then?"

Yes, for a country, a country of the future for the Virginians, and for Beausoleil-Broussard a country of the past. And all Acadie possessed as a fleet was this single schooner snatched from the enemy, this avenging, liberating, defiant schooner sailing the seas in the name of honor. She braved the winds and the waves, braved hellfire, braved the England who had stolen her home port. By her side the Virginia vessel defended a new land, a country yet to be founded. It was an unequal combat that opposed the two schooners with the greatest fleet afloat. But Robin Hoods of the Seas are valiant and bold and have salt in their veins. They stepped the masts again and the sails swelled anew. And the English fleet must have blinked its eyes. Especially since it was seeing double. For all of a sudden the four-master of the insurgent Americans that they had been chasing since the Virginia coast split in two in the trough of the waves and turned up both to port and starboard, a dizzying feat. And so it was that the Acadian captain, who had learned a lot about a lot of things on his long voyages and must have got wind of the sense of History, instinctively opted for the future and offered to cover the flight of the Virginia four-master.

Thus the *Grand'Goyle*, running a last-ditch opposition by a thousand kicks and pricks against her enemy, watched her twin sail off into the mists of oral memory. She never again had news of her sister ship. Except for a suspicion . . . There are some suspect it was the captain of the Virginia four-master who was behind what later came to be known as the Charleston Whiskey Carnival, an event the *Grand'Goule* had good reason to celebrate.

. . . It wasn't anything like the Boston Tea Party, why no, nothing like that! There was scarcely a skirmish; it didn't even come down in the annals of Carolina. It was more like a kind of Mardi Gras or April Fool's Day.

A night of hijinks and revelry, at any rate. Everyone knows that Acadie was never equal to defending herself in equal combat since she was never on an equal footing with anyone. She managed just the same, like Pierre-à-Pitre, by brushing up on the gift of the gab and by learning that the way out of an impasse is sometimes by way of a cul-de-sac.

And it was some cul-de-sac, that Charleston arsenal where the imprudent commander of the English navy locked up his prisoners. At first, when the four-master had finally surrendered to his cannon, he had been flabbergasted to discover not insurgent Americans but a bunch of ghosts from an ancient war, Frenchmen, nay worse, Acadians from Nova Scotia who had gone down with the ship in 1755, ragged phantoms of a ruined vessel, the *Pembroke*, declared lost with all hands a score of years before. It was enough to make the English captain think he was seeing things, especially since he was already overly fond of the bottle and inclined to believe in spirits. So he summoned Beausoleil-Broussard into his presence.

. . . And there, snug in his cozy cabin, he learned at length and in minute detail about the incredible, fabulous peregrinations of this *Grand'Goule*, alias the *Pembroke*, which had come out of polar seas like the early Christians out of the catacombs. Captain Broussard spared the Lord Commander, a lover of Swift and Defoe, not a jot. He led him off on adventures that would have made Gulliver and Robinson Crusoe themselves green with envy . . . For it mustn't be forgotten that Beausoleil-Broussard, like Bélonie, sprang from a people of storytellers and chroniclers who had produced Gargantua and his noble son Pantagruel, and that he remembered all the horrific and dreadful tales passed along from generation to generation while roasting chestnuts by the corner of the fire.

So Beausoleil told all: how the *Pembroke* and her crew had first been chased by a school of man-eating whales to polar regions; how the ice had encircled them and the cold congealed them; how through their envelope of hoary rime they had seen their own frozen words fall to the deck like hail; how for a quarter century they had been the immobile but still conscious witnesses of this solidified life where time stood still; how, when the winds finally blew them down to warmer climes, they had thawed out into life and time again, delivered, like ordinary mortals, back to the wear and tear and corruptibility of everyday.

"Amazing!"

And how! So amazing indeed that Beausoleil himself scarcely knew how to stop and galloped on, amplifying, doubling, tripling, ruminating, eking the story out, spinning it fine, explaining how, when the sailors had regained the use of their limbs and wits, they hadn't at first recovered their frozen words for a good six months more. Till one day a wind from the east-southeast-by-east had sent a hail of words raining on the deck, which the whole crew had gobbled up like garden peas. But, alas! They were French words, blown there by some mistral or tramontane. And from that day forward, on the *Pembroke* become the *Grand'Goule*, nothing was spoken but French.

The Lord Commander swallowed the last of this story with his last gulp of whiskey and was so delighted to touch, feel, and know an authentic reincarnated ghost that he lodged the whole of the phantom crew in the Charleston arsenal and gave orders to have the *Grand'Goule* reoutfitted and made ready to sail.

And that's not all.

Not all?

Beausoleil, whose throat was richly dressed in salt, had such a time slaking his ancestral thirst that he could, in a single sniff, ferret out every bottle and cask for three leagues around. So it was that he sniffed out the arsenal's reserve, Irish whiskey, closely guarded by the English navy. At that, he picked up his story again where he had left off, under the hail of frozen words.

. . . So the polar ghosts, to their great astonishment, found themselves speaking French. But they soon discovered that their maternal tongues came back if they warmed their gullets up. The proof lay in the whiskey. And Beausoleil supplied it in an

old aromatic English that got more perfect and pungent with
every glass. The reserve of Irish whiskey had such an effect on
the crew of the *Grand'Goule* that soon the Charleston arsenal
was ringing with words from every country on the Atlantic rim.
It was a real Pentecost. Or Mardi Gras. A veritable carnival of
the sea, which emptied casks and starred the heavens with fire-
works.

. . . Fire that got a little too close to the gunpowder, truth to
tell, for part of the arsenal blew up.

The crew of the *Grand'Goule* has been wrongly blamed for
this: All they had done was celebrate their return to the land of
mortal men. But mortals are so constituted that the least spark
fires them up and puts lightning in their eyes. And by the same
token, it seems, the light began to dawn in the Lord Commander's eyes as his brain began to clear a bit; ah yes, even in
the Lord Commander's eyes, so it seems . . . And Broussard-
called-Beausoleil saw it was high time to get under way.

Besides, Charleston stirred too many memories in him, all of
them driving him on to Baltimore.

But it was a long haul from Carolina to Maryland, and the
English fleet was more and more wary and vigilant. The
Grand'Goule mustered all her skill and courage, but in vain; she
arrived in Baltimore four months after the carts had left.

11

Thus began the race against time. Who would brave the winds best, those on land or those on sea? For while Pélagie whipped her oxen on and prodded the loins of her dawdling people, who day by day swelled the ranks of the carts, Beausoleil took the wind in his sails and the helm of the *Grand'Goule* in his own two hands.

To Philadelphia!

He'd catch up with his Pélagie in Philadelphia, city of love. And tack to starboard, and tack to port, and hey for the open sea! And don't let me catch a one of you spewing up over the side.

At exactly the same time Pélagie was urging her crew to pull to the right, toward the coast. The sea remained the surest link with Acadie-in-the-North. You could go astray in the forest or come up short on a mountain, but the northern sea could only lead back home.

Hue! Hue-Ho! Toward the sea.

But what Pélagie didn't know was that between the sea and the carts, with giant strides across this land of America, ran three young messengers from Beausoleil: Pélagie's Jean, Maxime Basque, and a certain Benjamin Chiasson, snatched from his home on Île Madame after the surrender of Louisbourg. The three couriers had received orders from their captain to overtake the marching exiles and direct them to Philadelphia. Also to defend them against possible attacks from insurgents bivouacking in the woods and in every nook and cranny between Virginia and New England where the rebellion was beginning to turn into an open war of independence.

"And that's how some of our people came to quit the carts and take to the woods."

"How's that again?"

So Bélonie, third-of-the-name, sitting before The Grouch's hearth told the circle of expectorators this unknown page of their history.

"A Léger called La Rozette, for example, and the youngest of the Girouards, and later on a Gaudet and a Martin . . . Why do you think they joined the ranks of the rebels?"

Dear God in Heaven! Rebels, too, is it?

Not rebellious rebels, insurgents as they called them; it was exactly like our *patriotes*.

"You don't mean to say so!"

"And why not?"

"On account of because."

"Would it be, then, according to you, that a country like America had no right to its own property and liberty? That Virginia didn't have the right to grow tobacco or Bostonians to drink their tea without paying tribute on it to the King of England?"

"Well, it was the King of England discovered the land in the first place and claimed it and planted it . . ."

"No siree! The English weren't the first. We got here ahead of them. Then before us were the Basques. And maybe even the giants from the north."

"What's he mumbling about now? Giants?"

"Well, whose leg bone was it we dug up at the end of the point in that case? Anybody ever seen a common man like you or me walking around on legs way over three feet long?"

The hearth held its peace. The tibia alone had indeed measured more than a yard. According to a Giroué of Sainte-Marie who was the only one to measure it. But what did that matter? The proof was there that giants had passed through the land; no one would dare doubt the word of a close relative of Sainte-Marie, now, would they?

"Which means the English of England can hardly go round claiming the world belongs to them, not even America."

"Tell us what you like about our ancestors' history, but don't go throwing in the Americans. That's not our cup of tea."

"Not our cup of tea! Not our cup of tea! Why, on the contrary, it was their tea we were drinking at the time and their land we were crossing on foot behind the oxen."

"Bah!"

"But let him speak, damn it!"

. . . So the cart swung its compass round to the northeast. But the farther they ventured in that direction, the more the war raged. To the point where the two enemy camps began to seek in the ranks of Pélagie's own caravan, continually swelling as it moved north, replacements for the corpses they left rotting in the hay.

"That war there's no concern of ours," Mother Pélagie clamored to her carts.

But that didn't keep young colts born in the years of exile from dreams of defending the motherland.

Célina raised her arms to heaven. The motherland! But where did those nitwits see a motherland? In this country of Red Indians and cotton planters? In this foreign land of drinkers of tea and Caribbean rum? Were they, those Giroués, Martins, Bastaraches, and Légers-called-la-Rozette, these sons of exile, these expatriates, going to die for a country that didn't even belong to them?

Just so. They were going to die for a country. At least death would give them a land they could call their own.

And once more Old Bélonie winked back at his cart, which came on, creaking its invisible wheels in the very ruts of the cart of the living.

Crack her whip and strain the oxen as she might, Pélagie was overtaken by the war at every turn in the road and at every spring where she brought her parched people to drink. War and its retinue of evils was added now to all the calamities that had hounded the cart since Georgia: famine, drought, rains, epidemics, quarrels, defections, and now a rabble of hotheaded renegades.

"Not all renegades, nor all hotheads. Some came quite loyally to ask shelter of the carts. The three Marylanders, for instance."

No, you couldn't take them for turncoats or criminals. They were hungry, that's all. For months they'd been hiding in the woods; betrayed, sold out, hunted down by the Empire, they had humbly come to ask refuge of this caravan of deportees even more miserable than they.

It was Pierre-à-Pitre who served as interpreter.

"Their Pennsylvania brothers are camped just opposite. They ask us to send messengers."

Three lost militiamen wandering around practically under the noses of the enemy, three handsome young fellows as hot-blooded as they were famished, already making eyes in the direction of Madeleine, Catoune, and the other girls. Charles-Auguste's fine gander snorted and P'tite Goule in one stride thrust himself between the soldiery and the Acadian maidens. And the soldiery scratched their necks and let it go at that.

At this point Pacifique Bourgeois drew Pélagie aside and acquainted her with her duties as mother, chief, and subject of a country that had welcomed and fed her for well nigh twenty years. These insurgents were traitors to their homeland and their king.

"The king? What king?"

"King George of England, you know that."

. . . George of England? The oath of allegiance one? The one who had summoned all the men of Grand-Pré one Sunday morning in September, then ordered the massacre, the burning of the

village, and the deportation of the survivors? The king who had
stripped them naked, her and hers, who had made her the
widow and orphan of Acadie?

She looked Pacifique-à-Jacques Bourgeois straight in the eye:

"Now here's three youngsters come knocking at our door. You
know our fathers never refused hospitality to the needy who
came asking it for the love of Jesus Christ."

"It's not sure those heathen come asking it for the love of
Jesus Christ."

"That doesn't stop them from being needy."

And pushing Pacifique Bourgeois out of her way, she bore
straight down on her guests and with her own hands offered
them drink from the so-called cup of hospitality, a ritual goblet
saved from the Great Disruption. And to accompany her gesture
she also pronounced the ritual words:

"Make yourselves at home."

Then she made room for the insurgents in the carts all the way
to Pennsylvania.

Later, Louis-the-Droll challenged his countrymen with:

"I hope the Americans haven't forgotten that we helped them
bring off their Revolution . . . Hee!"

Pacifique kept on insisting that King George couldn't be blamed
for everything, that he'd done nothing himself, that others had
done the dirty work in his name, but in vain. Pélagie replied
with a frown, but one that had a smile underneath:

"We neither, we didn't do anything ourselves, but I wouldn't
stop others from helping themselves to a little revenge on our behalf."

And she gave a good lash to her Corporals.

"It's not even sure," replied Pacifique-à-Jacques, "that England knew what Lawrence was up to in Acadie. Maybe he even
decided everything on his own, the good-for-nothing, without
consulting the ministers or the king."

Pélagie squinted an eye till the lid began to twitch.

"Mustn't go taking Governor Lawrence for a good egg, or the
king of England for a child martyr. What they did, they did.

And the way things stand, don't let anyone come asking me to fetch them a basin of water to wash their hands in."

And another lash of the whip to the Corporals.

. . . She wouldn't prevent either the insurgents or her own Acadian sons from fighting against King George—George-third-of-the-name by now, a little more George than his antecedent, executioner of Acadie, though Pélagie didn't know that. When you can hardly sort out the living from the dead in your own line, you don't go delving the dynasties of England. Even if she had known that the Georges were succeeding each other over there and passing the scepter on . . . Hmph! The fathers have eaten sour grapes and their sons' teeth are set on edge. What was true for her should be true enough for others.

"Whose fault is it now, do you think, that we're climbing America on foot?"

But before their homecoming, Acadie's poor people had a high price to pay for their resistance to the Georges of England and the reversals of History. It was as if the gods had resolved not to give the Acadians back their land till they had been forced to empty the cup to the dregs. In their thirst during those years of drought and famine they would have drunk anything, for that matter, and they'd have eaten their boot soles if they hadn't long ago fallen from their shoes. There were scarcely a dozen pairs of worn and battered boots left among them, passed down as the children's feet grew too big or their elders' bones decalcified. They would have eaten the straw of their hats or the wool of their socks; they would have eaten . . .

The oxen!

And the drama exploded.

The oxen were part of the daily fatigue, almost part of the family and had been for five years now, perhaps more, they'd lost track. At all events, along with the LeBlancs, Bélonie, and Célina, they were the oldest citizens of the cart. Then too, they had borne their burden without grouching, had pulled the carts with all their might, good weather and bad, their flanks flayed by the whip, their horns tangled in brush, their hooves sunk in the greasy bottoms of the swamps. Without a whimper, without balking like the Bourgeois's donkey or the Allains' mule. And now were they going to be sacrificed as their only reward?

"Well then! Let the hardest-hearted among us step right up and sharpen his knife on the bones of my shoulder blades. Here they are, naked as ever the Creator of heaven and earth made them one fine winter morning."

And Célina twined her withered arms round the horns of her Hussars to the snickering of the menfolk trying to peek under her blouse to see some sign of those blades the Creator of heaven and earth had planted between her shoulders.

At that, Jeanne Aucoin threw herself on her Corporals. Just who were they going to harness up to the carts in place of the oxen? Sure they were hungry, sure they were fading away before each other's eyes, all the more reason! And the weaker one gets, the more one needs a lift. Already a good quarter of the convoy, practically half, could no longer drag themselves along; which meant that without the oxen . . . Were there, by chance, any volunteers among the starving ready to stick their fannies in between the shafts and haul the carts from here on?

And everyone eyed everyone else's posterior.

Then it was the Bourgeoise's turn. Oh la! Step aside there! Here was a real Cicero coming up. She launched into a long diatribe on injustice and false privilege, accusing the Girouards, Célina, and even Pélagie of favoritism and blindness, with beams in their own eyes but picking out motes in the pupils of others, with their double weights and double standards for parceling out the beefiest parts for themselves and the leanest to the one, poor, weak-kneed Trooper left her. And she thrust her opulent bosom under the muzzle of the poor beast who must have been carried back to his days as a calf.

Pélagie cast a scornful eye on these grimaces and began to test the shanks and haunches of her own oxen. Five years already! They must feel worn out, the poor beasts, and be longing for rest, too. They had served their masters well, had accomplished a mission worthy of passing into the annals of their country. A country made in their image, at that: patient, stubborn, wilful,

vindictive. Vindictive against destiny, will set against history, patient with time. Acadie advanced at an ox pace. What did it matter if she arrived late, they had the whole future to catch up in.
Really fine animals! And Pélagie smiled to think of the funeral
tribute she had just sung them in the name of all her people.

Then she shook her mane and gave the sign to Alban-à-
Charles-à-Charles.

Of the five oxen, the Trooper was the most solitary and the
least solid. Its flesh, too, was perhaps less tough, fed as it had
been in secret by the Bourgeoise. It wasn't a question of choice.
The Trooper would have to be sacrificed for the children of
Acadie, who were dwindling day by day. Look at little Virginie,
nothing but skin and bones, or the young Allains with their rotten teeth, or the Melansons and the Boudreaus dragging their
rickety legs. Enough sentimentality! Anyway, the poor beast had
served its time; it must be longing for that animal paradise that
surely exists somewhere to stable the souls of creatures that have
been faithful to their duties and their masters all their lives long.

"Heretic!"

Jeanne Trahan-called-the Bourgeoise, not able to challenge
Pélagie's authority, launched an attack on her religion. A paradise for animals now! Why not a requiem mass while you're at it!

Why not?

Despite the lack of mass or celebrant, they carried out the
sacrifice within the rites, as though finding by instinct or a sort of
involuntary memory the primal origins of immolation. They
washed the victim, perfumed him with green hay, decorated his
horns with garlands, and decided to bury his yoke carved with
stars and half moons in the place of sacrifice. They prepared fire
and water, sharpened the knife on a rounded stone, sent the
other animals and young children to the fields, circled around
the beast caressing him while he turned on his masters a pair of
eyes that seemed to say: Come on now, get on with it, can't you,
flabby asses . . .

But the Hussars and the Corporals had to be led back to the
fields, for they tended to stick to the carts as though they smelled
death from afar. Then the ritual was begun again, Alban

Girouard turning the big knife round and round in his hands, till he let it fall. He couldn't do it, flabby ass or not, he couldn't. Might the ox forgive him.

And everyone breathed again.

And now Catoune stepped forward, Catoune guardian of the children of others, slim and white in her Cinderella rags, her hair as disheveled as on the very first day, her arm no thicker than an alder branch, Catoune bent down and picked up the knife from Alban-à-Charles-à-Charles's feet. She looked at no one, only at the victim who seemed to be saying tender and secret words to her, animal words that only this child of the wilds could understand. And before Pélagie, Alban, or the others realized it, she raised the knife to heaven and planted it in the throat offered by the last Trooper, who fell without a cry.

Bélonie, it seems, glanced over his shoulder to see if, in the circumstances . . . And sure enough, it seems the Wagon of Death was faithful to the rendezvous, even for animals. Pélagie could sleep reassured on that score.

Célina found the courage to read the entrails of the victim before the women made blood sausage of them. Entrails that for augury were a mixed lot and difficult to interpret. Those sails on the horizon, they were clear enough, no need of wizardry to understand; nor to be an oracle to guess those two armies squabbling over the land of America that year; no, it was the three figures like the Three Kings seemingly stepping along in the ruts traced by the cart that intrigued Célina. Who were they? Someone announcing a new Messiah? Bringers of good news?

Pélagie felt her eyes moisten. News!

More than three years now without news of the *Grand'Goule!* How much longer?

Long enough to let her scalawag son and his two fine companions traipse across half Pennsylvania in their tracks. And a leisurely journey they made of it, if the truth were known, for Bélonie's version would never admit that with a little more fire and steam the messengers might have arrived in time. Be that as it may. What's sure and certain is that they took plenty of time to eat well, the guzzlers, stuffing themselves on jack rabbit and porcupine and groundhog, which they snared in quantity.

So the three *coureurs des bois* enjoyed a liberty they took to strongly and would gladly have prolonged, had they not been charged with a mission that could not be set aside simply for the pleasure of eating hare and chestnuts and wild berries. And especially beechnuts, the fruit of the great American beech that tastes like apple seeds. But beechnuts are minute and very long to husk. And to get their fill the three woodland companions must have wasted considerable time.

Besides, they had to contend with the war, which was reaching its height by the end of 1775. Rebels and royalists crisscrossed the forests, and more than once our heroes found themselves pinched between the bark and the tree. For instance, one day, surprised bathing in a stream reserved for the baths of His Majesty's troops, they were conscripted on the spot. They argued in vain that they were innocently cooling their feet well downstream—as the lamb surprised by the wolf had argued long ago—and that consequently they couldn't have disturbed waters destined to cleanse the Empire. The Empire advanced the old argument that they certainly had ancestors somewhere who one day or other, by chance or design, had incommoded England, so it was up to the sons to make reparation. If ever anyone knew just how much those particular forefathers had got under the crusty skin of Old England, it was the sons in question. So they jumped feet foremost into the fable and were enlisted. But what the fable doesn't tell is the digestive disorders that assailed the wolf once he had greedily gobbled up such lambs.

Later, for the carts, Benjamin Chiasson of Île Madame provided two or three versions of the collective indigestion that hit the regiment that enlisted these *coureurs des bois*. As if the witness and storyteller himself couldn't remember the facts; or as if he hesitated among three variants: the most heroic, the most plausible, or the most true. Which led the Bélonies later on to say that our three heroes probably hadn't poisoned anyone, probably hadn't even managed to give the captain the colic, but that probably they'd simply snuck off before dawn the first chance they had, and skedaddled like wildcats.

But not for long. For not far from the royalist camp, if we are to believe Benjamin's story, another trap awaited them. No stream this time—after their adventure with the English army, our heroes swore on the heads of their ancestors not to wash again before rejoining the carts—no, not a stream but a trap, a real one, one the three dolts fell into head first and eyes shut.

It was a fox trap set by a young brave of a branch of the Iroquois tribe that had come down as far as New York and was scattered throughout the forest west of Pennsylvania. The three *coureurs des bois,* without thinking, helped themselves to the fox skin to make into a hat, which prompted Bélonie to tell Benjamin they certainly needed something to protect their brains with, they had so few of them. Emptying Indian traps! Did you ever hear the like! And Iroquois traps at that! They must have been really moonstruck, and that's no lie.

"Maybe the moon did have something to do with it."

Maybe. At any rate, more than one moon passed before their arms were unbound from the stake that held them prisoner. And without the devotion—some would have said the passion—of Pélagie's son Jean, they might have seen many more suns and moons revolve through the Pennsylvania sky and perhaps even the rays of the last sunset of all fading on their snow-white heads.

Had it not been for Jean-à-Jean LeBlanc of Grand-Pré.

Jean hadn't forgotten Catoune, or at least we suppose not, which is why he kept hot on the heels of the maternal cart. At the time of his trial in the circle of wigwams, that's the way he pleaded his case. They were just three innocent sons of a people martyrized by an enemy common to French and Indians alike, three innocents trying to overtake their families and their sweethearts. But on the way, hunger, cold, war, and a thousand other miseries had reduced them to such a state of indigence that they were ashamed to appear in rags before the eyes of their dear ones, which is why they had thought that a fur hat . . . a fox skin . . .

Anyway, they hadn't realized at the time that the animal might have belonged to someone, in fact they'd scarcely noticed the trap, on the honor of a Christian! It was just thoughtlessness, plain giddiness, no offense meant, and they were ready to pay the full price: a week's work in the fields.

Ha! Ha! Ha!

The circle of Iroquois roared with laughter. Work in the fields! That was paleface talk for you. Since when did the Indians of the Pennsylvania forests have to work in the fields? Didn't the Great Manitou supply their needs directly with water from the mountains, fish from the rivers, and game from the woods? And weren't the wild plants sufficient to dress their wounds and ward off evil spirits? And the feathers of birds, the skins of animals, and vines and the bark of trees, weren't they all that was necessary to keep well clothed and shod? A fat lot they needed the whites to come and upset the cycle of nature and the habits of a lifetime! They had lived thousands of suns in this Iroquois land before the usurpers renamed it Pennsylvania of America. A lot of use they had for America.

It began to dawn on our three heroes after this harangue that there would be no work for them in the Iroquois fields and that it would be in their best interest to make some new proposition.

Thereupon, Benjamin of Île Madame made so bold as to offer his services for hunting and fishing, claiming ancestral skills that Acadians had learned from the natives with whom they had been closely associated since their arrival on this continent. Why, his very grandfather, one Anselme-à-Pierre Chiasson, in his own day had been a great friend of the Micmacs, he could swear it . . .

Ha! Ha! Ha!

Poor Benjamin, he'd have been better off swearing nothing. Micmacs! Since he had only known this one tribe, he didn't know, the innocent, that Indians are fiercer amongst themselves than toward strangers, and that the least mention of Micmacs was likely to enrage the Iroquois chief far more than the theft of a fox skin from his son's traps. Micmacs! Great Manitou! All halfbreeds, sold out to the whites, living in wooden huts like Eu-

ropeans! Their skins were getting paler all the time and where
they walked their feet crushed the moss and the creeping plants.
They had forgotten ancestral customs and scorned the laws of
the Bird God. Never would the Iroquois deign to make a pact
with friends or allies of that degenerate tribe who had even
given up eating the hearts of their enemies.

The hearts of the three Robin Hoods of the Seas missed a common beat and Maxime Basque realized that he would have no
time, like his brothers in misfortune, to lose in useless palaver
that wasn't getting them out of the woods. So reaching into his
blouse he pulled out a reed flute he had carried with him from
the forests of Carolina and began to play.

One after another the Iroquois stifled their warlike whoops
and sat down cross-armed and cross-legged on the ground.

They say that night Maxime Basque drew from his flute more
notes than the reed had ever before contained, until even Jean
and Benjamin began to listen to the genius of the gypsy race is-
suing from their friend's lips. They heard the song of sirens on
southern isles, and the sound of the wind in the rigging, and the
laughter of young Acadian maidens on their wedding day, and
refrains sung by Acadian women carding wool and weaving
linen, and the voice of their ancestors calling, inviting them to
return home. At the same time, the Indians heard the squirrels
talking to the beaver and the woodpeckers tapping on the trunks
of the white birch and the morning breeze rippling the rivers
and the cry of the Great Bird, their Father Supreme, hovering
over the autumn clouds. The spell lasted a long time, a good part
of the night, and at daybreak the chief spoke to the prisoners.

. . . The gods must love and watch over whites to have given
them such a gift. So the Iroquois would not eat them but would
keep them as friends and brothers. They could come and go
within the tribe and share the Indians' food and shelter. But as
members of the tribe and guests of their new brothers, they must
not roam more than a day's journey from the wigwams.

A day's journey! That wasn't enough leeway to let them take
off without being picked up again next day. The three white
braves had no illusions on that score: The Redskins were fleet-

footed and knew how to run bending under the branches without leaving their ears behind. To be on a one-day's leash in Indian country was like having a three-foot chain in prison. Impossible to dream of desertion.

Not desertion, then, but seduction.

It was Don Juan who thought of it. Or was he prompted by someone else? Will we ever know?

It seems that in those days he still carried Catoune's image printed on his heart and pined after her in the wigwams. Unless he was already languishing for the looks of the young Iroquois princess who three times now had brought him drink in a wild plum leaf. She had black, almond-shaped eyes and a thick braid that ran down the length of her spine. And she was called Katarina.

Katarina was the Indian for Catherine, just as Catoune was its Acadian diminutive. What fate was it pushed Pélagie's son toward these Catherines? Was it the name Katarina, which Benjamin and Maxime heard him one day shorten to Kato, that drew Jean into this adventure that was still the talk of Acadie at the end of the last century? An adventure that's not even over today, according to my cousin Louis, and one that may still hold surprises for tomb-excavators, treasure-hunters, and rummagers in the secret history of our country. But at the time that Maxime Basque and Benjamin Chiasson told the carts the outcome of their expedition in the wilds, no one as yet suspected the importance the name of Jean LeBlanc would come to have in the story of Acadie. It was only much later, around Pélagie-the-Grouch's hearth, that the debate began as to the fate of the first LeBlanc of the American branch.

And all because of the beautiful eyes of an Indian maid!

He had got into the habit of paying a bead of his rosary for every leaf of water the princess brought him, the same rosary he'd been given by his mother as an heirloom the day he left on the *Grand'Goule*, the same that had belonged to his whole line of maternal forbears from Françoise to Madeleine to Marie-Josephe to Pélagie. So thus did Jean of Grand-Pré pass the only family jewel saved from the Great Disruption around the neck of his Indian sweetheart and transform an Acadian rosary into an Iroquois necklace. If Célina had only known!

But neither Célina nor Pélagie herself ever knew. For Jean explicitly told his companions to spare his mother and only serve her up part of the truth. With the result that the Bélonies themselves were left wondering . . .

And wonder on today.

"That Jean of Pélagie LeBlanc's was a lover boy, no hero."

"The one doesn't prevent the other."

"Maybe not, but it's less heroic to be a hero in love than a hero pure and simple."

"Less heroic maybe, but more fun surely. And anyways, it all worked out the same in the end, and that's all that matters."

"It was all that mattered, you mean, for our fine friends Maxime and Benjamin. They came out of it just short a few tail feathers, the rascals. But the descendants of Jean LeBlanc would like to know if their ancestor was a hero or not."

"They're a bunch of cows, those descendants of Jean LeBlanc, wanting to turn him over in his grave at any price a whole century after his death. And anyways, there's no such thing as descendants of Jean LeBlanc."

"No descendants of Jean LeBlanc? And what about the Le-Blancs of the Isaac-à-Charlitte branch, what about them, eh? And the ones connected to the Jos Coudjeau of Memramcook? And the David-à-Babées of Haute-Aboujagane?"

The fire on the hearth began to flutter and gutter and splutter blue blazes.

It was time to talk of other things.

All this while the carts struggled on against winter, famine, war, and the recriminations of the Allains and the Bourgeois, who found they were obliquing heavily to the northeast. Whereas Acadie was due north. Weren't they ever going to get out of this Pennsylvania? And the column of carts and cartlets snaked through forest and plain seeking the water courses and the fields of rusty wheat strewn with abandoned cannon and corpses.

That year Célina saw more old folk through their death pangs than she welcomed the newborn into the world. And returning Acadie was shaken in its fabric right to its roots. Was Grand-Pré still so far then?

And they asked those they met: "Acadie? . . . Yes, Acadie? . . ."

Never heard of it.

No one knew their country. Nova Scotia, yes, somewhere up north, a land of fresh water and green meadows so they said, but Acadie . . . The only ones who remembered Acadie were those who had issued from it, or their issue.

But Pélagie stuck to her route just the same, rending the American heavens with her cries of "Hue!" and "Dia!" echoing the "Helm aport!" of Captain Broussard-called-Beausoleil. And as if the cries of the Acadian leaders reached the ears of their deported brethren everywhere, clusters of cousins from Maryland and Pennsylvania came up out of their holes to cling to the racks of the cart.

It was in the midst of this embarking of new families for an old land that what was left of Beausoleil's couriers reached Pélagie's cart.

The oxen stopped of their own accord, nostrils flared, scenting a smell of home. It was Maxime and Benjamin who at last had caught up to the convoy and now tumbled their news out into the carts:

. . . the war seemed to be turning in favor of the insurgents . . .

. . . who gives a damn, what else . . .

. . . the captain of the *Grand'Goule* gives you rendezvous in Philadelphia . . .

. . . aaah! at last . . .

. . . and Jean . . . he stayed behind with the Iroquois.

"Jean!"

It was the price to pay for the freedom of the other two. A certain Iroquois princess called Katarina, or something like that, had persuaded her father to liberate two prisoners on condition that she marry the third.

"Jean?"

Jean had sacrificed himself, and in token of filial affection and undying loyalty to his country, he sent, the best he could do for the time being, ten red fox skins against the cold.

"Poor Jean!"

And Pelagie took the twenty-year-old face of her one and only daughter, Madeleine, in her hands and called out over the head of her child to all her progeny:

"Remember the sons, living and dead, I've scattered through seas and forest! And let them never forget where they came from." And harnessing her two remaining sons, Jacquot and Charles LeBlanc—who live on in the memory of Memramcook— to the cart, Pélagie sniffed back all her defiance for the continent and shouted out one last:

"Hue-Ho!"

No, not quite the last either. She still had half America to cross. And that spring Philadelphia to reach.

Philadelphia! The word sang in her ears like music. She let it soothe her. He had given her rendezvous in Philadelphia, beloved city. Quick now, carts and oxen, pull yourselves together. En route for Philadelphia.

But Alban Girouard came to speak to her. There was a river to cross and the ferryman wanted cash.

"How much?"

"More than we've got."

"We've already ditched our last souvenirs from home."

"Apart from the oxen we've nothing to barter but the crucifix, the chest, and the violin."

Pacifique and Jeanne Bourgeois gritted their teeth. Célina flapped her wings. The Allains clung to their cross, you couldn't sacrifice the crucifix, the last holy object left, a sacred symbol, you couldn't insult God and his saints like that.

That left the chest and the violin.

Everyone waited in the most complete impartiality, prodding Célina in the back and urging her to get into the Bourgeoise's hair. The time to choose had come: the chest or life.

"The chest."

No, impossible. Within reach of the goal, after six years' sweat and agony, the Bourgeois weren't going to compromise everything all over again. Impossible.

"So what's so great about that chest of yours? Have you got the crown of thorns in there by any chance? Or the sacred shroud with the Holy Face? Or our forefathers' treasure?"

Once again the Bourgeois plumped down on the chest and clammed up tight.

It was their descendants a century later who moved the chest though, passing it from one evening round the hearth to the next, each adding a doubloon, a pearl, or a *Louis d'or*. At that rate they'd have jammed the whole Valley of Port-Royal into the deported chest, if you'd given free rein to those storytellers of the next century. The chest was becoming an oratory, a church, a cathedral.

And that was its undoing.

. . . ?

It had grown too big. The more the deportees' effects dwindled, the more space the chest took up. By the outskirts of Philadelphia, it filled the whole cart. And yet, despite that . . .

". . . Just to show you what it is to have a Bourgeois head on your shoulders . . ."

The chest crossed the gangplank and left on the ferry for the other side. It was the violin that lost out. Not the crucifix, no siree, the Allains were as stubborn as the Bourgeois, and besides, a crucifix, that's religion. So they sacrificed the violin, the violin that had played at their weddings, tuned up their winter evenings and accompanied their ancestors to their eternal rest.

. . . How do you like that!

And Célina, forgetting her clubfoot, unleashed a kick at the impostor. What a shame, a chest for a violin! Pélagie had allowed that?

Pélagie had allowed life to have its way, because she well knew that in the long run they would sacrifice everything to life, the chest included.

"And today?"

Some claim the chest reached Boston, others say Tintamarre,

maybe even Memramcook. Just try to find out! One thing sure, the Bourgeois's heirs snooped into every corner of the nineteenth century trying to find the least trace of that treasure that was beginning to look more and more like a paradise lost. And when Pélagie-the-Grouch and Bélonie-the-Younger and Louis-the-Droll and all the descendants of the *Grand'Goule* and the carts get their hands on that treasure during those long northern nights by the fire . . . aaah!

The remains of a people wandering through plain and valley nibbling the last rotting roots and shreds of plants clinging by hazard in the clefts of the rocks. A tattered, foundering people sowing the land of America with young children and exhausted elders. Pélagie began to fear for Grand-Pré. If they were to lose the best seed on the way, what would be left to sow once they reached home? The carts now carried barely a quarter of each family, the scrapings of old Acadie.

"We're nothing but skin and bones," sighed Célina, rubbing her clubfoot till the nerves were raw.

And a skin that was shriveled, grimy, dried out like cod in the sun. Pélagie cast a harsh look at Old Bélonie, getting older and older, juggling with Death since the cart had left the swamps of Georgia. And for the first time she asked herself . . . which cart would win the race, hers or the old chin-wagger's?

On that July day in 1776 when all the bells of America burst out ringing independence and liberty, Acadie misunderstood and thought she heard the bells tolling death.

PROPERTY OF THE
PUBLIC LIBRARY
ST. MARYS, ONT.

12

Philadelphia, 1776.

The offspring of the carts would have two centuries to spin tales about this summery city where Pélagie and her people spent a season slowly catching their breath. A breath of salt air blowing in from the open sea. And Célina, hearing the prophetic birds pass overhead, reached up and caught their cries in handfuls to decipher them for whoever was curious enough to listen. Things were going fine, the oxen could safely rest a while.

"Just turn your skins round and let the undersides warm in the sun a piece. What you need's a good airing out the lot of you."

So spoke Célina.

And everyone slapped her on the back, the new Célina, that is, new ever since she'd smoothed the kinks out of her crotchety character by rubbing up against that jovial jumping-jack, Pierre-the-Fool. Hey! Cut that out.

So down they rolled, their wheels turning roundly, toward that

suave yet effervescent city of Philadelphia and its wildly pealing
bells.

"They're not ringing for the likes of us. Don't go getting excited now."

The bells were chiming out liberty and independence for
somebody else, but that didn't stop the exiles, like the dogs in
the fable, from licking up the crumbs under the table.

. . . Crumbs, you say?

Pélagie had got Maxime and Benjamin's message loud and
clear. And this time she was determined to stand up for her
rights. She would wait for the *Grand'Goule* in the port of Philadelphia day and night, from autumn to spring, for as long as the
good Lord, who spared her nothing, was pleased to let her. She
would wait, get that into your thick heads, Pacifique and Jeanne
Bourgeois. They had waited fifteen years in the south, hadn't
they, and had waited on those slowpoke clans detaching themselves in clusters from the seaboard colonies, and had waited for
the rainy season to pass so they could ford the rivers . . .

". . . so you wouldn't get the floor of your cart or the seat of
your chest wet . . ."

They would wait for the schooner and its new refugees till the
end of time if they must. Let that be understood.

The schooner appeared at the height of the summer. Praise be
Lady Mary, Mother of God!

The four masts had broken through the morning mist one at a
time; one after another they had loomed up before the startled
eyes of Old Bélonie, standing watch like everyone else. He had
had time to count them and to recognize the figurehead. The
Grand'Goule! A *Grand'Goule* weary and worn, but still proud,
the old girl, no mistake about that. She bore straight down upon
him, all sails flying, but this time without flames or phantom
sailors in the rigging. She was very much alive, the *Grand'Goule*
was, Bélonie had to admit that, and he stirred his near-century-
old bones and tottered off to get Pélagie.

Poor Pélagie! This time she was the one to feel her joints
stiffen. She stood there openmouthed, arms hanging, her heart

turned to foam. Bélonie had to tap her on the shoulder: Come on! Come on! so moved himself that he even forgot his "Hee!"

The celebrations at their reunion lasted three days, some would even say three months if you linked them up to the wedding of Madeleine and her fine gander Charles-Auguste.

Charles-Auguste must have heard the recommendations Pélagie called out over the head of her only daughter to her progeny for centuries to come. He screwed up his courage and pushed his mother into Pélagie's presence. And so it was that Agnès Dugas, Landry by her man, related to the LeBlancs through the males of the maternal line, asked for Madeleine's hand in marriage in her son's name.

Pélagie looked at the mother, known as the Magpie, looked at that fine gander Charles-Auguste, and her eyes misted over even before they turned to rest on her daughter. Already? . . . Why, sure, Pélagie! She was born in the hold of the *Nightingale*, not long into the year 1756. Twenty years, count them. At that age, Pélagie, you'd already brought all your children into the world, remember that. A girl who passes her twentieth birthday without giving her hand in marriage is likely to sit by the fire and spin, as the saying and sentiment goes in our country. No offense, Célina. And then, that Charles-Auguste's a gallant lad, resolute and resourceful . . . Who was it cleared the brush out of the oxen's horns the other day when they got stuck in the alder scrub? No skirt-chaser, he's proved that over the past two years, nor no numbskull neither, and besides, his father was first cousin to the first cousin of your own man, Pélagie, so this won't be one of those left-handed marriages.

Beausoleil came and stood by Pélagie's side. It was he who undertook to lecture the orphaned suitor. Young Acadians who'd survived the Great Disruption would themselves have to replace their own fathers. Alone and without masters they would have to learn a trade lain fallow for twenty years, without help or advice from elders either, since all had perished in the disaster. And it wasn't enough Charles-Auguste should be worthy of his father and ancestors. He would have to rebuild the line all by himself

and replant in the springtime as though the land hadn't lain
asleep for the twenty autumns before. He would have to rebuild
aboiteaux abandoned to the gulls and seaweed, build himself a
fishing boat, add outbuildings to the farm, and perhaps one day
take up arms against an invader always prowling around its pe-
rimeter fences. More than that: The head of an Acadian family
couldn't be satisfied with just an heir or two in the next hundred
years, for the dead cried vengeance and the hearths were empty.
The upcoming generations had only a century to make up the
century lost and to prevent the race from dying out. Only the
cradle could avenge Acadie.

Charles-Auguste opened a pair of wide moist eyes at all this,
eyes that had often fondled Madeleine's milk-white skin, and
throwing himself at the feet of Captain Broussard-called-
Beausoleil, he blurted out in a strangled phrase:

"I love her, I'll do anything, I love her!"

Robin Hood of the Seas burst into a laugh, then pulled the
Fine Gander to his feet, and Charles-Auguste understood that
the gods were on his side and that the cry he'd choked out was
one Beausoleil and Pélagie could fully appreciate that summer.
So in all due pomp Charles-Auguste Landry received the hand
of Madeleine LeBlanc, the only daughter of Pélagie, in marriage.

The announcement of this match put all the carts in heat. The
oxen, so serene and reasonable till now, began frisking around in
the grass and mooing sweet nothings through the picket fence to
cows who, since the Declaration of Independence, could justly
call themselves American. As for Célina, there was no end to her
burbling under the tickling attentions of her cavalier who was
forever pinching her . . .

"Eeeee!"

Meanwhile, the two fugitives from the Indians went sniffing
and snooping around the collective petticoats, dropping a pro-
vocative phrase here, and an evocative pinch there, willy nilly.
Mainly nilly. Yes, the day fine-feathered Maxime, who thought
the disappearance of his rival Jean would give him a free hand
with Catoune, tried to reach under the thick cloth of the bodice

protecting the forbidden fruit beneath, he discovered he'd been prodding more nilly than willy.

Catoune hadn't reacted to the story of Jean's misfortunes and his union with the Iroquois princess, hadn't budged. But from that day on she trembled at the least breeze like an aspen leaf, or flinched at the slightest whimper from the children, although they had all adopted her as guardian and governess, the little Virginie first among them.

For Virginie Cormier had survived in a time when three children out of four perished. And had even become mascot and darling of the caravan. On the sly Catoune took bread from her own mouth to slip between the milk teeth of her little charge, who prospered from it visibly. She was pink and plump with *joie de vivre* as if at three she already knew what a privilege it was to be alive in times like these. And she laughed and babbled from morning to night under Catoune's wing.

But since the news that Jean was definitively gone, swallowed up in the wilderness, to their amazement Catoune had more than once scolded Virginie and the other children. And to Pélagie's consternation, she sometimes disappeared for days on end.

"Go look for her, P'tite Goule," she would order the giant.

And he would execute her orders as if on Crusade in heathen lands. Catoune would be led back, submissive, on tiptoe, into camp and Pélagie, without harshness, would look at her as if to say, "You know very well he won't come back. Be reasonable."

Reasonable? Catoune? But reason was precisely the one gift the gods had denied her. And with reason. Catoune knew, without ever having learned it, that a clam is a clam, and man is a man, and to square the circle is nothing at all. She knew all that by instinct, so why go asking her to be reasonable?

Any more than P'tite Goule. But he was so reasonable from the word go, poor giant, that he needed no urging. Every time Pélagie turned her eyes in his direction, he would pull on his seven league boots and slip off in search of something or someone. More often than not, Catoune.

Without knowing it, he was getting tame.

Beausoleil noticed this the day he proposed that the giant

rebecome his cabin boy and set off to sea with him again. P'tite Goule blinked, tried to understand, and his eyes brimmed with a salty flood that was sad to see. At which the captain broke into a hearty, reassuring laugh. They wouldn't go off alone, either of them. He had come for Pélagie, and Catoune could come along with the baggage.

At that P'tite Goule opened his giant eyes so wide Beausoleil could see his whole schooner reflected in them.

"And, we'll be happy to the ends of the earth," concluded the captain, whistling a sea shanty.

Agnès Dugas came around with a chip on her shoulder, looking for Pélagie. On a question of protocol. Were they planning to go ahead with their children's nuptials without the sacraments? Charles-Auguste was the son of Charles-Auguste-à-Charles-Auguste-à-René Landry, fervent Roman Catholics all of them since the Seigneury of Aulnay.

"Are we to have my boy's marriage blessed by a Quaker?"

Pélagie was left to conjure with that all the rest of the day. It was her daughter's wedding too, a daughter of Jean LeBlanc descended from first generation colonists as much as the Landrys. But how were they going to find a missionary in Pennsylvania? It was dreaming to think they'd find a second Baltimore on their route. Even a justice of the peace was better than some heretical official, if they wanted properly constituted grandchildren to dandle on their knees one day. Just think of the Antichrist born with a full set of teeth. And Pélagie was left scratching the back of her neck.

Then one morning she approached Bélonie:

"I know you're stronger on funeral services, Old Bélonie, but couldn't you, maybe, just once, change your skin?"

"Hee!"

"I've a daughter to marry, and you know the custom: When we're short a priest, we fall back on a patriarch."

"Hee!"

"If my late father's memory was good, you'll soon be rounding your hundredth year. Age brings certain rights with it among us.

When we come across a real live priest, we'll ask for his rebenediction."

"Hee!"

Had she spun out her arguments the length of New England, that day Pélagie would have got no more out of the old boy than his "Hee!" Yet she was sure that on the wedding morn Bélonie would lay his hands on the heads of the future man and wife without grouching. So off she went to see to the preparations.

The whole of Philadelphia was celebrating that summer, so the deportees could organize their own festivities without attracting attention. And they jumped to it with a vengeance. A wedding! A wedding feast besides! And the Holy Virgin herself a part of the party.

"Can't you leave the saints out of it, Jean-Baptiste Allain, for once we don't need them?"

But Jean-Baptiste Allain with his stigmata in his palms and his crucifix in his bag was already running out his litany of matrimonial advice for the benefit of the betrothed . . . As spouse and mother of your children, you are taking to wife a virgin made in the image of the Mother of God who will love, honor, and obey you, since you are the chief who in the Garden of Eden received the baton of authority over the whole family . . .

Pélagie cocked an eyebrow at this authority and, picking up the whip used for the oxen, unleashed a crack on the trunk of a poplar standing there lifting its head to heaven. Then she smiled to herself. Her daughter Madeleine hadn't known the old ways before the Great Disruption. Most family chiefs had perished in the catastrophe, carrying their batons of authority received in the Garden of Eden with them to the depths of the woods or seas. As a result, the women had to face the enemy and adversity alone and wield the scepter of the head of the family. As posthumous child of her father and ancestors, Madeleine knew only this regime. Pélagie could count on her to continue the line.

Then it was Célina's turn to hold forth, the Célina of grand occasions.

"I warned you, I warned you all that one day we'd pay dearly for that chest."

The chest again.

"Now what's up with the chest?"

"It's still there large as life, that's what's up."

"And did it drop on uns little tootsie, eh gimpy?"

Célina's nose veered to crimson. Not content to stick up for their chest after all the trouble it had given everyone, they were even going around now sticking names on people, those money-grubbing, penny-pinching misers.

"All on account of this chest we've been dragging from south to north with us like the Cross of the Lord Jesus Christ, we had to pay the price of a violin."

And then, triumphantly, leaning on every syllable:

"And didn't I hear some talk of a wedding today?"

So that was it. At last you could see where the wind was coming from. Just the same, Célina was right to lament the fiddle. In times past, Acadie had seen winters that froze the cider, and spring breakups that carried off the nets and the fish traps, and southeasterly winds that lifted the roofs off the houses, but never once had they been without music. Weddings without a priest they'd seen before, but not without those magic strings to give the tone and their rhythm to set the time for the rigadoon. The Bourgeois had made the carts pay a heavy price for their chest.

François-à-Philippe Basque dared suggest to Pélagie that they might delay the ceremony a few weeks. With a little luck, who knows, they might track down an ash in the forest, or a bird's-eye maple.

"Not on your life!"

This cry escaped Charles-Auguste, the Fine Gander, coming right up, unbidden, from the hot, vital depths of the impetuous fiancé's being. And he blushed at the knowing laughter of the men.

Pélagie put her hand on her son-in-law's arm and told the Basque to make do without the fiddle, to find something else, to invent something, anything. If you've got a beak and hands and feet, surely you can put them to use, can't you? You'll never get me to believe at this late date that you have to go borrowing music from trees.

"I make do, I do, feeding my gang without pots and pans and practically without utensils."

Utensils . . . the word didn't fall on deaf ears. And François-à-Philippe Basque went on his way already whistling brand new melodies.

The festivities could begin. For Madeleine and her brides-maids, that's to say all the women of the carts, they had brought out the silks, laces, and cashmeres lifted from the ladies of Balti-more in circumstances now familiar and preserved snug under the secret treasure of the Bourgeois's chest . . . Petticoats, cloaks, bonnets, neckerchiefs, bibbed aprons, and silk garters. Before such a parade of red-and-indigo-striped finery, the men's eyes gaped and all were afflicted with Saint Vitus's dance.

"And what about us?" Maxime inquired of François-à-Philippe.

So they marched down to the stream to scrub their shirts and breeches.

But happiest of all were the children, decked out in leaves and flowers to hide their indigence, scampering between their mothers' legs and earning a volley of smacks distributed at ran-dom without much attention paid to whether they landed on the rightful recipient or not. It was the first real Acadian wedding feast since the Deportation and they were bound and deter-mined not to be short of a thing. For the occasion they had just about emptied the hold of the *Grand'Goule* as well as the carts' reserves. Tomorrow could look after itself, or the devil take it!

"Ho, ho, ho! . . ."

And each family made a contribution according to its inspira-tion: freshly snared rabbits, porcupines, and groundhogs run to earth with sticks, preserved Indian corn, lamb's quarters, fiddle-heads, hawberries, currants, gooseberries, and chokecherry and dandelion wine and . . .

"Phew! How hot it's getting!"

. . . and a kid found by chance wandering around at the top of the field looking for its mother . . . and some turtle doves laid out in front of a baker's shop where the inattentive baker was too busy talking politics . . . and a barrel of molasses just

unloaded from a Dutch ship fresh from trade with the isles . . .
and chickens, geese, and ducks aplenty, for in those times the
streets were full of them on market day . . .

"Stop 'im! Stop 'im! He's got my rooster!"

And Pierre-à-Pitre takes to his heels and disappears into the
back lanes.

They had waited so long for this first great joyous picnic that
after twenty years they weren't going to wait a single hour more.
So even before Pélagie had managed to push Bélonie up to the
canopy formed of sails and masts, Madeleine and Charles-
Auguste had already said yes and all Acadie had tucked in to the
grub.

. . . And sling me a wing and I'll whizz you the gizzard . . .
and don't swallow the stew spoon there . . . and hey, you mon-
keys, get your heads out of that molasses barrel . . . and pass the
pancakes up this way and I'll slide you the giblets down the
other side . . . and I'll have another little swig of the grog . . .
and don't all talk at once . . . and get your hands off me, you
devil, heel heel . . . and let the wine piss and the bread stuff us
and puff pastries pop out my belly button . . . I can't take any
more!

Acadie was dead drunk.

Drunk on chokecherry and dandelion wine, drunk on tenderness, mirth, and music.

. . . Music?

Why sure! You didn't imagine that folks would go marrying off
their eldest without striking up a tune and dancing a cotillion,
did you? So what if life has done you out of your bagpipes and
Jew's harps, and even your fiddle in the last skirmish, you've still
got spoons and thighs to accompany your warbling, haven't you?
What say, ladies and gents?

The Basque clan again. This time they had helped themselves
to the kitchenware and went banging out tunes by knocking
spoons against their thighs and knees: *Et j'ai du grain de mil, et
j'ai du grain de paille, et j'ai de l'oranger, et j'ai du tri, et j'ai du
tricoli* . . . Everyone was *tricoli* now, high as kites, the lot of
them.

"Hee, hee, hee! . . ."

"Ho, ho, ho! . . ."

And beating time with feet, hands, heads, bums, beaks . . . *et le bec, alouette, savez-vous plantez les choux* . . .

And shit to His English Majesty!

Greet your partner ladies, greet your partner gents, now everyone, switch partners . . .

Yahoo!

Watch it, Benjamin! You can tell he's new around here, can't you? Nobody'd go pinching Célina unless he was called Pierre-à-Pitre and had a long pair of legs under him! Ho, ho!

That's enough out of you!

> "Split the wood, lay the fire,
> Sleep on my beauty in your fine attire."

. . . And shit to His English Majesty!

All of a sudden there's a new note, booming like a big bell, coming from the platform at the foot of the canopy; a new rhythm to attune the spoons to, a half-time, quarter-time syncopation like a beating of crow's wings caught in an alder bush.

"It's Célina!"

Clubfoot Célina, red with fermented dandelion, drunk on gooseberries and stew, high on tenderness and fraternity, tapping the club of her clubfoot on the planks, a clubfoot playing the left-hand melody three octaves lower than the right . . . Tum-ti-dee, Tum-ti-dee . . . and the planks reverberating, creating rhythms so lively and novel that since then, passed down from generation to generation and from wedding to wedding, the reel named "The Clubfoot Reel" has enlivened accordionists' repertoires from that day to this.

Not all melodies came from Orpheus's lyre, and Acadie of the hard times is living proof of that. For this one wedding feast for Madeleine and her Fine Gander gave rise to a good half of the refrains and a quarter of the roundelays in our oral patrimony. Yes, and if they'd had no musical instrument at all, Pélagie's people would have tooted tunes out of their own tubes, and that's no lie. So it was lucky the Basques dug up the spoons and Célina shook loose with her clubfoot.

At dusk the oxen were led to the field, their horns still garlanded with red festoons and copper bells tinkling wavering melodies.

"Drop their halters," called Pélagie, "and let them pasture in the Quaker minister's field. On a day like today anything goes."

Anything indeed, especially for those who had unjustly borne the enemy yoke for half a century. Had the whole world been forced to pay for the wrongs done her people, Pélagie would have felt no remorse, not that day. Back home, before the Great Disruption, the LeBlancs would have given their daughter a wedding worthy of her heritage and her ancestral line. Too bad now if they happened to take back a few crumbs of the booty the persecutors had stripped from them. And let no historian in centuries to come stand up and proclaim that Pélagie and her clan short-changed anyone.

"Nor anyone, nor his neighbor. Just returned to an orphaned girl a bare quarter of her rightful due." Beausoleil-Broussard laughed aloud. Even anger was becoming in this woman.

And shit to His English Majesty
Who declared his war on you and me!

The two lovers disappeared into the field behind the animals. That night many a fine and tender thing was said between them with only the oxen for witness. Do you mean Bélonie stayed behind at the banquet the whole while? Bélonie, usually so curious about the least tremor in the life of the carts . . . had he been mixing his drinks, the dandelion and chokecherry?

That shows how little you know Acadie if you can think for a second Bélonie, or even Célina, capable of following a pair of lovers the likes of Beausoleil and Pélagie up into the ox field. Capable, moreover, of letting others, or their posterity, in on the words and deeds of two people who themselves had decided to tell you nothing. In our country, love stories and love songs are sung in a minor key and practically always in a whisper. Which makes my cousin say the curious must needs keep their ears clean.

What hour of the night was it when suddenly Pélagie cocked an eye open and perked up her nose like a watchdog?

Catoune? Where had Catoune made off to? No one had seen her the whole day long.

"Charlécoco! P'tite Goule! Pierre-à-Pitre!"

Catoune's disappeared. In the middle of the party. Hurry up. Don't waste time on galloping fears. Come on! . . . What was troubling her anyway?

"Try the woods! Search there!"

Now who would have thought it possible! And Jeanne Aucoin prodded Agnès Dugas who prodded Célina to come up with some notion as to what in the world had got into Catoune's head.

Madeleine went wild and wanted to stop the wedding, annul the marriage, and return to her maiden life till her foster sister was found. And she tore off her fancy linen cap and started across the fields at a run. Poor old Charles-Auguste was so staggered that when he finally did come to he never could catch up with his bride-of-an-hour who by that time had disappeared into the edge of the forest.

"Dear God in Heaven! Stop them! Stop them all for the love of God!"

And for the love of God, or Catoune, Célina hoisted her club-foot and clumped off as best she could after the newlyweds. Then it was the Jeannes—and Acadie of the time boasted almost a dozen of them—then the Maries, the Annes, the Marguerites, then the whole clutch of kids, scurrying off between the men's legs before they had even decided which direction to take.

The giant, all on his own, wringing with sweat and emotion, laid low the alders, ripped up bushes, strode over fences and jetties, and sinking his huge sabots into the sand of the dunes, churned up lakes and sandbars, so say the chronicles. They even say it was lucky for Philadelphia that Catoune came home by herself before Orion came out, for it seems the giant was getting ready to make a foray into town. As it was, he was practically the only one in camp, along with Bélonie, to welcome Catoune back when she returned with a celebrant.

She had slipped away at dawn without anyone knowing, and had gone straight to the hermit's hut. Yes, a priest, the ex-chaplain of one of La Fayette's regiments. Where had she learned of the monk's existence? How had she found him in the forest? . . . Come on now, everyone knows Catoune could never go astray in woods that had fed and sheltered her from earliest childhood. She had true north in her bones the way others have perfect pitch. And if we can trust Bélonie, that day she was the only one of the lot to carry a compass in her eye.

"Hee!"

This time Bélonie had every reason to snicker. For he had seen them all take off, one after another, in search of the lost one, and one after another get lost in turn in the fields and forest. From under the wedding canopy you could hear the shouts bouncing off the trees: "Charles-Auguste! Madeleine! Agnès! Marie-Jeanne!" Calling each other, the lost ones wandered around in circles through the woods, retracing their own steps, cursing, bawling, and unsettling the bleary-eyed owl. When everyone had breathlessly regained camp, the only one missing was Célina. They fished her out an hour later, soaked to the butt, hurling imprecations to all the saints in heaven, her clubfoot wedged between a couple of rocks in a streambed.

At last they could count heads and discover that they had added one, the hermit's. Whereupon began this preamble to the religious ceremony:

"A priest! A real Roman priest!"

"Is it, dear God, possible!"

"What's this? You mean to say monks sprout up under the trees around here like mushrooms?"

"Show a little respect there, you young fry. Anyway, it's not a monk, it's a hermit."

"Is that more or less than a priest?"

"He's a poor servant of God."

"Praise the Lord! What's more he speaks French. We'll be able to hear the Latin in our own tongue."

"Excuse them, Father."

And the good Father excused them with a smile and let them finger and sniff and question him while the women busied themselves under the canopy brushing up the crumbs of the wedding feast.

. . . Quick, children, go get spruced up again, and you young folk, help your mothers get the platform set back up, and come on everyone, get a move on, we've a real priest to celebrate a real ceremony for us, Lord bless us all!

Jeanne Aucoin la Girouère hadn't been so busy since the day of her father-in-law Charles-à-Charles's funeral. And as if the two events met somewhere in the depths of her subconscious memory, she said to the late patriarch, with a sigh:

"To think you never lived to see your second-degree descendants hitched in marriage, Father, to think you never saw it in your own lifetime."

But raising her eyes to the stars, she noticed the Pleiades twinkling like so many glowing embers. So she winked back and whispered just for him:

"Don't worry, I'll fix it up so as one of yours chooses a wife who'll be a credit to his ancestors. I'll fix it. Count on me."

Yes, he could count on his daughter-in-law, Charles-à-Charles could, living or dead. For that matter, nothing in Jeanne Aucoin's manner had changed after the old man's death. Every night she still gave him an account of her day and asked him, in the name of the family who had taken her for wife and mother, to approve her conduct and the decisions she had taken as moral chief of the clan. Then she would wait for a sign from the deceased, usually a tug on her big toe, before falling asleep. That had gone on for five years. But tonight they had a monk handy. So Jeanne Aucoin proposed that the assembled flock kneel before God's representative to ask him for a retroactive celebration by proxy.

. . . How's that again?

Nothing simpler. Jeanne Aucoin was just requesting the hermit to remarry fathers and mothers united in exile, to rebaptize newborn babes, most of them going on four years old now, and to rebury the dead rotting in American soil from Georgia to Maryland. All that with the full pomp of Gregorian chant and the purest of Church Latin as spoken formerly on the shores of the French Bay.

The poor monk consented to everything: remarriages, rebaptisms, long distance funeral services. But when the Allains came along to ask him for a Solemn High Mass, the priest judged it time to get on with the marriage of Madeleine and Charles-Auguste, which, after all, was why he had torn himself away from his forest retreat in the first place.

Go right ahead, Father. He could take up the ceremony from where they'd left off, on the brink of the sacrament. A sacrament in right and due form this time, with its blessed bread and its *ora pro nobis*'s, with a sermon that rankled Jean-Baptiste Allain because he had missed giving his, and with the laying of hands on the heads of the young couple, who exchanged rings swearing fidelity till death did them part.

Beausoleil came close to Pélagie. It was the time for exchanging vows, the hour of the evening star.

"Don't say anything," she said.

"Is it because Jean didn't come back?"

"They're more than thirty families now, all clinging to my skirts."

"But those families aren't yours. They all have their own heads."

"None of them knows the way in the dark, you could see that just now in the woods. Besides, none of them's got the image of home in the gut."

"What about those twin sons of yours, and your newly-married Madeleine?"

"So soon! It's hard to get used to the idea."

"If they don't know how to handle the oxen after six years, they never will."

"The oxen, sure. But the people of Beauséjour, Port-Royal, Rivière-aux-Canards, and Grand-Pré, that's another kettle of fish. When poor Catoune ran off today, you saw the hullabaloo."

"But one day Catoune, and the twins, and the whole of Acadie are going to have to grow up and take their lives in hand."

"One day, when we reach home."

"Could it be, Pélagie, that you've fallen out of love with life; that the *Grand'Goule* was too long at sea?"

Pélagie felt the pain of it in her bones and soul.

"If the *Grand'Goule* went sailing off for eternity to the ends of the earth, I'd spend the rest of my days with my eyes glued to the open sea."

Broussard-called-Beausoleil took the woman he loved in his arms and bending over her covered her with all the stars that are mirrored each night in the sea.

Then, taking a breath of salt air:

"Who can they be, those devils of saints set by heaven to watch over Pélagie and Beausoleil?"

"Saint-Marin and Saint-Jacques of Compostela, the patron saints of wanderers . . . First let me take my children home, then together we'll go and rebuild the land of Beausoleil."

"And of Grand-Pré," added the captain.

Sitting apart from the celebrations, Catoune crooned a song to quiet her heart and soothe the children she would never bear. And when Pélagie came over to offer her a drink of nuptial wine, she heard lamentations rise up out of the cup the very instant Catoune touched it to her lips.

They say in Acadie that the cup has never ceased to lament any time anyone tries to drink from it. It's my cousin from the Bélonie side who claims to have seen and heard it in the garret of one of the cart's descendants a few years before his house went up in flames.

PROPERTY OF THE
PUBLIC LIBRARY
ST. MARYS, ONT.

13

"The party's over. Get back in your rags."

And once again the lid of the chest creaked open and laces and oriental silks were swallowed up in a gulp. Everything was ready, they could pull up stakes. To oil the cartwheels the Negro went off into the fields snake-hunting. In three years Jeanne Bourgeois had got used to these barbarous habits and no longer threw up every time. Now she settled for a dainty eruction and "I'll never become accustomed to slaves," which gave the rest of Acadie a good laugh when they thought of the generation they'd just come through in exile and slavery.

"Think yourself lucky, Jeanne Trahan, that you don't have to eat the Negro's snakes."

That morning Célina should have kept a sharper watch on her tongue. That at least was the opinion of Old Bélonie who wagged on about either you were a sorcerer or you weren't, and whoever has the gift, be it as healer, blood-stauncher or seventh-of-seventh, you should never tempt fate. For fate, being touchy, malicious, or simply playful, is quite likely to take soothsayers at their word.

And the year following the Philadelphia celebrations, they ate snake.

Yuk!

"They ate cow flaps and ox dung, the old folks used to say, and slept piled up on one another to keep warm. One of the worst winters of the century by all accounts, one that froze what little grease was left in the marrow of our forefathers' bones. Even Jeanne la Girouère, it seems, had a whiff of her own death.

. . . Jeanne Aucoin? You don't say.

"But she didn't die."

And to treat me to the rest of the story, my cousin put on the enigmatic ancestral smile:

"Jeanne Aucoin was as familiar with the dead as Old Bélonie in person. Only she resisted them, you see, never got taken in. Seems she had the knack of sticking her foot in the eye of any cheeky visitor from the other side, apart from Charles-à-Charles, who had the nerve to come round at night pinching her toes. Indeed, I've heard say that even the deadest of the dead would keep a good ten feet away from Jeanne Aucoin Girouarde . . . Hee!"

So The Girouarde came out of her agony fresh as an onion, ready to toss her winding sheet into the wash on Monday morning along with her old man's underpants. For Jeanne Aucoin was washerwoman the way Célina was healer and midwife. Even more so. In any regular army she'd have held the rank of quartermaster. Pélagie had, in a manner of speaking, entrusted the housekeeping to this woman who in troublous times had learned how to keep a leaky boat afloat and how to grow wheat in the bottom of a cart. And invent the mobile clothesline, to boot.

It was the day after the wedding and she had just caught the two embarkations out in a flagrant display of pigheadedness. Neither the schooner nor the cart would consent to be first to leave. No, not us, we're not budging I tell you, we'll wait till doomsday if need be, that's our last word and that's the way it's going to be, yah-yah-yah, blah-blah-blah. Schooner and cart stuck there face to face, each waiting for the other to tire out or give in.

"We're waiting for an offshore breeze."

"We're letting the oxen rest."

"We're getting our sheepshanks unshackled."

"We've got our axles to grease."

"We've got sails to hoist."

. . . And other such arguments.

But when Jeanne Aucoin heard:

"And our clothes to dry in the sun . . ."

. . . She judged that excuses had dragged on long enough. When things had gone so far as to delay the return of a people to their ancestral home on the pretext of half a dozen shoulder capes and three petticoats to dry in the sun, it was time for Jeanne Aucoin to act. She cut short the debate by hoisting the foresail with her own hands and by installing her mobile clotheslines in the carts: bushes solidly fixed to the sideboards, each capable of carrying a whole family's laundry on its branches. Jeanne Aucoin had too much organization in her system, and above all too much heart in her chest, to let the two most eminent figures of her time go on destroying themselves a second longer. First sear the abscess; worry about the scar later on.

So it was, on the morrow of Madeleine of Acadie's wedding, that the caravan of carts lumbered on again, remounting America, garlanded in festoons, ribbons, the leftovers of the wedding feast, and the underclothes of a people who had nothing left to hide.

A hard year followed. For if north winds and black frosts could be foreseen, no almanac of the time had predicted the freezing rains, tempests and tornadoes, and the floods that followed these perturbations. For the carts and the oxen, New England was a catastrophe.

Yet, they resisted.

But thanks to what miracles from Célina! Attacking fevers with slabs of salt herring and slices of onion applied to the soles of the feet, with doses of senna, wildcherry, and witchgrass root,

with frictions of green oil also called wood tea, with cataplasms
of leaves soaked in infusions of goldthread or sacks of camphor
tied around the neck against mumps or other throat ailments,
with linseed poultices for breaking abscesses and yarrow to en-
courage the breaking of wind, and frogspit for all the rest. Ah!
Let me tell you, without Célina's love and stubbornness in that
year 1777 . . . Bélonie had already predicted it: too many sevens
in the year. Why 1777 alone contained the seven years of lean
kine and the seven scourges of Egypt.

. . . The ten scourges of Egypt.

Ten if you wish, but let me tell you, the Acadians had their
hands full with seven and would have passed up the other three
without a whimper. It was high time, on the first of the year
1778, to take on Boston, a Boston, alas, that was ready and waiting for them.

The carts had forgotten Captain Beausoleil's warning about
the perverse memory and the vindictive nature of the Bostonians. After such a wretched time wrenching themselves out of
the clutches of winds and tides, you could hardly imagine men
crueler than the elements. And yet . . .

"Everyone's got his ugly days," one of the Bélonies was to
venture later on, not looking at Pélagie-the-Grouch.

Hmph! When someone dished up twisted words like that, The
Grouch didn't have to be stared at to know who they were talking about, if you please, so she turned the hasty phrase back on
the brazen speaker.

"And some get uglier every day," she said.

On one point, however, they were agreed. The Bostonians
had gone too far in persecuting a poor ragtag people tiptoeing
up the continent. A fine thing to pile on when destiny turns
against you and go beating up folks already on their knees.

To that, the Bostonians would have replied that these ragtag
Acadians were the sons of the scourge of their fathers a century
before, and that now it was their turn to pay. Thus they thought
to avenge the past by spitting their bile and venom on complete
strangers. And thus the deportees, who had already paid the
price of exile for a squabble between two kings, neither of whom

could have found Acadie on the map, now found themselves maltreated in the name of a war in which neither they nor their fathers had fought.

But just try explaining that to American Loyalists now fleeing before the triumphant insurrection. The beaten slave beats his dog; and the defeated Loyalist drubs the deportee. And to think that soon they would both be finding themselves face to face in the ancient land of Acadie where the drubbing would go on all down the next century. If Pélagie had been able to foresee such a future so close at hand, she would doubtless have redoubled her zeal in this skirmish between the carts and the Boston chargers . . . just to get a bit of an edge in the battle between fox and wolf that will never end.

It all began with the winter yokes.

. . . ?

The winter yokes against the ice.

. . . ?

Why, everyone knows winter yokes. Everyone knows oxen suffer from frost and icy pavements too, and that no iron shoe or cleat ever invented can stop them from dancing on slippery roads. The poor animals rear, wobble, crash into one another, and end up with their horns locked, it's a known fact. That's where the winter yokes come in; they're better adapted to the dance and keep the oxen from strangling themselves. They were used all the time in old Acadie. But where to find winter yokes in Boston? And horn yokes besides, in the Acadian style, quite different from your English neck yokes.

Really, you'd have to be thick-witted to think the English would stock horn yokes; and still more thick-witted to think that even if they had them they'd hand them out to the French; and even more witless than thick-witted to step right up in broad daylight and waken the sleeping bear.

Worse still, get him right out of bed.

Pélagie tore her hair.

"Just what's the big idea this time?"

This time the big idea sprang from the Allains, themselves

sprung from Adam and Eve, and it came with the best intentions in the world, of course. Ah yes, Jean-Baptiste, we know it's the intention that counts, but it helps to throw in a bit of judgment from time to time. Just imagine! This zealot, not satisfied with asking a local merchant for foreign yokes, goes on to sprinkle him with the holy water of a flood of pious sentiments to the effect that The-Lord-Is-With-Us and No-Salvation-Outside-The-Church and the like. A doctrine that had the effect of heating up the Presbyterian's bile so much he ousted the Papist from his shop with a series of well-placed kicks.

And there on the sleety cobbles of the public square, each clutching his faith in one hand and the collar of his enemy in the other, they engaged in a combat for their respective churches that soon had all Boston on the *qui vive*. In less time than it takes a Bélonie to say it, blood spurted, teeth flew, arms locked and twisted, and cries of "Stop them for the love of God, they're going to hurt themselves!" rang out to heaven. Pierre-à-Pitre hastened to find Pélagie who rushed to the scene to find the whole town in a circle around the combatants shouting, "Hit 'im, Tom! Hit 'im!" Hatreds two or three generations old surged up in everyone's memories and hearts. The French from New France, Papists and enemies in 1633, in 1709, in 1744, and so many other times, had attacked them savagely. "Hit 'im, Tom! Hit 'im!" And again in 1755 all along the Massachusetts coast they had unloaded schooners full of skeletal, wild-eyed beggars who by night had eaten the grain sprouting in the fields. "Hit 'im, Tom! Hit 'im!" And Tom pounded poor Jean-Baptiste, who was no match for him, all soused in the Holy Spirit though he might be.

Pélagie had never felt any particular sympathy for the Allains, be they first-favored of God the Father or no. But she couldn't let the massacre continue. She was as responsible for the Allains as for the others, whether she liked it or not. So she whistled for her giant.

On perceiving P'tite Goule, Boston understood that every Bostonian would be needed to set the balance right. So all together the Bostonians jumped on the giant like flies.

And then? . . .

In a twinkling the Basques threw themselves on the heretics, the Protestants on the Papists, the Landrys, Giroués, Cormiers, and LeBlancs on everyone else and . . . My God! What a splendid brawl! And no one took time to pick up teeth or wipe bloody noses either. With fists and kicks they drove through to the giant, who was standing there alone monopolizing the shower of Bostonian blows. Don't let them get away with it, stick up for yourself, P'tite Goule, a blow for a blow, squash them! Mounted on her Hussars, shouting to her men and her Jeannes, Pélagie issued commands, led the attack, charged with horns lowered and cart racks rattling. Olé! Hue-Ho!

Suddenly the fight froze, locked in suspended animation. The evening sky was glowing with an unaccustomed light.

"Fire!"

A cart was burning. Two even. Help!

They managed to save the Allains' by practically throwing themselves on the flames. But the Belliveaus' cart was a total loss.

"Not one plank left joined to another."

Summoning up all the breath left in her and all the fire in her eyes, Célina let fly:

"Ye Sons of Satan! That was their home!"

The Sons of Satan must have been ashamed, for they fell apart like a broken string of beads. It was even said that one big blond fellow, some think the Tom in question, came back the same night with a full cartload of victuals for the disabled crew. It seems that Pélagie let him know that she'd have preferred a cart to a cartload, but the Bostonian didn't appear to understand the lingo.

"Isn't that just our luck," Pélagie said. "First we're reduced to sleeping on straw; now it's ashes."

But it was Célina who was kept hopping that night, for the healer had to ransack her apothecary stores.

"What a shambles!"

By dawn there wasn't a single leaf of wood tea or flower of camomile left in the whole of the perambulating pharmacy. Nor a single Acadian intact. But as one of their heirs was to say later

on, a people who can come through the holds of Governor
Lawrence's schooners with all their bones should be able to
come through a Boston rumble with most of their teeth.

Which didn't prevent Jean-Baptiste from making the most of
his martyrdom and broadcasting, for the benefit of any of his descendants willing to listen, that his broken bones would be num-
bered in paradise and nothing forgotten in the waiting. And
caressing his wounds, Jean-Baptiste Allain cast a scornful look on
the bunch of unbelievers, the LeBlancs and others, who came
from the low lateral branches of defenders of the faith and who
had not, like the Allains, participated in Saint-Bartholomew's
Day.

. . . In what?

He went digging far afield for his history, that Jean-Baptiste,
all the way to the forgotten little town of Saint-Bartholomew in
the Old Country. Would you believe it! And Bélonie gave a good
snicker.

Hee! . . .

But it was no time for laughter, Jeanne Aucoin made that perfectly clear. For as luck would have it:

"It had to be the biggest family to go up in flames."

Sure enough, of all the clans the Belliveaus were the most
numerous. Seventeen children in all, without counting the
granny and three daughters-in-law. And all direct descendants
too, for by some miracle none had perished in the Great Disruption. This was no time to give in, practically on the doorstep of
home. Jeanne Aucoin consulted Charles-à-Charles, Bélonie his
cart, and Pélagie her sea captain, and all the absent ones gave
the same reply: "Share the victims."

So the next day they proceeded to parcel them out.

Jeanne Aucoin perched on a barrel and started the auction.

"Here she is, the old granny, first to go. Who'll give a place in
their cart to poor Anne-Marie-Françoise, widow of Joseph-
Mathurin Belliveau, formerly of Rivière-aux-Canards? There she
stands, Anne-Marie-Françoise, just a little loose skin twisted
round a few sticks of bones, with her rosary twisted round her

fingers. There she stands, Anne-Marie-Françoise, with seventy-four years on her and still got all her teeth and hair . . ."

She was laying it on in proper style, La Girouère was, for everyone knew old Granny Françoise, with all her names, as well as her age and her ailments. But it's not every day you get to have an auction, so best make the most of it. And Jeanne Aucoin continued, with improvements:

"Seventy-four years of Christian life come rough, come smooth, and never a whine or whimper over her lot."

"We'll take her!"

All heads turned.

"Done! To the Cormiers. From this out Anne-Marie-Françoise rides in the Cormier cart. First come, first served."

"Thank you."

"Think nothing of it. After the granny, the babes. Two of God's little angels just freshly arrived from their mother's belly both on the same day, a prettier pair of twins you'll never see. Who'll take them now, along with their mother, if it's not too much to ask . . ."

A hand goes up.

"To the Landrys. Much obliged."

"Aaah!"

"And now folks, who'll take little snotnose here, a kid without a scrap of malice or mischief in his nature, a little shaver, Marguerite Bourg, who'll keep the mud scraped off your wheels, just see if he won't, and see me if he don't . . . Thank you, thank you, Marguerite-à-Pierre-à-Céleste Bourg . . ."

And they pass little snotnose from hand to hand over the heads of the crowd to Marguerite-à-Pierre's cart where she squashes her own crew a little closer together along the sideboards.

"Mama!"

Then came the girls, all in a row like so many onions: Angélique, Marguerite, Rosalie, Isabelle, clambering over the tailgate into the carts of the Légers and the Basques who pitch their last souvenirs of a bygone age overboard to make room.

Jeanne Aucoin caught her breath again.

"And now Henry and Marie-Louise, joined by God as man and wife, twice escaped from the flames with all their brood and reunited to their family after the calamity . . ."

"Stop!"

Oxen and carts together ceased their lowing and creaking.

"Stop . . ."

It was Pélagie come to join Jeanne Aucoin at the foot of the barrel.

All Acadie lifted their blue, prayerful eyes to their chief, who now had taken over the tribune. Drawing in a long breath, as though all the air of America could never quench the thirst of her nostrils, Pélagie lovingly took in her people with a single sweep of her head.

"Once already our fathers saw their families torn apart and dismembered. Well, it was once too often. Some are still wandering over a hostile world seeking each other, and God knows when they'll be knit together again. What the barbarians did to us without God's consent, we will never do to others. Henry and Marie-Louise, collect your own around you again and come to my cart. Let it never be said by those who follow after that even without wishing to we dismembered the only family saved intact from the hands of the King of England . . ."

And she stepped down from the tribune draped in her cloak like a Roman consul in his toga.

That day Pélagie was fit to be crowned with laurels, if laurels had been in season.

Three days later the caravan took off again north, a little more cramped in their carts, a little heavier on their thirty-six wheels, but singing thanks to God that they hadn't lost a single soul in the skirmish.

Out there on the open sea the news of the battle of Boston rushed into the sails of the *Grand'Goule*, careened to the deck, and struck Broussard-called-Beausoleil full in the heart.

"Set the helm nor'nor'west," he shouted to his crew, "and every man to his post."

Robin Hood of the Seas was beside himself; he was ready to swing round on Boston and put the town to the sack; ready to make anyone who had raised a hand against his people, his brothers, his beloved Pélagie, walk the plank.

. . . He'd give no quarter to the heartless herd who had harried the homeless.

The winds and crew had all they could do to calm this captain now more furious than the ocean waves and stronger all alone than his full ship's complement. A complement more complete than usual, more complete than ever before, yes, Bélonie . . .

A young recruit stepped up coolly before the ship's master after God. Beausoleil had fished him out of the sea, or from the islands, or some even claim he had snatched the lad from the jaws of the sea monster who for untold ages has swum the ocean deep. Only one thing is sure: He spoke in French and in the accents of Acadie.

"I've a great desire to find my own kin again," said he to Beausoleil with neither a flutter in his eye nor a catch in his voice.

The captain looked at his cabin boy and little by little his jaws unclenched.

"Your own kin's not much of a people," he replied, "but that's no reason to deprive you of them."

And then to the crew:

"Due north," he shouted. "And the first to spy four oxen harnessed to a cart gets a double ration of bread for the next three days."

Due north was not to be all that due all that long, for soon the *Grand'Goule* had to bear east to bypass Cape Cod which held a bay longer than the French Bay itself. It was there Boston lay, nestled in the crook of its arm like a sleeping paramour. Once more Beausoleil dropped his eyes to his newly recruited cabin boy, the survivor of the deep, the latest of his race to search for his ancestors, and he swallowed the bile that rose in his throat and turned away from Boston. Henceforth he would think only of catching up with the carts to help tend their wounds. And, who knows, perhaps try his luck one last time. What wouldn't he have given to hear from the mouth of Pélagie, Pélagie his woe, Pélagie his hope, his Pélagie of the long nights at sea, the one cry he'd been longing to hear for the past five years.

But the cry he heard came from the young recruit at the top of the mast:

"Salem! The port of Salem lies west-by-south."

But when Beausoleil tried to question him further, he found his cabin boy in a trance, like a prophet possessed by a demon.

"Salem!" he yelled till he was hoarse, as if Salem had brought him into the world.

Well! As he himself was to tell his own son's son at a later date, it had been predicted that a town on the coast of Massachusetts, a town the size of this one, a town with closed dormers in black roofs like these, would one day render him more than life. So it had been predicted by the witches who murmur in the swamp winds by night. It was the name of Salem that was carried in the reed's song.

"More than life, you say? What can be more than life to a man?"

"The life of a man's bloodline," answered the cabin boy.

And Captain Broussard-called-Beausoleil turned the helm and made full sail west-by-south.

PROPERTY OF THE
PUBLIC LIBRARY
ST. MARYS, ONT.

14

The Salem marshes were flooded.

"We can't get through," shouted Charles, twin to Jacquot, Pélagie's son.

But his brother Jacquot went on whipping the oxen.

They'd seen worse and had got through muddier marshes. In Georgia, along the Savannah River, in the Carolinas and in Virginia too, come on, push!

"In Virginia and the Carolinas we weren't so many, and every cartwheel still had twelve spokes. We can't get through, I tell you."

It was the first time Pélagie had seen her twins in disagreement, each pulling his own way. A bad sign. And you could hear the hubs cracking with the strain.

"Everyone out, except for Granny and the babes. We're going to try to make it across the fields."

. . . You men, put the children up on your shoulders; you

youngsters, haul and heave; you women, hitch up your skirts and petticoats over your knees; come on now, Hue! Hue! Hue!

They can't get through.

No, they couldn't get through. Better accept it as fact and not keep doggedly on. Pélagie mopped the back of her neck and throat. Over there lay the sea, just over there beyond this swamp flooded by the hardest spring of the century. They were still struggling in the throes of a slowly rotting winter that nipped the buds and split the tender April sprouts. They were struggling still under a malediction.

"What cries are those?"

. . . The winds, Pélagie, the marsh winds. At the heart of the breeze where the nor'easter twines into the sou'wester. The marshes wail in the April winds, you know that, Pélagie.

"The winds, is it? Then why is Catoune worked up like that, staring into the sky? There's a moaning comes from afar, from beyond the sand dunes, I can hear it."

. . . It's the ocean surf breaking on the pebbles of the beach, that's all. The sea is high with the flow of ice drifting down from the north.

"Stop! I hear the screams of witches burning at the stake and the groans of the shipwrecked swirled in the foam. Stop!"

. . . No, Pélagie, you mustn't take the voices of swamp and sea for witches hanging on a gibbet. A century of winds has cleansed Salem now. All Catoune hears is the sea and the northeast wind.

"Calm yourself, Catoune," says Pélagie, "it's nothing but the cry of the gulls following ships out at sea."

And they whipped the Hussars who plunged their forefeet into the mire.

Alban-à-Charles-à-Charles came over to Pélagie.

"If you ask me . . ."

Pélagie stared at him hard. But he went on.

"If you ask me, we ought to change course and veer a mite more nor'west."

Pélagie cast a glance at the sea on the other side of the marshes and dunes.

"Nor'west will take us a long way off course," she said.

Off course? What course? Since Boston they'd more or less given the oxen their heads, letting them pick their way as best they could through the ruts plowed in the melting snow. So as to a course . . .

"If we reached the sea we'd have a course. All we'd have to do would be follow the coast leading due north."

Alban-à-Charles-à-Charles's voice grew gentle.

"That's true enough. But maybe we should wait a mite till the marshes are passed so as not to take any chances."

"And quit the coast?"

"The way it is now, we risk quitting our very lives. I have this premonition that . . ."

But he hadn't time to state his premonition before reality seized them both by the throat like a prophecy fulfilled.

Mooo! . . .

The oxen! The oxen stuck, sinking, bawling themselves hoarse, dragging the lead cart, Pélagie's, down with them into the sinking mud.

"Save the babies and old Françoise!"

"Get them out of the cart!"

My God! My God! Stop the earth moving like that, keep the wheels from sinking, for the love of God, block the wheels!

Meantime, at sea, a young ship's boy aloft at the top of the mast called down to his captain:

"The carts! The carts! Over there in the marsh, not a half a league from shore!"

Beausoleil scrambled up the rigging like a squirrel, back bent double and knees and elbows flying. Sure enough, he could count them, carts and animals too, five oxen, a donkey, a mule . . . The *Grand'Goule*'s latest hand would get his three-day's double ration of bread all right.

The quartermaster, whose ears were sharpest of all, was the first to hear the cries.

"Hark! Something strange is happening over there."

"It's the wind whistling in your ears, matey, or else they're calling us over to a feast."

"They're calling us right enough, Captain, but to no feast."

"Strike the sails! Quick!"

And the *Grand'Goule* dropped her sails, furled them on the yards, maneuvered between the anchored ships and landed at the port of Salem like a vessel of mercy.

Catoune is the first to see the schooner, to hear its sea horn and to catch the salty smell of home. She tugs at Pélagie's skirt and draws her up the hill to the top of a pile of fieldstone.

"God be praised," sighs Pélagie to the heavens she'd been invoking all morning long.

And now they can see the seamen approaching in their seven league boots, their broad shoulders cleaving the haze floating in a band level with the reeds.

"Yoo-hoo!"

"Halloo!"

"Hurry up! This way!"

On the sailors come, rowing with their arms through the thin layer of fog already dissipating in the wind. Then, as they near the carts:

"Good Lord!"

Pélagie cups her hands and shouts to Beausoleil not to approach the cart from the southeast where the muck is too soft.

"Go around. Go around by the north."

Beausoleil takes the measure of the five hundred feet separating him from Pélagie and decides he doesn't want to go around. On he comes, bogs down, but on he comes again. Then, suddenly, as he comes within earshot:

"I've a present here for one of you, from the Old Country."

A present? From the Old Country? Who for?

And thrusting his hands under the armpits of his youngest cabin boy, Beausoleil lifts him overhead and shows him to the astonished carts.

"Bélonie's his name, son of Thaddée, son of Bélonie, rescued from the deep!"

Heaven itself must have registered Captain Broussard-Beausoleil's words that day, then sent them bounding down on the head of Old Bélonie who took them like a kick in the stomach. If ever, since the beginning of time, a man has borne a ghost of the pangs of childbirth, it was Old Bélonie of the cart. At a hundred years or nearly he had just brought his own lineage into the world.

And Pélagie had just time to see a tear run down the old man's right cheek, the right side being the side of luck and happiness in life. She had just time to follow the tear's course down into his beard, for at that very moment a clamor broke out in the swamp.

"The oxen!"

All morning Charles and Coco had been striving to calm and reassure the two Hussars . . . steady there boys, steady on there, we're going to get you out of there . . . but the poor beasts couldn't hold out any longer, and unable to stop sinking, they suddenly let go and took the bit in their teeth. Their feet float, they no longer touch the ground, nothing solid anywhere, everything moving under them, the earth itself caving in with the oxen.

"Not the giant! Don't let the giant near the cart. He's too heavy."

No, P'tite Goule, don't go. You'll just get bogged down with the oxen and the cart.

"You, Pierre-à-Pitre, go ahead, you'll float."

"No!" yells Célina-the-Clubfoot, "you're sending him to his doom, you heartless brutes!"

Back comes Pierre-à-Pitre. Then suddenly he sniffs, blinks both eyes, and disappears into one of the carts. Out he comes in a jiffy with a long cord draped round his neck. And then, quicker than Célina can follow, he climbs up on to the giant's shoulders, fixes one end of the rope round the giant's forehead, then throws the other end which, as if by magic, knots itself round one of the Hussar's horns.

"Aaah!"

"Now where did he ever see that trick?"

No one had ever seen it before. Not yet. It would still be another century before cowboys invented the lasso. Pierre-à-Pitre was a genius. And before adventuring out on the tightrope, he cuts a couple of capers while balancing on the giant's head, just to loosen up his muscles and relax his public's nerves.

"Like the days when I was court jester," he declares, sliding one foot out along the rope, "left foot first and make a wish."

"Better wish you don't break your neck, jester."

. . . Court jester? What court?

And while the Basques chortle, and Célina probes her hero's past, and everyone else holds their breath, the Fool's feet move forward one after the other toward the cart.

"Watch out!"

"Lord a' mercy!"

Over he goes, back he comes, there's one.

"Holy Mary, Mother of God . . ."

Back he goes and returns once more. There's the other.

"Gentle Jesus hanging on the Cross . . ."

Pierre the Fool has just snatched the two Belliveau babes from the doomed cart. Their mother and Anne-Marie-Françoise are still there, but Pierre-à-Pitre's not up to that.

"Keep the oxen quiet, they're up to their bellies now!"

By this time the seamen have circumnavigated the sinking sands and here they are, at last!

"Beausoleil!"

But it's no time for effusiveness. The granny and daughter-in-law are prisoners of the cart. Pélagie tells her Captain this the same way that once at a wedding feast in Cana a mother told her son they were short of wine. So at a glance the captain measures the breadth and depth of the sea of mud.

Pélagie watches him and hardly dares breathe.

"Stand back everyone and don't budge. Even if I call out, don't come near."

Do what he says. On dry land or on his ship's deck Captain Broussard-called-Beausoleil is master after God. And everyone steps back and stands stock still.

"Pass me the jack."

The jack?

"The jack, Jean-Baptiste, you jackass. How do you expect him to lift the cart?"

And Alban passes the jack to Beausoleil who straps it to his belt like a sword.

"Now you men, form a chain and pass me out flat stones, one at a time."

They make a human chain from the pile of fieldstone to Beausoleil and pass along flat stones, one by one.

"What's the captain going to do?"

He's building a road over the slippery mire and moves cautiously along it on his knees toward the imperiled cart.

"Take care, Beausoleil-Broussard!" calls Pélagie, as one says in Acadie when wishing someone safe journey.

And, without moving the rest of his body, Beausoleil-Broussard slowly turns his head toward Pélagie, and his smile lights up the horizon. Then he grits his teeth: The blasted stones will hold, don't worry, Pélagie, even if he has to make them float like planks on the water. Was he remembering from his childhood by the ocean those mornings he spent skipping flat stones across the water?

. . . They'll hold, the blasted stones will, they'll hold.

And hold they do, and Beausoleil crawls over them on his hands and knees, eyes and nose nervous as a wildcat's.

Pélagie peers around the circle of faces seeking Catoune's. There she is, the wild thing, but her eyebrows are relaxed and her forehead unruffled. Pélagie can breathe again.

"Fetch me thinner ones, thinner and larger."

"He's going to sink!"

"Do what he says!"

And they fetch him thinner and thinner and larger and larger.

. . . Only a couple more fathoms, Beausoleil. Keep it up. Imagine you're walking across the ice floes to the deck of the *Grand'Goule* rocking on the deep. Only a yard or two more, Beausoleil.

"He's made it!"

He grasps the spokes, the cart's sideboard; now he's hoisted the daughter-in-law over his shoulder . . .

"The old lady, Beausoleil, take the old lady first!"

. . . No, first the mother with milk for the babes.

"Let him be. He's in charge."

. . . And back he comes, as he went, on all fours, this time with the young woman hanging round his neck, across the stones encrusted in mud.

"God be praised!"

"What a hell of a man, that Beausoleil!"

"Thanks be!"

But there's still Anne-Marie-Françoise. Nobody moves. Once more Pélagie looks toward Catoune. She hasn't changed. Or hardly. The merest shiver flicks across one eyelid. Already the valiant captain is down on all fours again. He's moving a little more quickly and boldly now. Don't exaggerate, Beausoleil. Easy does it. The stones are moving. Sometimes he stops to test the marsh on either side, then on he goes, crouching lower and lower to the ground, spreading his weight. He reaches the cart and grasps the only spoke left showing above the surface of the mire. Whereupon the wheel sinks and disappears.

"Ah! . . . Ah! . . ."

François-à-Philippe cups his hands and calls:

"The grub hoe, there's a hoe in the cart!"

Beausoleil eyes the handle sticking out between two of the sideboard stakes, and now he frees his arms from the mud, and now . . .

"He's got it!"

He's hanging on to the handle and speaking swift and low:

"Come on, grandma, come on, quickly now. Drape yourself round my shoulders."

With wide, startled eyes Anne-Marie-Françoise stares at this black stranger and flattens herself against the back of the cart, her fingers fumbling the beads of her rosary while she mutters Hail Mary . . . Hail Mary . . . Hail Mary . . .

From the hillock they're calling:

"Anne-Marie-Françoise! Granny! It's Captain Beausoleil, one of us . . . he's come to save you!"

Anne-Marie-Françoise listens hard, distends her nostrils, then

screws her whole face up in distaste at this black pirate struggling in the ooze.

. . . Who's yelling like that? What do they want with her?
What's going on?

"Come back, Beausoleil!"

"Carry her off by force!"

By force! He has barely enough of that left to keep him from
going straight to the bottom of this shifting mud that's trying to
suck him down like a gaping mouth . . . the old lady had better
not balk to long . . . because . . .

"Françoise . . . Françoise, for the love of God . . ."

. . .

". . . for the love of your children . . ."

. . . Her children? Mathurin and Marguerite? . . . Someone is
bringing her back her children?

She leans out over Beausoleil to inquire:

"You know Marguerite? The English took her away with three
of her children, little Pierre . . . Joseph . . . and . . . I forget . . ."

"Come with me, Françoise."

"And Mathurin? You wouldn't have seen him at sea off Cap-
de-Sable? He never came home. They say he was lost at sea. You
wouldn't have seen him?"

". . . Yes, surely . . . Didn't he wear a medal round his neck,
your Mathurin?"

Anne-Marie-Françoise leans out even further to hear the
sailor's news of her boy . . . and of his medal . . . and Beausoleil
grabs her just before she topples overboard.

"He was far out at sea, way past the islands . . ." Beausoleil
tells her, struggling to keep his head out of the mud ". . . out
with the whales in the Great North Sea . . ."

Thus the old lady consents to let herself be carried, stretched
out flat on Beausoleil's back while he tells her about her son as
he scrambles over the floating stones.

When the sailors and carters at last lifted the mired couple to
their feet, Célina exclaimed that you might have taken them for

Adam and Eve as fashioned by God on the first day from a handful of mud.

Then all together they leap on the old lady and her rescuer and, to clean them up, lick them all over like dogs. They cluck and stroke and pet them and all talk at once gurgling and jumbling their words: What d'you know! Flat rocks, think of that! Did you ever! And the old lady bouncing along on his backbone! Everyone saved!

"And a new Bélonie to boot!"

A Bélonie escaped from limbo, true descendant of old chin-wagger Bélonie-à-Thaddée-à-Bélonie. And where did he turn up from? Not from Belle-Île-en-Mer, surely? What was he doing there? Make room, quit shoving, give him room there.

Pélagie feels Catoune's heavy breathing on her neck. She turns brusquely and peers into Catoune's eyes staring at the animals stuck in the mud up to their flanks. The cart and oxen are still in danger . . . No, Catoune, we can't do anything about them, be quiet now . . . The oxen and the cart . . . No, Catoune. And just as Pélagie is about to take Catoune's frantic face in her hands, she feels her own head caught in the broad palms of her captain who looks into her eyes saying:

"Now we must save the ship."

And before she can grab him or block the way he has leaped to the first stone and then galloped on like a stallion. No more crawling for Beausoleil-Broussard; he runs, he flies from one stone to the next, his boots barely brushing the moving earth.

All morning long Old Bélonie has stood there, his eyes clamped on this offspring dropped in his lap like a heavenly joke, but now he removes them an instant and stares open-mouthed at this stag bounding fearlessly toward the enemy . . . three times is too much, Captain, you mustn't tempt Fate. You mustn't tempt Death with her three dice, the ace of spades, and the seven of diamonds in her pocket.

Jeanne Aucoin clutches La Bourgeoise, who hangs on the Clubfoot's arm. And without meaning to, the Allains crowd nearer the Landrys and the Bastaraches. The clans draw close together, burying their chest, their violin, and their crucifix as all eyes focus on the cart hitched to a pair of oxen floundering in a sea of mud now perilously approached by the intrepid sea captain.

. . . Aye, perilously. Come back, Beausoleil-Broussard, don't be too bold.

But our intrepid hero has drawn his courage from the eyes of the woman of his life, enough to send him to the ends of the earth. Others before him plunged into the shadowy depths of the sea all for a golden ring in an old Acadian song. And how could our Beausoleil be less valiant than the heroes of old?

In the other direction, in the centuries to come, Bélonies from father to son went on polishing and embellishing this episode of the chronicle, which they called the combat of the carts. For there wasn't a soul that day but knew that Death in person had entered the lists and had drawn her sword against life. And if someone knew it beyond the shadow of a doubt it was he who had Bélonie blood in his veins.

Flying over the stones sunk in the mud, Beausoleil has reached the cart. He has reached it and is clinging there. Now what's his plan? How does he think he can, with only his bare arms, free a cart and two oxen not even touching the bottom. You can see him, almost swimming through the sludge, circle the cart three times as if seeking leverage for his jack. But what can a jack or a jack-tar do in this muddy ocean?

Now Pélagie hears Catoune's breathing blending with the groaning of the wind. Once again the witches' cries arise from the reeds of the Salem marsh.

Wououou! . . . Wououou . . . !

Pélagie digs her nails into Catoune's shoulders. Cut it out! Keep still! Stop squirming!

Catoune hears neither Pélagie's supplications nor the cries of the people of the cart. She has neither eyes nor ears, just gaping pores, her whole body straining to swallow in the strange waves hovering between heaven and earth.

"Aaaah!"

The cry goes up from every throat. Beausoleil has slipped. He is caught between the cart and the oxen. He struggles . . . he claws his way up . . . falls back . . . No, P'tite Goule, don't go out there! . . . Stop him!

"Wait till he surfaces again . . . Wait!"

. . . God save us!

He comes to the surface, tries to unhook the shafts . . . strokes the oxen's rumps . . . Gentle Jesus, have mercy . . . lifts one shaft and leans it back against the box . . . feels around in the mud for the other . . .

"Heeee!"

That cry was Bélonie's, the first he's uttered since the fatal day of the Great Disruption when he lost all his kin in a single slurp of the sea. Since then, all he had ever addressed to Destiny were a few feeble groans or the occasional wink. Yet if he were still alive at almost one hundred today, it was to see his cart brought safely home and his lost offspring in full possession of their souls again. As for his own, he'd settled that score long ago.

. . . But today, today, you slut, there's something more at stake, says he, focusing his eyes and soul over there on that little wooden bridge crossing the stream. A high-humped, narrow, wooden bridge rumbling with a hollow sound that only Bélonie can hear.

The Wagon of Death.

Pélagie watches the old man and understands. The Reaper is there. She couldn't miss such an occasion, could she? For twenty years she's been feeding off Acadian seed, and here she is now sniffing around the parent plant with its roots plunged in the clay of the marsh between earth and sea. This time Pélagie-the-Cart speaks no word to Bélonie, just watches him, her living eyes planted in his beyond-the-tomb gaze.

"It's Beausoleil, he's gone down for the third time!"

The group squeezes up so close to the giant they almost crush him.

Bélonie keeps staring at the little bridge.

Suddenly the giant shakes himself free of them. It was he, it seems, who first had the idea. Or maybe it was François-à-

Philippe Basque who was the first to throw himself down flat on his belly in the mud. The other men catch on fast. And one by one, walking over the body of the man ahead, each throws himself down at full length in the mire. Human stepping stones, if you please, living bodies paving a road for the giant. And the giant, naked as a babe, jumping from one body to the next like a lumberjack hopping across a bunch of floating logs, rushes off to the cart.

Bélonie keeps his eye on the wooden bridge.

The women, standing there hugging their kids to their skirts, are speaking to their dead . . . Charles-à-Charles, you were a warmhearted man during your life, weren't you Charles-à-Charles? . . . Remember your son and daughters today, my Fine Gander Charles-Auguste.

Catoune stands apart, her voice joining the monotonous chant of the wind, her incantation blending with the voices of the witches, which little by little are getting tamer now.

Pélagie alone is speechless.

Suddenly she sees Bélonie take off. Away he goes, around the heap of flat stones and straight toward the bridge. Bélonie . . . Bélonie, what are you up to?

He's entering the fray like the rest, that's all, Pélagie. It's his turn. All the men, young and old alike, are wrestling with the moving slime, and the women are invoking the heavens, and Catoune is exorcising the evil spirits, and P'tite Goule, alone out there with his captain and the cart, has encircled them both in his gigantic arms and is holding them up above water. Are his giant's feet touching rock bottom at last?

Old Bélonie has reached the little bridge, mounts it, stops halfway, stretching out his right arm before him. He is smiling, almost chuckling.

"Now it's between the two of us. None cross here."

There she is, sure enough, large as life, black, no doors, drawn by six black horses. Old Bélonie takes the squealing of the wheels and the whistling of the whip through the air like a slap in the face. Already she's begun to mount the bridge, you can hear the wooden trusses cracking; then she halts; he can hear the axles groan. She seems to hesitate, as if surprised.

. . . You, Bélonie? My faithful Bélonie?

"No, not him."

. . . Everyone is mortal, old man, even him.

"Not today."

. . . I don't make any difference between today and yesterday or tomorrow, I'm beyond time.

"Well, you'll have to make a small exception for a man with a mission."

. . . All men have a mission. And his is done.

"Not finished yet. He still has family to take back home."

. . . He should have hurried more before. One can't delay one's hour.

"Just one little hour, just a tiny sliver of life, for pity's sake."

. . . Pity? What's that?

"It's true, you don't know. My late father told me as much. You'll find neither heart nor reason, he said, beware."

. . . Your father was a wise man. Very few know me well.

"Admit it, you don't always play fair; it's not easy to get to know you without leaving one's skin behind."

. . . Heh, heh, heh!

"Do you really get any pleasure out of your wickedness? Have you ever tried, just for once, to be good?"

. . . Good? . . .

"It's no use, you don't know what that is either. I've just one card left to play."

. . . What's that?

"The joker. I'm going to catch you off guard."

. . . Just you try and see.

"It's already done."

. . . What . . . ?

"Hee!"

. . . ?

"Hee! Hee! You've wasted too much time jawing with me, old hussy. The time it took Beausoleil to slip between your wheels. Look over there in the swamp, your victim's got his head up out of the water. It's P'tite Goule who's holding him up. So I managed to distract even you for a second, one little second, all that's needed to slip through between time and eternity . . . Hee! Hee!"

The Death Cart, it seems, stood there blinking blankly.

Pélagie contemplates this scene from afar. She can clearly see Bélonie, his arms outstretched, his back arched, as if making a flying buttress to the horizon. She can guess the rest . . . Hold on, Bélonie, she calls to him with her whole soul. You can do it, and all alone too. Don't give in, Bélonie.

The chroniclers of the last century swear that Pélagie didn't move during the whole episode, that she stood there straight as a poplar, its head in the wind. She neither called out, nor prayed, nor raised her fist to heaven, as has been claimed. And no one saw her throw herself down on her knees and grieve, that's not true either. And no one heard her hurling insults at the saints or pleading with them for the love of God.

"Well, what about her cry, then?"

"She never uttered but one word, a single word. But such a one, it seems, as struck fear into someone standing not far from there."

Pélagie's single word, in fact, struck fear into the Wagon of Death trying with all its might to take revenge on Bélonie.

"My life!" was the cry that mounted from the Salem marshes and rolled over the reed beds to the wooden bridge.

And the wagon must have heard it, for it squealed in every joint and axle. Twice in one day someone had impudently come and barred the way! Who dared!

"Hee! . . ."

Bélonie kept on chivying her with his splendid grinch and the gleam in the corner of his eye. He had the old hag squirming, but he wouldn't let go.

"You missed your rendezvous for once. You'll never make it up again. Tough luck. You haven't time now to reach the mudhole before they've pulled Beausoleil out of the mire and got his head above water. Too late. You've lost."

. . . You weren't talking in that tone yesterday or the day before, old chin-wagger, when you needed my help to get your kin back home.

"Yesterday and the day before aren't today. Between the two, life turned up an heir, sprung from the depths of the sea. You cheated me, old harpy. You hadn't carried off my whole line in your wagon after all. So now be off, I don't need you any more."

. . . And if my wheels rolled over your body, by accident?

"My line is assured without me from now on, do what you like."

. . . You don't feel more concerned than that?

"Listen, you stale old jade, have you forgotten I'm going on a hundred?"

. . . You'll pay me for this one day, braggart, so be ready to cough up.

And Bélonie heard the four wheels roll down again, and the mares' shoes clattering against the shafts, and the wagon, the only one in the world that had never in its death gone backward, clumsily bumping against the guardrail of the little bridge, which rippled with laughter in surprise. The story even has it that Old Bélonie, hoisting a great kick at the muzzles of the mares, let fly a fart right in their faces. A corrida with Death like this was well worth a life. He would be ready.

At the same instant a new clamor arose from the carts:

"Beausoleil is safe!"

The giant, like an Easter Island colossus, was bringing back his captain and half the cart, holding them up at arm's length. For throughout the combat with Death, Beausoleil had never let go the box of the cart, had never renounced the trophy he had gone out to get for Pélagie at the risk of his life. It was when he realized this that P'tite Goule made the supreme effort to save the cart along with his master.

The giant's feet must have touched bedrock at last, for you could see him arching and pumping like a living jack. The mud had slurped, burped bubbles, sucked in all the air in the sky, and then let go. The giant's offspring had just robbed the swamp of its double prey. And now the men, a living chain, had brought back the captain and the cart in triumph to Pélagie's feet.

It was the grandest moment in the heroine of Acadie's life. For the first time her cart had vanquished the other. From now on she could lift her head and look the north in the face.

"The north is due north, Bélonie."

Heel . . . Eh? Oh yes. He wasn't, my God, sure of anything. And anyway, he was looking straight ahead of him from now on, never again would he turn his head to see . . . to be sure she was following along behind, the dirty slut.

Heel . . .

In the combat all they lost was the oxen, the Hussars, whom they finished off right there in their muddy grave, out of pity. The witches wailed all night long in the swamps of Salem. But when morning broke, the sun leaped up from the horizon and struck the sky like a gong.

PROPERTY OF THE
PUBLIC LIBRARY
ST. MARYS, ONT.

15

They took what was left of the spring to rebuild a cart on what was left of the first one and thus give Pélagie back her primitive home. Gave the Belliveaus back a home too by building them a brand-new cart. Land and sea united through the arms of carters and sailors in a building bee the like of which hadn't been seen since they left Acadie. *Et j'ai du grain de mil, et j'ai du grain de paille, et j'ai de l'oranger, et j'ai du tri, et j'ai du tricoli* . . .

By the end of June they were ready to turn their eyes northward again. They were at the door, on the very doorstep of home, hang on there, Bélonie. Now there was only the state of Maine to cross, just one small state. And hiding just on the other side of it was Acadie, just on the other side. Hang on, Bélonie.

Bélonie was hanging on all right, hanging on very nicely, so what's worrying you? Never had he been so talkative, so chin-wagging, as if determined to pass down all his knowledge to his descendance in one breath. For hours at a time you could see him taking his grandson, second-of-the-name, to one side and instilling a memory in him, drop by drop. And the second-of-the-name, opening wide his eyes, eager disciple that he was, swallowed down everything: the raw and the cooked, the old and the new, the true and . . . the rest. The forefather kneaded the boy's memory and imagination the way a baker works up bread dough. And every day the offspring came out of those sessions his mouth and eyes wider open than ever.

"He's going to drive the lad crazy," complained one of the Jeannes one morning.

But not Célina. Célina had no time to waste on this kind of observation. Ever since that spring's accident she'd been busy replenishing her stock of herbs on the one hand, and refurbishing the battered skin and bones of her menfolk on the other. For everyone, not just Captain Broussard, had come through the Salem swamp in terrible shape. They had all floundered around in the moving mire and had all lent their backs to those giant feet.

"Everyone took a giant beating," the old chin-wagger chirped with a brand new grinch, as though he knew precisely what he was talking about.

"Except for old centenarians," Célina chipped in, taking time from her flasks not to miss such a fine occasion to add her pinch of salt.

A pinch too much, Pélagie thought, raising an eyebrow, which told Célina they were hiding something from her. And the Clubfoot fretted in a fit of pet all the rest of the day.

"If things have gone so far you have to go whispering them to yourselves, might as well open up another chest to keep them secret."

"Might just as well . . . Heel!"

Now they could move northward again, draw a deep breath, and tackle the last leg of their journey. This time, no more rendezvous between land and sea before they reached Grand-Pré. The carts were striking off through field and forest.

On the last day Beausoleil-Broussard tried, without much conviction, to change Pélagie's mind. He was sure she wouldn't leave with him. He knew it by her looks, by her silences, by a new feeling that seemed to emanate from her, a sort of tranquility of soul. Every morning she would caress her cart and the only oxen left her, the team of solid, stubborn Corporals. And she wore the triumphant smile of a king's messenger bringing home news of a victory. In Charleston and Philadelphia, Beausoleil's rival had been Acadie; in Salem, as he grew to understand, it was the cart.

. . . But your sons have grown up, Pélagie, and you've married off your daughter.

. . . !

. . . And all the men have picked up the knack now after such a long trek.

. . . ?

. . . Even the women, Pélagie, the Jeannes, Célina, Agnès-Dugas-the-Magpie, the Marguerites, the Maries . . . isn't that enough to lead your oxen?

Pélagie laid a hand on Beausoleil's forearm and with the other caressed the rough wood of her cart. Eight years already? It was a custom in Acadie to bring your man a cart as dowry. The cart as sign of constancy. And if you needed proof, just look at the damn good show the little devil had made in the mud; she hadn't lost more planks in the fray than the men tail feathers. She'd turned in a damn good fight.

"It's maybe time to pass her on to your daughter Madeleine who'll know how to take good care of her."

. . . such a good fight that even when she was mired to the hubs she kept on sparkling in the sun and singing in the wind.

"Others, too, put up a good fight," said Beausoleil-Broussard almost between his teeth.

Pélagie came to.

There he was beside her, her captain, her chevalier, her hero, the man who had thrice risked his life for her, who had gone down in the moving slime for the third time—always the last time—for her, for hers, and yes, in the end for her cart. It was he who had finally saved her cart, who had hung on to the chassis come life or death.

She pressed close to him, cradling her head in the crook of his

shoulder, murmuring tender sounds and words he didn't hear
. . . He had risked his life for her and in exchange she had
offered her own. Their double life offered as hostage, one for the
other. Nothing would ever erase that from the record. The cart
would always be the pledge of that.

Next stop, Grand-Pré. So the schooner disappeared over the horizon, without farewells, without anxiety, but replying on her sea
trumpet to the refrains sung by the carts:

> *Je lui plumerai la queue*
> *. . . Et la queue!*
> *Et le dos*
> *. . . Et le dos!*
> *Et la tête*
> *. . . Et la tête!*
> *Et le cul*
> *. . . Et le cul!*
> *Et le bec*
> *. . . Alouette!*

> And shit to His British Majesty
> Who declared his war on you and me!

"Hue-Ho!"
"Let's go!"

"Every cloud has a silver lining," exclaimed Jeanne Aucoin,
pinching her man's fat thigh.

A summer of fine weather such as one rarely sees had put the
Corporals and the rest of the caravan in high spirits. A caravan
that continued to accumulate deportees clinging to the Massachusetts hills: Breaus, Comeaus, Héberts, LeBlancs—even more
of them, Pellerins, Melansons, d'Entremonts . . . the Mius
d'Entremonts? We're not choosy, climb aboard, any branch will
do, straggling, broken off at the trunk, strewn by the four winds
to the four corners of the continent . . .

Maine! Maine at last, the last lap. A state with ill-defined and disputed boundaries. Where did Maine end and Acadie begin?

"Acadie? Never heard of it."

And Pélagie realized that their homeland would have to be rebuilt.

"Repossessed, acre by acre."

But the others weren't in the least upset at the somber thought of having to reconquer their own front yards. The autumn was too beautiful and the yellows and reds of the Maine woods melted without boundaries into the ochers of the Acadian forest. How did you go about dividing that up? Where was the median tree between red ocher and flame red? None of these homebound exiles could have told you by what channel they were entering the country or when, precisely, they had crossed the border. Between the stormy autumn sea, the brilliant forests with their complete palette from yellows to flaming reds, between the warm, singing inland winds and the smell and rustle of dead leaves beneath their feet, somewhere in the midst of all that, Acadie lay concealed, every son of a son of this land could recognize that.

"Man changes, but nature never. The Rivière-aux-Canards will be there still."

"But what's to say King George isn't watering his mare there now?"

"As long as he don't just take it there to shit."

"François-à-Philippe, mind your tongue."

"Ha-ha!"

. . . The rivers will still be there, and the valleys, and the French Bay, which even now they're beginning to call the Bay of Fundy. But go on changing the names of our lands and waterways and you risk changing the color of the times . . .

"Come on, these are good times. Quit complaining. Just a huff and a puff more and we'll be there."

About All Saints' Day the sky clouded over, oh ever so little, just long enough to make them think of offering flowers to their dead and collecting pumpkins and acorns to store in the back of the carts. Then the warm weather returned and they plunged headfirst into Indian summer. Eight days' reprieve. Eight days of thumbing your nose at winter . . . Nya, nya, you can't catch me, just try to get me! . . . Watch out, children, don't be cocksure, winter will soon be here with its long drifts and numb fingers.

But in the meantime, the warm wind of Indian summer made fun of the frost.

. . . And shit to His British Majesty!

One morning the carts woke to the cries of migrating birds flying south in formation.

"Fall is done," declared Célina, weather prophet as well as ancestor-delver. "Get your woollies and furs out. Saint-Martin's day is past."

So they rummaged around in the old clothes trying to dig out something warm.

"The further north we climb, the harder the winters are going to be," warned Pélagie. "This year I really think we should make camp for a few months."

The head of the Bastarache clan came over worried and fretful:

"You don't mean to stagnate here?"

"No, not stagnate, but catch our breath while the bad weather passes. We haven't enough snowshoes to go round. And none at all for the oxen, it's mainly that. Where would you get snowshoes shaped for a two-wedged ox hoof? Acadie's not Carolina, you know, François-à-Philippe Basque.

Not Carolina, no sir, nor Virginia nor Boston neither. You can always keep your chin up out of floods, torrential rains, tornadoes, and hurricanes, but just go trying to drive your way through a snowstorm in an oxcart.

"Mustn't imperil our little ones or make our old folk suffer. Can't do that."

Bélonie raised his head.

For the months he had been initiating his grandson into the storytelling trade, he'd neglected the carts and had forgotten to tell them tales. This autumn they had had to fall back on Pierre-à-Pitre who spun yarns just for the fun of it and talked just to

hear himself babble. Pierre-à-Pitre's stories were pure invention, everyone knew that and only listened for entertainment.
But Bélonie's tales were something else.

So as the last day of autumn sidled over into winter, Old
Bélonie, sitting in Pélagie's patched-up cart, cleared the rust
from his throat and so doing drew around him just about everyone in the caravan.

"Gather round everybody. The old chin-wagger's going to give
us a tale."

And round they came from the Cormiers, Landrys, and Belliveaus, from the Babineaus and Bourgeois and all the northbound
clans. Old Bélonie was storytelling. Already he'd entered into his
trance and was staring out fixedly over the heads of his audience
and now was asking permission to begin.

At first they thought he was going to pick up the story of the
White Whale where he'd left off after their escape from the
Charleston prison, for it was a story with countless variations
and infinite ramifications. Yes, there he went, mumbling the pet
names of the White Whale and other denizens of the deep. In
fact, however, he was feeling his way and was quietly priming
his pump. And sure enough, they soon saw the Whale turn into
the Ogre, and the Ogre into the Giant Lady of the Night. Now
where had he gone and dug her up? But Bélonie's repertoire was
inexhaustible, you should know that by now. And if he hadn't
fished this Giantess out of his bundle till then, it was simply because he'd been saving her up for a special occasion. For it was a
story like none other.

Listen and shut up.

. . . It's the true story of one of our ancestors, one of the first
of the race, who lived before the Tower of Babel when all men
spoke the same tongue. The hero wasn't a wicked man but bore
the name Ti-Jean Fourteen because of the fourteen tricks he'd
played on his father. One day he decided to take a wife.

"At long last," everyone sighed. "That'll sober him up and
give the rest of us a little peace."

"Go ahead, marry," said his father, "and the sooner the better."

So our young man went off to ask for the hand of the girl of his choice.

"And what would you like for a wedding present?" he asked.

"A ship," she replied.

"A ship?" said he. "Is that all?"

If his fiancée wanted to sail into marriage that was her business. So away went our hero to find her a ship.

He went straight to the carpenter's to order her a fine vessel made of wildcherry planks, caulked with pine resin, clear-decked, well provisioned, and rigged out for a honeymoon, all ready to set out to sea and sail to the very ends of the earth. The carpenter replied that to complete such an embarkation he would need three magic words.

"Three magic words?" said the young man in surprise.

"To finish your ship I need three words that only a sorcerer can help you find."

So Ti-Jean Fourteen, fearless and blithe, went off to see a sorcerer.

He was a solitary old sorcerer who lived in a deep cave and rarely came out in the sun. He was so large and so still that a tree had grown on his shoulder and birds were nesting in it. That tickled Fourteen—who hadn't sobered up that much yet—and he started throwing stones to knock down the nests to get the eggs, as he had when a boy.

The sorcerer scowled but said nothing and waited for our friend Ti-Jean to ask his question.

"I'm looking for three magic words," he said, "to finish a ship to get me married to start me out in life."

The sorcerer glared at him and said in a voice that seemed to come straight from the tomb:

"And where do you wish your ship to take you?"

"To the end of time," said Fourteen, laughing and twirling around on his toes.

"Very well," said the giant sorcerer, "I'll show you the way to go to get the magic words, but as for the way back, you'll have to fend for yourself."

"I'll fend," said the beamish young man, "I'll fend."

So the sorcerer showed him the road to take to get to his distant forbear called the Giant Lady of the Night.

The giantess was sleeping, stretched out in an enormous field. She was so big Ti-Jean had to walk three days and three nights to measure her.

At the end of the third day he hailed her.

"Great Lady of the Night," he yelled, "it's me, Ti-Jean, your great-great-great-grandson. I've come in search of the three magic words I need for my ship to set me on the road to my new life. Help me find them, Giantess of the Night."

The giantess slept on and didn't stir. Fourteen then noticed at the level of her head what appeared to be two mountains moving up and down. He approached and discovered that the mountains were the jaws of the giantess who lay there snoring with her mouth open.

"Well," he thought, "here's my chance. The three words are certainly hidden in there somewhere."

So he climbed up her chin to peek inside at her boulder-sized teeth.

Suddenly he heard singing overhead. It was some birds watching him and seeming to say "Go ahead, Ti-Jean! Go ahead!"

"Why not," said he to himself.

So in he went, with never a backward look, straight through the jaws of the Giant Lady of the Night.

He searched the whole mouth: between the teeth, under the tongue, at the back of the gullet. The three words weren't there.

"They must be further down," he said to himself, becoming soberer and soberer and bolder and bolder. "I'll continue my journey."

So cautiously placing one foot ahead of the other he stepped forward on the wall of the throat and then slid down the length of the esophagus.

And there he stood dumbfounded. The insides of the giantess were so large and so broad you could have tilled fields and planted cabbages there. Fourteen rubbed his eyes. He could see lungs as big as chimneys and a stomach as deep as a well and intestines as long as underground tunnels. He guessed he must be standing at the opening to the bowels of the earth and decided to explore further. So he made himself a raft out of bits and pieces of tree root rotting in the giant stomach and sailed from one end of the gut to the other, holding his nose and retching at every bend in that stagnant, stinking stream. Yuk!

At last he arrived at the end. But just as he was about to step ashore, he perceived in his path the open fiery jaws of a dragon, one of those monsters the world produced in the days before men learned to till the soil and plant the earth with seeds. Ti-Jean trembled but didn't draw back. And just then he remembered the jackknife his father had given him for his twelfth birthday.

"What's to lose?" he thought to himself.

And he pulled out his knife.

The dragon gnashed its teeth and spewed out bright red flames. Fourteen clutched his knife in his fist. And at the very moment that the monster reared up to attack him, our young hero saw a white spot under the dragon's throat, a little patch no bigger than a basswood leaf, where the skin lay bare of scales. Ti-Jean drew in his breath and gave a mighty blow with his knife right in the dragon's heart.

Phew! . . . Not a moment too soon.

Blood spurted forth. And to his amazement Fourteen saw a stream of pearls and diamonds spilling out at his feet. The dragon was none other than the very one who, since the beginning of the world, had kept in his belly—which lay at the bottom of the belly of the Giant Lady of the Night—the famous treasure that all mankind had been seeking since the beginning of time.

But Ti-Jean had thoughts for nothing but his three magic words, which he suddenly saw dancing in the midst of all those precious stones. Spurning the riches, without a moment's hesitation he seized the three words and stuffed them into his pocket.

Then he started out on the road back: the big intestine, the small intestine, the liver, the stomach, the esophagus, which he

climbed hauling himself along its humid walls, through the arch
of the uvula and under the palate lined with a double colonnade,
two enormous rows of teeth planted there like colossi in white
limestone . . . And at this point he remembered the sorcerer's
words: "I'll show you the way to go, but as for the way back,
you'll have to fend for yourself."

He clutched his three words in his pocket, those three words
that would let him finish the ship that would take him to his own
true love who would stay with him to the end of life, a never
ending life . . .

Alas! Life always ends and no one has yet returned from the
longest journey of all. No more Ti-Jean Fourteen who thought
himself immortal but who didn't know he'd been vulnerable
since baptism on account of the fact that by mistake they'd put
three grains of pepper on his tongue instead of salt.

So as a result, when he was trying to get past the teeth of the
Giant Lady of the Night, Fourteen slid through feet first, which
made the birds laugh, for they'd been waiting to see him come
out, but not ass backwards, and the birds' laughter woke the
giantess, who clamped her mouth shut in surprise and bit our
hero in two.

"Aaaaw!" went all the carts who'd begun to take an affectionate
interest in good old Ti-Jean.

"Did he really have to finish up that way?"

Heel . . . Then Bélonie concentrated as though he were going
to go into one of his trances again and, without looking at anyone in particular, cast out:

"Never you mind. Even with only half a body, and the best
half at that, Fourteen was still plenty alive enough to give his
ancestor the Giantess of the Night a good run for her money . . .
a run for the rest of eternity. You can take my word for it."

And everyone swore afterward that they had with their own
eyes seen Bélonie turn around as though looking for his Wagon
and shake his fist at it, as if the bitch were drawing too close.
And it seems that the very birds of the air must have sensed
something, for they all flew up in a bunch, making a devil of a
racket. Célina was ready to take her oath on it.

"The wind's come up mighty fresh," Pélagie noted suddenly. "Better take shelter before the night dew falls."

Pélagie prowled back and forth like a cat looking for a place to drop its litter. It was getting very late and the old man hadn't returned to the circle of carts yet. It had become a habit of his to take a little walk in the woods before turning in, to talk to the animals, to feed the birds, or consult the state of the moss or the bark of the white birch as to what the weather would be tomorrow. But on this first night of winter all the carts were so preoccupied with the change in climate they forgot old chin-wagger Bélonie.

All except Pélagie.

Finally she went and roused Alban-à-Charles-à-Charles, then François-à-Philippe Basque, then the Cormiers, the Landrys, and her sons. Célina turned up of her own accord, grumbling that she had a weight on her stomach that was giving her bad dreams. In the end everyone got up, right down to little Virginie, and they all began to beat the bushes and search between the rocks and in the underbrush.

"Was that a wolf?"

"No, no."

"Then what's that I hear?"

". . ."

"What do they call the north winds around here?"

"Maybe it's dogs baying at the moon?"

"Maybe it is."

But it was neither wolf, nor dogs, nor the wind. A strange, distant sound it was, coming from the depths of the forest.

Célina, wishing to distract everyone, was saying whatever came into her head.

"If Bélonie was here, I'd say it was him still talking to that cart of his."

Pélagie gave Célina a strange look, then sunk her chin on her chest.

They searched the rest of the night and the three next days. Then Pélagie began to reason thus:

"He's told us many a time before not to worry about him, saying he'd lots of family and relations hidden everywhere."

No sense being obstinate, Old Bélonie always had the last word. Best way to get the upper hand this time was to leave. You could be sure he'd follow.

Every chronicler since has had his own version of the end of Bélonie the storyteller. Some speak of wild animals, others of deep creeks in the valleys. But the Bélonie line has always stuck doggedly to their own fixed idea. On that November night in 1778 what they heard was neither wolves nor dogs but the distant creaking of the wheels of the Wagon of Death. Like the well-bred, courteous man he was, Bélonie had gone out to meet it, like the proud man he was above all, like a man going to have the last word. He wasn't one to wait around to be picked up with the rest of the batch, not him; he would climb aboard while he was still with the living, he would, and he hailed the six horses himself.

"It's his 'Hue-Ho!' rang out in the night, not the wolves."

And the proof of that is that never in two centuries since has anyone in the whole of the American line of Acadians that stretches from Louisiana to Gaspé ever found the least little wooden cross on which you might read:

Here lies Bélonie, son of Jacques,
son of Antoine Maillet: 1680–1778.

But the best proof of all was furnished by the carts camping that first winter in the woods. Bélonie was everywhere, with everyone: With the Arseneaults, the great bear and moose hunters, who provided the skin tilts to cover the carts and make tents. Hee! . . . with the Cormiers, setting snares for jackrabbits to fill the famished travelers' bowls up over the brims. Hee! . . . with the Girouards, fishing through the ice for smelt and tommy cod. Hee! . . . with the Belliveaus and Babineaus, the lumberjacks, hauling logs for firewood over the snow. Hee! . . . with the Landrys, those skilled craftsmen, making snowshoes with deerskin thongs. Hee! . . . with the creaking of the hinges of the Bourgeois's chest, with the prayers and litanies and lamentations of the Allains, with the merry twang of the Jew's harp and tapping of the spoons of the jigging Basques . . . Hee! Hee! Hee! Everywhere! All nature was invaded by Bélonie. His wink, his grinch, his mouse-trot walk, his mocking little smile aimed at men and gods alike, his complicity with the cart that obstinately trundled along behind in the ruts of the other . . . Bélonie's century left its mark everywhere.

And it was a winter, despite the snow, the cold, and the sudden breaking up of the ice in the middle of February, when the Acadians camping at the very door of their homeland didn't bury a single child.

Thanks, Bélonie.

Hee! . . .

PROPERTY OF THE
PUBLIC LIBRARY
ST. MARYS, ONT.

16

For all one winter and all one summer Bélonie's shadow hovered over the carts. To the point where the Allains practically forgot their *ora pro nobis*'s and directed their litanies straight to the deceased . . . deliver us from evil, Bélonie; to the point where Célina neglected to consult the thickness of squirrels' fur and the height of hornets' nests to predict the weather but asked the old chin-wagger directly, without beating about the bush; to the point where the Bourgeois, let me tell you, did unheard-of things, and the Basques, ah! the Basques spent the year making musical instruments out of branches and reeds and composing a thousand dirges to the memory of the centenarian bard:

> Now listen here, both large and small
> To a story as true as it's ancestral
> Of a man of a hundred who'd no heirs at all.
> For all his kin went down one day
> To a watery grave, it's sad to say,

Yes, storm and shipwreck had their way
And schooner and crew, they perished all,
So weep for them now, both large and small.

But springtime came and a brand-new day
And on the horizon a sail, hooray!
It's the *Grand'Goule* entering the bay
With a young man aboard not very tall,
Just a cabin boy to tell you all
But bold he is and brave withal
And Bélonie is what he's called
So give a cheer, both large and small.

The summer passed, then came the fall
And at last the ancestor of them all
After years of exile heard the call
And without a word simply slipped away.
But ever since that fateful day
You can hear his "Hee!" in the clouds and the way
The seagulls utter their grinching call,
So sing his praises, large and small.

They were at the gates of their country. They'd be in Grand-Pré before winter. Tum-ti-dee, tum-ti-dee went Célina's clubfoot.

Pélagie hadn't made many mistakes in calculation in ten years of returning, so we must forgive her this one. The rigors of Acadian winters had faded from her memory during the fifteen years in Georgia. And to make matters worse, the previous winter had been so mild they had imprudently taken it for granted. So you must make an effort to understand and excuse the carts. The winter of 1780 fell on them at the beginning of November, premature by forty days, jumping in ahead of Indian summer and Saint Martin's Day, opening before them without warning and without mercy like the jaws of the Trojan horse.

The storm fell on marching Acadie like a monster the day after All Saints' Day. What a trick to play, Bélonie! On the Day of the Dead, no less! No time to finish collecting the winter's store of hazelnuts and acorns, or to salt down game and herbs, or to dry herring, or to wrap apples, or bury spuds in root cellars hacked out of the soil. No time to bundle the children of Acadie into their woolens and animal skins, Bélonie. And the children of Acadie took a beating.

You could see them clinging to their ragged mothers; bowing their heads under the lash of the wind whipping their faces; opening their mouths wide to gasp the air that barely filtered through the snow. You could see them at once amazed and dismayed at this stranger: a northern winter.

They barely had time to take shelter under the carts, tying tilts to the sideboards and wheels and digging holes into the earth, which, in mid-November, hadn't had time to freeze yet. Pélagie could hardly believe her eyes. She had thought that after the first snow the mild weather would return at least long enough to let them set up a winter camp. But this season didn't follow the normal course and baffled her predictions. Especially the grandest one of all: that they'd reach Grand-Pré before the cold set in.

"Yet I'm sure we're just about there."

Just about or almost just about. But a just about makes all the difference when it comes in wintertime.

The snow flew so hard and heavy they could dig tunnels through the drifts without ever touching the ground. Then they forced the animals into them so they could warm themselves on the beasts' breath and sweat. The oxen's, that is, for neither the Allain's mule nor the Belliveau's donkey had northern winter in their blood, and the poor beasts perished, frozen stiff.

Every day the men sallied forth from their igloos to hunt what little game there is that doesn't hibernate between the feast of Saint-Nicholas and mid-Lent, to wit: the hare, the prickly pig or porcupine, the beaver, with a lot of luck a deer, and with a lot of risk a bear sleeping in a hollow tree. To awaken a bear in January is like challenging a cannon with a slingshot, like setting out to sea in a birchbark canoe, like refusing to take the oath of allegiance to the King of England. But the Acadians were used to all that, to England, to the sea, to cannon; so they turned the bears out of their holes.

"It's your skin or mine," they laughed, just to keep their jaws from trembling.

When The Grouch tried to find out how many of her ancestors lost their skins that winter, Bélonie would change the subject and begin to carry on about the cold and snow. Storms were Bélonie-third-of-the-name's weak point. They were a weakness with Acadian chroniclers in general, for they could go on end-lessly about winds whistling, blizzards blustering, snow swallow-ing up trees, and frost freezing one's saliva before it hit the ground.

"Is it, Dear God, possible!"

"Sure as I'm standing here."

"Their spit froze in their throats?"

"At fifty below the spit you spit rings like a marble on the crust of the snow."

There's worse still.

"What now?"

"Maxime-à-Maxime's Jean, true descendant of François-à-Philippe, swears that last year in February he saw with his very own eyes an icicle standing straight out in front of him.

". . . ?"

"He was taking a pee at fifty-five below."

"Don't tell me!"

That and plenty more. Their fathers had all seen such things the year they lived buried in the woods slinking around like mar-tens between the trees, covered in skins and wearing boots cut right out of moose shanks, wild boots as they're called in Acadie.

"Winter has claws and teeth the same as animals," says my cousin Louis.

Which still doesn't stop him from clamming up when it comes to talking about wild beasts, just like his forbears Louis-the-Droll and Bélonie-the-Younger. Those tenderhearted chroniclers were all mum when it came to talking about the cruelty of animals, despite the brave airs they put on. So in the long run neither I nor Pélagie-the-Grouch, nor even Pélagie-the-Cart, first-of-the-name, ever knew the number of victims that fell prey to bears or lynx in the forest. When a trapper or woodcutter failed to return, his companions would talk of the sudden thaw or wheeling snowstorms.

But the animals paid dearly, the widows could take some consolation in that. For every woodsman who didn't come back, what a lot of skins came in, bearskins two yards long and more, and only marked by a single shot. Yes indeed, a single shot! The Acadians' new masters had forbidden them the use of firearms ever since the Deportation, so they didn't go around taking pot shots.

. . . Let sleeping bears lie.

"So that's why they hid their rifles and made up stories instead."

And that's what lies behind the vast repertory of bear stories, drawn from the common stock of animal tales but converted and adapted. For it was safer in those somber days for an Acadian to stick his tongue in his cheek and tell the English governor that he'd slaughtered his bear with a table fork than admit he owned a gun.

. . . And as a result, the English governors believed Acadians capable of anything, and locked up their wives and children.

"Your skin or mine!"

So the Acadian hunters and trappers managed to bring just about everyone through this hardest winter in their history . . . Just about, but not all. Some infants were lost and some old folks, among them Anne-Marie-Françoise, the survivor of the Salem mudhole. But, as Célina said, she'd left a good bit of her wits in the swamp anyway and had spent her last days asking Beausoleil to bring her back Marguerite and Mathurin, disappeared in the Great Disruption.

"So it was good of the Good Lord to come and fetch her."

But one morning the Good Lord . . . be quiet, Célina . . . One morning it was little Virginie's turn. She had really been great, the cart's mascot, ever since leaving her native Virginia. Walking at ten months, talking her head off at two and getting washed all by herself in the running brooks, and by four able to tell good mushrooms from bad. By the age of reason she already knew how to do everything for herself, and her mother could confidently think of bringing more children into the world.

But that morning Virginie ran up a sudden, fierce fever. Was it the lungs, the throat, or the bowels like little Frédéric? Catoune, Célina, and Marie Cormier all rushed over to Pélagie together. They weren't going to let that happen, no, not that, the Cormiers had taken more than their share of miseries, they didn't deserve that, no, Pélagie.

Pélagie shook her head and tried to rise to the surface. Wasn't it enough that she'd rescued them all from the clutches of the enemy? Was she supposed to save them from death now? What wouldn't they be asking her next?

. . . Just who do you take me for? she asked them.

But neither Célina or the Cormiers would listen to reason. And Catoune, her eyes starting out of her head, clung to Pélagie's skirts so tight you'd have thought the nails would split. At the end of her tether, Mother Pélagie took a deep breath:

"Go get me Jean-Baptiste," she said.

So they brought round Jean-Baptiste, stumbling between ostentation and consternation at suddenly finding himself so important. But when he realized what Pélagie required of him, he abruptly stopped pluming himself and put on a miserable air. He was devout, true, no one would contest his piety . . . but a miracle, Pélagie . . . it was nothing short of a miracle she was asking . . . to obtain the cure of a child by the laying on of hands and the touch of a crucifix . . . At that moment he must have regretted snatching it from the flames at the peril of his life in the Church of Saint-Charles of Grand-Pré.

Pélagie insisted:

"All we want, Jean-Baptiste, is for you to replace the priest, who in a case like this would have implored God and God would have answered his prayer."

But Jean-Baptiste stuttered:

"I'm not a priest . . . he-heaven didn't want it s-so . . . I'm afafraid that . . ."

"We'd have asked Bélonie if he'd been around. From this out, you're the eldest."

Poor Jean-Baptiste Allain choked on his own saliva at that. They were asking him as the eldest and not as the most devout. His Adam's apple slipped halfway down his gullet. The saintly man had to swill deep from the cup of humility that day. And some hold it's because of this that heaven took pity on them. All the story does say is that under a flood of tears and *libera nos Domine*'s, little by little, Virginie began to move her eyes, her head, her legs, then to call for her mother. The fever died down of its own accord and, like a mushroom growing out of the night, the child came out of the shadow and lifted her head to the sun.

They threw themselves on Jean-Baptiste the healer's neck, they kissed his hands and asperged him with gratitude. Seems as how he stood there all confused and benumbed, quite dumbfounded by such a happening, not knowing how or where grace had come out of him. It even seems he remained humble and generous for the rest of his days, Jean-Baptiste Allain did, never showing off his stigmata, nor pulling out his crucifix, nor grabbing the whole of heaven and shoving it down into his heart for himself alone . . . so it seems.

But as far as the line of storytellers is concerned, it was all Old Bélonie's doing. They claim that at the very instant the child favored by the miracle opened her eyes, a little "Hee!" came out of her mouth. The Bourgeois and the Belliveaus swore to it.

Whatever the case, Virginie was saved, and they offered up thanks to God. But it's not God's way to go around repeating himself every other day, and the healer had used up all his charisma in one go. Other children afflicted in the lungs or throat never did pull through.

It was a hard winter.

When at the end of February they were finally turfed out of their hibernation, crouched at the end of their ice tunnels, frozen stiff under the floorboards of the carts buried under the snow, or huddled down in the crotches of tree roots, you could count every knob on their backbones, on all of them.

It was a Godin who unburied them, a Godin of the Beauséjour

branch, a hunter, trapper and *coureur des bois* Acadian-style,
that is, chiefly a guide. He was Acadian like them but one who
had stayed behind in Acadie, hunted into hiding for all the years
of the Great Disruption.

So at the beginning of 1780, Pélagie realized that she had
finally come back home.

The eyes of the deportees grew wide with the effort of understanding, and their stiff, chapped fingers reached up to touch the
face of the huge man standing there under the branching pines.
He spoke their tongue, he was alive, they were all alive. The
longest winter in their lives had just come to an end, a winter a
quarter-century long.

And Pélagie LeBlanc-called-the-Cart, bowed low at the feet
of Pierre Godin-called-Beauséjour, wept one-hundred-year-old
tears.

It had been a long journey to the south, yes, but the circle was
closing again. The deportees and refugees of the woods were
reunited after a generation, almost at their point of departure. A
generation of survivors. They were survivors from life in the wilderness, survivors from exile, survivors from History.

"It's handsome Lawrence who'll have a cat fit when he finds
out!"

"He's had it already, and for the last time, don't go troubling
yourself over the likes of him. Seems he even had it at table, the
glutton, trying to stuff down a goose before they'd plucked it.
Life's a mortal affair for everyone."

"Except for them as they've tried to kill over and over and
their heads always keep bobbing back up again."

One after another heads bobbed up seeking the light, like
sunflowers. Just a little gulp of air, just a little glass of light to
cheer our bones. Just give us time to get our memories back, to
limber up our eyelids and grease up our wits. You'll see we'll
have heart and stomach for anything, yes, gumption and ginger
galore, just give us time.

. . . So the Landrys and the Cormiers and the LeBlancs
rubbed elbows with their cousins the Godins, Godins called

Beauséjour, Godins called Bellefontaine, and Godins called
Godin. All descended from an ancient family from France who
claimed to trace back to Godfrey de Bouillon. Godins who might
have been called Godfri, Godfrei, Godfrain, Godfrin, or Godain
before settling down into the Godins of Acadie, the very ones
who had fled to the woods at the time of the Great Disruption,
had hidden there during the torment, and had saved the carts
when they were ready to yield up the last breath, buried under
the snow of that terrible winter of 1780.

So the two branches of Acadie recounted their double odyssey.
They even claim that it was there in the Godin's square-timbered
cabin that young Bélonie, second-of-the-name, made his first
pass at arms and astonished everyone. This novice already knew,
hold tight now, how to spin a tale just like the old chin-wagger,
without skipping a line and in the very same accent and style. He
could even reel off the history of the carts better than the carts
themselves, it's Célina who'll vouch for that, though she can
scarcely believe her ears. It just doesn't make sense anymore!
Where'd he go and pick all that up?

Heel . . .

Ah no! I must be hearing things! He's the spitting image of his
ancestor, not a wrinkle or tic out of place. And to think he barely
knew the old boy, would you believe it!

"It's in the blood," said Alban-à-Charles-à-Charles who was an
authority in such matters. "And maybe he picked up some scraps
of the past floating around in his mother's belly."

To match storyteller Bélonie, the three branches of Godins
offered Bonaventure-called-Bellefontaine, son of Gabriel, son of
Pierre Godin-called-Chatillon. And the old man told them stories
even gloomier than Bélonie's. How, just for fun, the English soldiers had left open the cellars of families in flight to let their
stores freeze or rot; how furniture, tools, even family books had
been confiscated to prevent the Acadians' descendants from trac-
ing and recognizing each other; how Acadians had been used for
target practice during military exercises by new recruits from the
American Loyalists.

"What's that?"

"Bostonians newly arrived in the country who'd taken refuge along the Saint John River around Sainte-Anne. And to give his soldiers rifle practice, the colonel . . ."

Pélagie was taken with stomach cramp.

"Quiet now, Bonaventure-Bellefontaine, that page is turned. If we've breath left, let's use it to sort out our families, since they've burned our books, and build them up again."

Then she remembered her first encounter with the Loyalists in Boston. Were they going to follow her all the way home?

"How many days are we from Grand-Pré?"

Bonaventure stared at Pélagie.

"Grand-Pré?"

"Yes, we're going back there."

". . . ?"

"How many days?"

"A month or two by foot. But . . . The English are everywhere and it seems they haven't pardoned yet."

The word hit hard, and Pélagie struck back:

"Pardoned?" she said. "Is it up to them to pardon now?"

The Godins lowered their eyes and spoke no more. And Pélagie realized that the fugitives from the woods probably knew more than the exiles about the mentality of the new masters of the place.

"It's high time to take off again," she said. "Let it never be said of me that I failed to get my head up out of the water one last time. They'll never say that. Hue-Ho, the oxen!"

Alas, Pélagie had forgotten that they'd eaten the remaining oxen during the winter and sheltered under their hides. She'd forgotten that the carts had lost both racks and wheels, and that her tattered people were in shreds.

François-à-Philippe Basque and Alban-à-Charles-à-Charles looked at each other and together went over to Pélagie to propose that the families be split up again amongst the roadworthy carts. Pélagie consented to any arrangement except giving up her own. Alban went on arguing with her while the Basque tried to patch up her moribund cart . . . Square me up one of those branches there with the axe, and set that wheel back in place, and go find me some farm animal able to pull this contraption.

The Negro took the Basque at his word. He set out to find a beast of burden to replace the oxen.

"For the love of God! If he goes and brings us back the colonel's mare, we'll never get out of the woods."

"Or the lieutenant-governor's cow . . ."

"Who is it let him take off like that?"

"It's sure to bring us bad luck, all this."

The Negro returned with an Indian.

He never did manage to explain to the carts how he had made this Micmac understand. But he was thinking straight anyway. In the spring thaws and squalls they needed a guide to keep them out of the spongy marshes far more than some heavy animal stuck up to his flanks. Remember Salem. And the Negro harnessed P'tite Goule to Pélagie's cart.

So it was that they set out on the last lap, this time really the last. Less than a hundred leagues to the basin of Les Mines. All aboard everyone, and take a deep breath. You'll be eating your wild strawberries at Grand-Pré.

Wild strawberries, apple trees in blossom, fresh cod, and smoked herring . . . the springtime that had been stolen from Pélagie twenty-five years before was there waiting for her on the shores of the French Bay. Just a hundred leagues more and she'd forget, she'd pardon, she'd rebuild her vandalized home.

"Hue! Dia! *En route!* And don't let me catch a single one of you scrimshanking."

But at the very moment Pélagie herself stepped out into the cart tracks, she felt her back seize up and refuse to unlock.

"Hey!" she exclaimed. "It's no time to start playing the old woman, Pélagie. Your life's beginning."

And she made another effort to straighten up. Without success.

The men reached her up by force into the cart, ignoring her cries of: "I can walk! I can walk!"

Alban-à-Charles-à-Charles gave the sign to the giant who swung into motion.

Célina collected an armful of old-time plants that day, her dear herbs whose scent had stayed in her nostrils for a quarter of a century. Let them come now, mumps, toothache, inflammation of the lungs or bowels! Célina was in her own territory in the woods of Acadie.

But the next night she didn't sleep a wink, trying to read the cry of the wild geese passing over, a little late, on their way home.

PROPERTY OF THE PUBLIC LIBRARY ST. MARYS, ONT.

17

Pélagie had heard the cry of the wild geese coming back from the south; they could begin to turn the earth again and set their traps in the sea. They could already start to measure off the arable land, mark out the fields, and cut larch poles to build up the *aboiteaux*.

"Bestir yourselves, you bunch of loafers, don't you hear the call of the wild geese? Can't you hear the crickets and the weet-weet of the tadpoles in the cattails?"

There's plenty of lost time to make up, and a long exile to end, so hurry up. Can't you see Grand-Pré burning yonder?

Jeanne Aucoin and Célina once more dove into the young ferns. How could they draw some new medicinal concoction from the spring woods? Mix fiddleheads and sarsaparilla? The juice of honeysuckle and quicklime? Raspberry root and ginger? Boil white birch bark stripped from top to bottom on the side of the rising sun?

But Pélagie was far beyond herbs and the medicines the

healers were concocting. Her malady had roots the roots of the raspberry couldn't reach. And again she whipped the men as in the old days she had whipped the oxen.

"Hue-Ho!" she called. "Open the gate there. We're at the back fence of home. We've a story to tell our descendants."

Alban-à-Charles-à-Charles, then François-à-Philippe, each in turn, came over to Pélagie to tell her to spare herself, to save her strength for the last lap, still a month to go, we're only in April yet, you'll still have to put your back into it . . .

. . . The back, that's where the seat of her pain was, as if she had dragged a cart across the continent all by herself. A back bent under its burden, bowed to its destiny, eaten away from within. Don't stop. Keep going. Home is that close.

But they had to stop, despite her will.

"If only we had some cherry stems!"

Cherry stems in April? What are you thinking of, Célina?

Well, no, she wasn't exactly thinking that, but she was saying it, just like that, like you might say: "If only I had Paris in a bottle . . ." Catoune heard and left the caravan before dawn, followed by her giant.

The couple marched all day through the woods and at evening reached a river that seemed familiar to P'tite Goule. A rusty river with glistening clay banks. But the sun had already set and he didn't recognize it. It was only the next day at dawn that opening his giant eyes he discovered the Petitcodiac, the chocolate river. And drawing himself up to his full height he began to laugh and to cry giant tears.

"It's her! It's her!"

And he sniffed her like a stallion a mare in heat. It was his own river, the river of his giant childhood, both rising somewhere in the past in the red clay lands of Petitcodiac.

So P'tite Goule carried Catoune on his shoulders to his secret hiding places, untouched since the Deportation. And there they found, intact as in an ancient tomb, his treasures of herbs and seeds of wild plants.

And so it was that two days after they had disappeared, Catoune and the giant brought Célina cherry stems that had been twenty-five years drying . . .

. . . So you could put Paris in a bottle after all!

After the cherry stems they tried compresses and plasters and frictions and urine baths and salt crystal necklaces and the cones of the female hop plant, and this time they peeled the bark of the white birch from bottom to top on the side of the setting sun, and they were just about to wash Pélagie in spring water collected before dawn on Easter morning, when the Indian came to warn the carts that he had spied a colony of Palefaces, newly installed on the land and English-speaking.

"Many hunting rifles," he said. "Vamoose."

Yes, go. That's also what Pélagie's Madeleine advised, for she had taken the reins from her mother and transmitted her will to the rest. Grand-Pré, head for Grand-Pré. And so Pélagie, lying in the bottom of her dislocated cart, once more moved on through the forest on the road back.

Then one day they broke into a clearing in the forest, a field flooded with morning dew quickly being drunk up by a bold, resplendent sun.

Spring! Almost summer well before its time. A month of May trying, all alone, to make up for winter. And about time, too. And Jeanne Aucoin lifted Pélagie's head to let her sniff the perfume of the tender leaves that had burst from the buds overnight.

"If I can trust my eyes, I think I see a clump of dandelions."

Just about, just about dandelions all right, new grass anyway, and pussy willows, and mayflowers. Yes, Pélagie, mayflowers! I swear it.

"Everything's rising up this morning, Pélagie. You'll see, there's nothing better for a bad back than the dews of May."

. . . You've got it mixed up, Jeanne Aucoin, it's not the dews but the miraculous snows of May that cure all ills.

What matter.

"Everything's springing up, Pélagie. You'll soon be up yourself."

Up, that's it, up. Pass me my sabots, Madeleine, and my shawl
. . . no, the cashmere, the one we lifted from the ladies of Boston . . . no, Baltimore . . . would he never come then? . . . pass
me my fine linen cap, Madeleine . . . have to arrive in Grand-
Pré in full pomp and finery.

"Hurry up there!"

Dust the kids off, straighten the cart coverings, get out the
laces and oriental silks, we're coming home like a bride to a wedding.

The caravan crossed the golden field singing almost, pulling
the carts by hand, rocking, limping, yawing like a schooner on
the open seas, eyes riveted on port.

> *Et j'ai du grain de mil,*
> *et j'ai du grain de paille,*
> *et j'ai de l'oranger,*
> *et j'ai du tri,*
> *et j'ai du tricoli,*
> *et j'ai des allumettes,*
> *et j'ai des ananas,*
> *j'ai de beaux . . . j'ai de beaux . . .*
> *j'ai de beaux oiseaux.*

Pélagie has hoisted herself up off her straw pallet and is walking,
yes, walking, her arm hooked through one of the stakes of the
rack as around a mast . . . Yonder on the high seas, he's coming,
her Beausoleil is, he's coming back to her, back to Grand-Pré.
His long voyage will finish there in his native land where he'll be
with her again, he promised so. She will wait for him under the
blossoming apple trees in this new springtime of their lives. And
this time nothing will tear him from her ever again, for she has
accomplished her task, she has answered her ancestors' will. Yes,
this time . . .

Her daughter Madeleine, Catoune, Célina, Jeanne Aucoin,
Agnès Dugas, all these Acadian women have eyes only for that
smile of well-being that triumphs on Pélagie's face, on the face
of Pélagie-the-Cart who with her whole strength is taking the

last few steps that separate her from the land of her birth. One more, just one more small breath and Grand-Pré will be there across the French Bay which they now call the Bay of Fundy.

A few days later Pierre-à-Pitre climbed into the top branches of a solitary oak and yelled down:

"The sea!"

At last! . . . There it was, the bay, the bay that mirrored Fort Beauséjour on one side and on the other all the basin of Les Mines. Pélagie pushed forward with a step that was almost firm, ahead of the others, panting deep breaths. Tomorrow, Beauséjour. The Cormiers and Girouards squirmed with excitement. Jeanne Aucoin gripped her stomach.

"First thing, we'll hold the ceremony for the burial of our dead," she said. "I'll never believe they won't give us back our dead after twenty-five years."

"And our cellar foundations to build back upon," added François-à-Pierre-à-Pierre-à-Pierrot.

And the fields and boats and *aboiteaux*. They'd start back over again from zero if need be, but they'd start again in their own land and tie the future to the past.

Already the Basques had their instruments out and all Acadie was coming home in song, when the Indian, who had been scouting on ahead, came back with this news: Beauséjour was occupied, permanently. Likewise the whole Chignecto Isthmus.

At that blow the carts stopped breathing. Pélagie was the first to catch her wind back to ask:

"And Grand-Pré?"

Grand-Pré was deserted. Burned and deserted since that fatal day in September 1755. Out of superstition or fear of God, they hadn't dared settle anyone there. They had left Grand-Pré abandoned to the gulls and the wild grass, this formerly flourishing, lively town on the French shore.

Like an ancient cemetery.

Like an abandoned cradle.

All eyes turned from the south-southwest and faced the north. Except for Pélagie.

She stayed there, like a sphinx of stone, murmuring to herself words that were inscribed in the heavens . . . This Grand-Pré that was not to be for her children would never be for the children of others either. No one would build a nest there, ever . . . ever.

Then, raising her head and a fist to heaven, she called out, for generations to come:

"You'll return there to flower the graves of your ancestors. So say I to all LeBlancs, Bourgs, Bourgeois, Landrys, Cormiers, Giroués, Belliveaus, Allains, Maillets, and all the sons of Acadie who have come out of exile in the oxcarts. And this I say to all the children of Acadie: Never touch Grand-Pré, but forever keep its memory green in your hearts and blood."

And to illustrate these words of hers to her people crouched at the foot of the carts, she tore off the kerchief she wore round her neck, opened it to the wind, then folded it by the four corners and stuck it back in her apron pocket.

"I'm carrying my Grand-Pré with me in my apron," she exclaimed. "No one is going to snatch it from me a third time."

And into her apron pocket she also stuffed a stock of words, ancient words sprung naked from her grandsires' gullets, words she wouldn't leave as a heritage for foreign throats; and in it she stuffed all those legends and tales, marvelous, terrifying or prankish, that her line had been passing on since the beginning of time; and in it she stuffed beliefs and customs hung round her neck like a family jewel, which she in turn would leave her heirs; and in it she put the history of her people, begun two centuries before, then whirled around by the four winds and left for dead in the gutter . . . till one day a passerby picks her up and brings her back to life and leads her, by force, back to her own country; and in it she stuffed her fathers and her sons swallowed up in the Disruption and her son Jean lost in the wilds of the Pennsylvania forests and who all alone might never discover the way home; in it she put the Captain of the *Grand'Goule*, her hero, her impossible dream who would never reach her now on the shores of Grand-Pré . . . for, you see, Beausoleil, they've taken our Grand-Pré from us, with its apple trees in flower and its fresh cod and its wild strawberries. They've taken our lands and our boats. And once again we must wrap our Acadie in homespun cloth and bury it deep in our chests and move it on a bit more to the north . . . But you Beausoleil, you'll keep warm here in my pocket next my belly, Broussard-called-Beausoleil, you who inspired my march home at the head of my people.

. . . Her people. For the first time Pélagie realized it. Now that the family who had left Georgia by cart had reached Acadie, they had become a people. In ten years she had made a clean sweep of the land of exile, bringing back whole tribes of her countrymen and women to their own lands by the back door.

Above all, let sleeping bears lie.

So back we go, each to his own, on tiptoe, to wait as long as need be. They'd waited, hadn't they, in Georgia, in the Carolinas, in Maryland, throughout the whole length of New England, waited for the first cart to pass by so they could hitch their own behind. So they could wait again on the doorstoop of their own home till the door should open and the house empty itself again. Wait till the land warms up, till the sea grows calm, till memories grow less sharp. Wait till the plants sprout again in the ravaged fields and gardens.

Alban-à-Charles-à-Charles let Pélagie follow her thought through to the end. Then, wiping his brow, he ventured:

"Where we are here is the Tintamarre marshes," says he. "It's no place to dig cellars or sink foundation posts for cabins. We'd maybe better think about moving on."

"Yes," she says, "move on further north."

"The Indian says there's many of our folk up there at the heads of creeks and bays and in the woods, hiding out."

"Hiding out in their own land, in Acadie?"

Alban-à-Charles-à-Charles lowered his eyes and held his peace. But Pélagie heard him just the same. He was telling her Acadie didn't exist any more, that henceforth there would never be more than Acadians.

Pélagie lifted her head and smiled at Alban Girouard:

"And what does that matter," says she. "It's men who make the land and not the land makes men. Wherever it is we end up on our march, they'll have to give some name to the place. And I'll call it Acadie. On account of because we're going to rebuild it, just you wait and see, we're going to rebuild it as big as the country."

Alban took Pélagie in, then raised an eyebrow in a little Hee-Hee!

And then it was she who called out:

"Get the carts moving again!"

But when she went to move her own, she found the four wheels mired in the marshes of Tintamarre.

And Pélagie remembered the Salem swamps.

At Salem her cart was snatched by miracle from the mud of the marsh. Coming home out of exile, Acadie was really born, like the first man, from a handful of mud. In Tintamarre . . . Would Beausoleil arrive in time to save her and her cart again?

But at Salem it was above all Bélonie who had saved the cart and had saved Beausoleil, Pélagie knew it, she had seen him . . . both Pélagie and the old man had offered their lives in exchange for the other's. And the heavens had heard them . . . Yes, Bélonie, it's true. Beausoleil had come through the mire alive thanks to the old chin-wagging, story-telling tale-spinner. The Cart of Life had vanquished the Wagon of Death that day. But today at Tintamarre . . .

She had sworn to her forefathers she would bring her people home. She had kept her word. And more. She had brought back the roots of a people. Her broken-down cart surely deserved a rest. She didn't have the heart to rescue it from the mud a second time.

. . . Her cart, her home, her witness, her sister-in-arms. Her cart that had worn out six oxen, crossed a continent, sheltered her family and saved a people. Her cart that would be her grave.

Jeanne Aucoin left Pélagie alone with her reverie, alone to her combat with the Angel, without ever suspecting that the Angel was so near.

. . . Bélonie . . . I hear you Bélonie . . . I know . . . I know . . . At Salem I wanted his life at the price of my own. We all

wanted that. You didn't fool me, Bélonie. I know what you did, I
saw you. It's on account of you that my cart won . . . Because
my cart did win, Bélonie, despite everything, yes, she won after
all against yours: We reached home. And now it's finished, she'll
go no further. She deserves rest . . . You can come now, my
back is shattered but I'm still game. Enough to catch up to you
on foot anyway, Bélonie. And once there, watch out, I'll still be
called Pélagie-the-Cart, it so happens. And I'll know how to
stand up to that Reaper of yours, I'll know how to hold back her
arm if she dares raise it too soon against one of the children of
my country . . . or against families torn apart seeking to join together again . . . or against navigators on the high seas carried
away on the tide.

. . . Don't pine, Joseph Broussard-called-Beausoleil, don't pine
. . . each night the stars will shine to guide your four-master,
and every morning the winds will swell your four-and-twenty
sails, and in the evening the gulls will sing for you . . . for you
and you alone . . . don't pine, Beausoleil . . .

. . . Go ahead and show yourself now, Bélonie. I can hear you
already anyway. I recognize the creaking of the wheels and the
whip whistling through the air . . . I'm used to the movements of
a cart, you can't fool me there. And get this straight in your
head, Bélonie, your Pélagie's not one to go sneaking off in the
woods like the wolves, not her, get that straight in your noggin.
She'll climb aboard your cart without even using the handgrip,
left foot first for luck, standing, straight-backed, without looking
over her shoulder . . . eyes wide open.

At dawn it was Catoune's cry that woke the carts. A cry that ran
like a wave through the salt hay of the Tintamarre marshes.

They buried Pélagie the same day in the ruins of her cart.
Madeleine had remembered her mother's words at the death of
old Charles-à-Charles Giroué . . . I'll not quit my cart, she had
said, till it falls into pieces the day I need planks to set up a cross
on my grave. A single cross standing there in the Tintamarre
marshes, in the cradle of the country, there where they fell together, Pélagie and her cart.

The next day Captain Broussard-called-Beausoleil landed. He

had arrived too soon at Charleston, at Philadelphia, at Salem, for Pélagie hadn't finished bringing her people back to Acadie. At Tintamarre, he arrived too late. And he set to sea again, the captain did, with his giant and his fool in his four-master without flag or home port, absurd, intrepid, heroic, swooping like an albatross over the scud of the waves, flying toward impossible horizons, toward lost kingdoms, entering upright into the legends of his land.

Célina watched the *Grand'Goule* and her captain vanish.

"Whosoever steps down from the Wagon of Death once, will nevermore set foot therein," says she.

And everyone understood that the root-delver had just immortalized him.

Then she turned her face from the sea and followed Madeleine and Pélagie's sons north.

It was hard by, in the valley of Memramcook, before the startled eyes of her man and the disbelief of her brothers, that Madeleine LeBlanc felled her first tree . . . Come on, you flabby asses, it's here we're digging our cellar and throwing up a roof! . . . So spoke Madeleine, worthy offspring of the cart through the female line.

And the carts spread out to the four corners of the land of old-time Acadie, pushed by winds from the south, southeast, southwest, northwest, and northeast, climbing the rivers, jumping from one island to the next, digging into the hollows of creeks and bays.

And that's how the Cormiers wound up high on the Cocagne River and married into the Gagnons and the Després . . .

. . . and the Bourgeois sunk their roots around The Bend . . .

. . . and the Allains, the Maillets, and the Girouards on Buctouche Bay . . .

. . . and the Légers at Gédaique called Shediac . . .

. . . and the Godins, the Hachés, and the Blanchards more to the north, right up to Caraquet and Île Miscou . . .

. . . and the Belliveaus and the Gautreaus at Beaumont looking across at Saint Mary's Bay just opposite . . .

. . . and the Poiriers at Grand-Digue . . .

. . . and the Bordages and the Richards at Richibucto . . .

. . . and the Robichauds at Barachois . . .

. . . and the Basques in the islands and on the dune spits . . .

. . . and bits of LeBlancs here and there and everywhere.

Célina waved her arms to the carts disappearing one after the other through the wild hay of Memramcook. And once again it was she, delver of lineages and relationships, who had the last word:

"I do believe that this time the Deportation is over and done with, and it's the Dispersion that's about to begin. And to my way of thinking, it'll be quite some time before we see the end of it."

Then suddenly she turned around to discover that she'd lost sight of the Negro, that child of the Good Lord!

. . . But never you mind, clumpy Célina, all this time the Negro was laughing as broad as his fine white teeth. For he'd followed the Indian back to the Saint John River valley, and the Indian had made him a headdress of the tribe's feathers before presenting him to his chief who had never seen a black man before. It was the first time this Redskin couldn't call a stranger a paleface, which left him fairly perplexed, so it seems.

And Catoune?

The carts looked for Catoune in the Tintamarre marshes and waited for her two full days as they had done so long ago in Georgia. But this time in vain. She didn't reply to the calls of Madeleine or Célina or Jeanne Aucoin. She didn't reply to the cries of any of the carts. But three generations of Acadians would later swear that Catoune answered the call of Acadie from Pélagie's tomb. Because, for a century, every night of high wind you could hear Catoune's voice singing in the marshes of Tintamarre.

And some claim you can hear it still to this very day.

EPILOGUE

According to my cousin, old Louis-à-Bélonie, the Acadie that crept out of the woods a century later, pop-eyed, disheveled, huffing and puffing and sniffing the air and the weather, that Acadie, trying to transplant wild perennials dug out from among the roots of the forest into the sleek lands of the coast, lifting their heads and blinking at the sun, spitting in their hands and calling to their neighbors over the back fence gate to take care now . . . according to old Louis, that Acadie, crawling out of the woods and laughing with their eyes and rolling their rrr's . . . wasn't exactly a virgin race.

The wild geese had gone over, the high tides had washed the dune grass and the marsh hay, they could turn the cattle into the fields, they could hang winter up to dry, and air out their feelings and memories. A century had passed over the heads of this Acadie hidden deep in the woods and they hadn't said a word in a hundred years.

. . . Let sleeping bears lie.

But in 1880, a hundred years after the return from exile, on

tiptoe, in by the back door, Acadie stepped out into the front
yard to sniff what the weather was and to get news of the family.
From all the creeks and all the bays and all the islands, they
perked up their heads and cocked their eyes open.

And that's how they came to rediscover each other.

Those from Grand-Digue yelled across at those from Cocagne
who called to those from Buctouche who let those from Prince
Edward Island know that they'd dug up cousins in the northeast
called Lanteigne, Cormier, Landry, and Godin, just like everyone else. And these in turn poked their necks up out of their bur-
rows, peered off to the south, and waved their arms to those
from Shediac and Memramcook, who replied they'd found more
relations in Cape Breton and in Pubnico and all along Saint
Mary's Bay in old Acadie.

Yes, they'd reached as far as that.

Along the shores of the French Bay, called Fundy, all around
the basin of Les Mines, just about right up to the gates of Port-
Royal. And too bad if it was now called Annapolis. They'd got
as far as that, without really meaning to.

Only Grand-Pré remained deserted, solitary, mute, like some
ancient temple haunted by the gods. As Pélagie had predicted.

Without really meaning to.

Like the wheel of a cart, like the helm of a ship, the new
Acadie had spread the spokes of its compass points to the four
corners of the country, without knowing it. Playing blindman's
buff with Destiny, Acadie had, in the long run, reopened all its
fields and replanted roots everywhere.

Without really meaning to.

And so it was that one day it would hear its own names echoing all at the same time from southeast, northeast, and southwest:

"*Salut*   Jean - à - Maxime - à - Maxime - à - François - à - Philippe
Basque!"

"*Salut*   David-à-Gabriel-à-François Cormier of the Pierre-à-
Pierre-à-Pierrot branch!"

"*Salut* Alban Girouard, son of Alban, son of Jean, son of Alban-à-Charles-à-Charles!"

"*Salut* Fine Gander of a Charles-Auguste!"

"*Salut*, Louis-à-Bélonie-à-Bélonie-à-Thaddée-à-Bélonie-le-Vieux Maillet, the old chin-wagger!"

"*Salut* Pélagie-the-Grouch, daughter of Pélagie-à-Madeleine-à-Pélagie-the-Cart, *Salut!*"

"Bestir yourselves, you bunch of flabby asses! No one here's going to spoon-feed you or tuck you in bed. Come out of your holes and take your place in the sun. The wild geese are back from the south, time to start turning the earth again and casting our nets into the sea. Come out, you lazybones, the weather's veered to fine."

Yes, the weather was fine in 1880, Bélonie himself says so. Hurry up there! It's no time to be starting late again.

Acadie had a whole century to catch up.

> Buctouche, June 23, 1979
> in this year of the 375th
> anniversary of Acadie

CANADIAN CLASSICS

new press

Add to your Canadian literature library with these
outstanding Canadian Classics!

STACK

Maillet, Antonine   A-F
                                     Mai
                                     PB

Pelagie

STACK

PROPERTY OF THE
PUBLIC LIBRARY
ST. MARYS, ONT.